ETERNITY'S ESCAPE

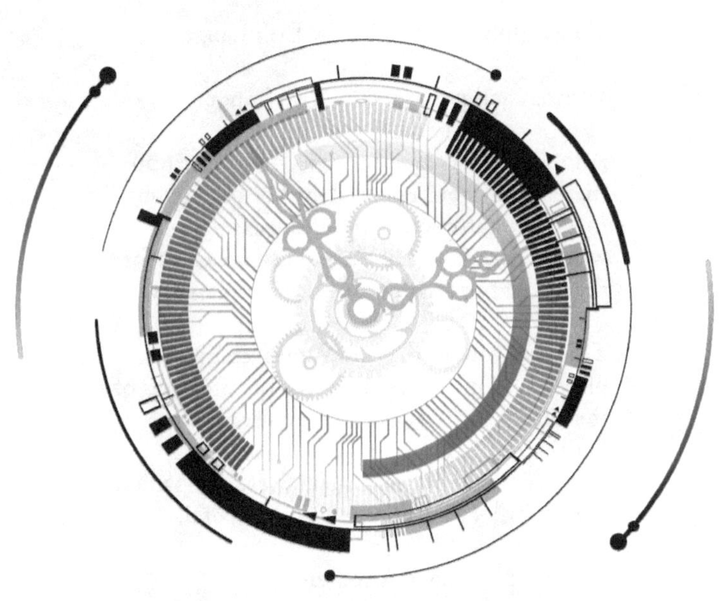

ETERNiTY'S ESCAPE

THE KARL LARK CHRONICLES

ERIK LANGE

Cover art by Shane Almgren

First Printing, 2022
First edition, *Escape from Hy-Brasil*
Second edition

ISBN 979-8-9869779-1-1 (paperback)
ISBN 979-8-9869779-0-4 (ebook)

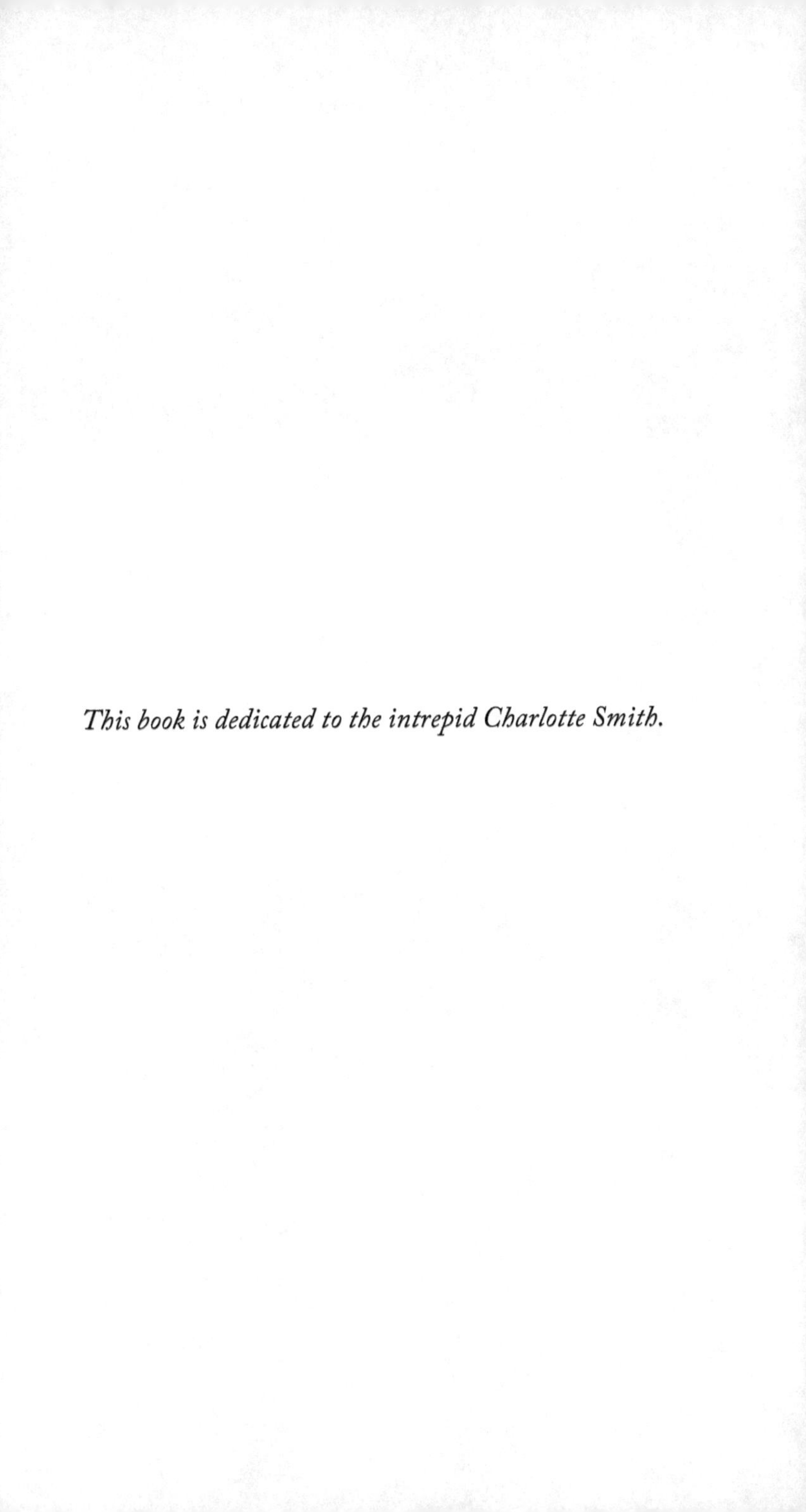

This book is dedicated to the intrepid Charlotte Smith.

CHAPTER ONE

"Higgebotham, I thought you were never going to call me again? Your exact words were that I was *persona non grata*." I say this to the man on the other end of the line.

Keith Higgebotham is not a bad sort, but he is still being an ass. A few months back, one of my clients made a private purchase of a rare text. Unfortunately for Keith, he had been lobbying the same owner to donate it to the British Museum. Keith and the museum lost, and I won. The commission had been quite handsome to boot.

A big pile of money beat out philanthropy. Go figure.

Higgebotham's tone is hostile, "Thomas, this isn't how I like to start my Monday's either. Nothing has changed. I still don't want you here, but the curator wants your opinion. This is your area of expertise and the request comes from her."

"Why are you calling me then? Why doesn't she call me?" I ask the question already knowing the reply. Dr. Elizabeth Chatzas is an archeology purist. She disapproves of my commercial activities even more than Higgebotham.

"Because she's my boss, and she told me to."

Between Higgebotham and Dr. Chatzas, I do not believe a visit will be pleasant, or even all that civil. Whatever they want me for, it is to look at something that is museum property. So, there is no commercial opportunity to be had. I am not seeing my motivation in what Keith is asking.

After a long pause, Keith, speaking in a more persuasive tone, says, "Thomas, we found something unique. It is a book. Or at least sort of a book, and it is very old. No one here has any idea what it says, or if it is a hoax. For your own sake, you should see this."

I'm still not feeling convinced, already having a significant workload to deal with for my paying clients. Spending a day, or even a couple of days, on museum business is not really part of my near-term business plan.

"Will I be getting paid for this?"

"Dr. Chatzas feels that when you see what we have,

you won't be worried about the money."

That was an odd thing to say. It took years of study, hard work, and travel to get me to where I am in my field, and I am always keen on getting paid. The bills don't pay themselves, and time is money, as the Americans say.

Keith, sensing my hesitation, continues pushing. His next words surprise me even more than being asked to do something for free.

"Dr. Chatzas told me to tell you 'please'."

What had they found? Dr. Chatzas is a career archaeologist who, at a relatively young age, clawed her way to one of the most prestigious posts a person in her profession could hope to achieve. Prior to this conversation, I would not have thought *please* part of her vocabulary.

What the hell. It would not hurt to take a look and maybe get some good will out of it.

"Okay Keith, you sold me. I will come and take a look. But you need to give me some background before I visit. What will I be looking at?" He can't be expecting me to show up blind.

"Until the museum is sure this isn't a hoax, nothing can be public. You will need to sign a confidentiality agreement when you get here. Nobody is going to risk their careers on this. Dr. Chatzas is not even allowing photographs at this point."

The plot thickens. So, I would be going in blind. Normally, I would prepare before I look at something. Keith is telling me that is not going to happen.

Now that I had agreed I would participate, it was time to ask, "When should I visit?"

"Dr. Chatzas' invitation is immediate. We would like you to come as soon as possible. Today even, if you could."

That explains why this call is at 8am on a Monday morning. They're in a hurry. That is a red flag. Nobody in archaeology is in a hurry. *Glacial* appears in the dictionary right under *archaeology*. Not literally, but the expression is true nonetheless.

"I have to tie up some urgent tasks. How about after lunch?" This gives me more time to think about this phone call and its implications.

"Fine, right after lunch. Call me when you are close to arriving. Remember, there are things to sign first when you get here. Goodbye, Thomas," The tone of Keith's closing words reveals how my agreeing to take a look at the find made his day. He successfully dodged going back to Dr. Chatzas empty-handed and incurring any potential unpleasant consequences.

Hopefully, whatever it is waiting at the British Museum is as interesting as Keith implied, and not a waste of my time.

The rest of the morning until my museum appointment is spent on work for clients. As noon approaches, I make a light lunch, clean up, dress semi-professionally, and take a taxi to the museum. I call Keith as the taxi pulls away from my flat, giving him at least a twenty-minute warning.

Higgebotham is waiting for me by the information

desk at the main entrance of the museum. Keith is a man of average height and slim build, with the coloring of a Caucasian man who spends most of his time indoors. He also dresses like a professor who does not own an iron. As we approach each other, I notice the manila folder in his hand.

Having made sure to be on time, so as not to give him something else to complain about, Keith not only smiles at me, he also shakes my hand and thanks me for coming.

Such a positive greeting is somewhat surreal. The last time we had seen each other was also at the museum. Keith had been an angry, red-faced Neanderthal, his words less than professional and spoken with such force I was sure his spit was on my shirt by the time I left.

The manila folder contains the confidentiality agreement, which I quickly sign. With the formalities out of the way, we head straight to a lift and down into the bowels of the museum. Keith swipes a card through a reader and enters a code to start the lifts downward drop. The card and code meant our destination is the fourth sublevel, high security. I knew it existed but had never been there.

There is no small talk on the way to wherever we were going. Keith is happy I was doing his boss's bidding but I can still sense his dislike of me.

The lift is slow, and Keith calls Dr. Chatzas on his cell, to let her know we are in the museum and on our way down.

We arrive, deeper under the museum than I have ever been before. Leaving the elevator, we walk for some distance down a long hall, passing rooms on our right and left. The air is dry; the humidity kept low to protect the artifacts. The décor as bland and lifeless as any warehouse. As we walk, our footfalls echo down the hallways. Apparently, we are alone. There are no signs of other people, and most of the lights in the hall and in all the rooms we pass are extinguished. It is dark, with just enough lighting to make our way to our destination.

Deep in the museum, poorly lit, no people around, for a fleeting moment the ambiance has me wondering if there really is a book. If Keith wanted to do away with me, this would be the place.

I look at Keith and shake my head, clearing my mind of the paranoid thoughts. Keith is an archaeologist, not a murderer. *Get a grip,* I think to myself.

Finally, we enter through an open doorway to our destination, a small, brightly lit room.

The room is empty, except for a heavy-duty steel table standing in its center. About the table are adjustable spotlights and a large magnifying lens on an arm that could be repositioned for viewing from different angles.

In the middle of the table is a box, apparently made of black stone. The surface facing up had been painted at some point. The paint had mostly chipped away over the years, with only small patches to show something had been there.

It is, however, not a book; it is a box.

I feel the need to point this out to Keith, "That does not look like a book."

"The book is inside. The box is made from andesite stone, super hard stuff. The paint on the top is how we dated the find," Keith continues, "Put on the gloves, you know the routine." He pulls a pair of linen gloves from his pocket and hands them to me.

While I put on the gloves, Keith does likewise and we approach the table. He opens the box with a careful gentleness. The painted top cover is hinged and sweeps upwards and back when opened.

So far, I am impressed, "It appears the hinge is part of the stone box. All carved from one piece?"

Keith nods, "That is one of the mysteries. How could something this old have been built like this? Carving stone this hard, into a complex shape, would be almost impossible even today. There are similar examples that exist, such as the Incan site at Pumapunku or the Schist Disk in Egypt,"

"How old does it date to?"

"Close to twelve-thousand BCE, give or take."

Inside the box is what looks to be a shiny copper tablet, stamped with Sumerian cuneiform. No corrosion or green oxide, just shiny copper. I look closer and comment, "This copper tablet is in Sumerian."

"Yes, the stamped cuneiform matches a known Sumerian form. And this is not a tablet," Keith reaches into the box and slides a finger into a groove on the inside of the box. Hooking the edge of the copper, he lifts to reveal it to be a page that could be flipped up, just like the cover. Underneath, another copper page with cuneiform writing can be seen.

On the backside of the thin copper sheet, you can see the text stamped out the other side.

"I am not an expert on all things Sumerian, but to my knowledge, everything discovered to date is only on clay tablets." Elation fills me, this find could be groundbreaking, if it is real.

"How many pages?"

"Seven."

"So instead of pressing characters into wet clay with a stylus, they used a punch on copper sheets? I have never heard of this."

A woman's voice carries over from behind me. "Yes, we have never heard of it before either, and our hope is you will have more to contribute to our understanding."

There is no need to turn and look, I know the voice.

Now turning completely to face the new arrival, I say "Hello, Dr. Chatzas."

She is tall, almost six-foot, brunette and pretty. If I had to guess, she is in her early forties, like me, but she has that classical bone structure and good looks that makes placing her age difficult.

Professionally dressed: skirt and blouse, tasteful jewelry. Her hair is down. Dr. Chatzas does not just look good, she looks almost perfect: clothes, makeup, hair.

To sum up her stance and gaze, I would use the word imperious. She could look down on someone, even if they were taller.

Yes, beautiful, intelligent, successful, and arrogant. She is very difficult to like.

She also has a reason to dislike me. Not just the reason Keith hates me for. There is another reason. A few years back, a politically connected sponsor donated a rare book, an original. I was paid to provide a third-party valuation for the insurance company.

I visited the museum to perform my due diligence. Except the book was a fake. After documenting the forgery, I followed protocol and turned my report over to Dr. Chatzas.

Because of the donor's political ties, nothing could be done. Publicly announcing the forgery would have caused a scandal. The museum buried the donation, never to speak of it again. It was a brilliant move on the part of the donor. He received a significant tax credit for his charitable donation and coincidentally disposed of a valueless forgery.

Even though I was not responsible for the forgery, I was still the messenger, and Dr. Chatzas firmly believes in shooting the messenger. She has been barely civil to me since. The museum still employs my services, but only begrudgingly.

After realizing there had been a long pause after our initial exchange, I decide to err on the side of diplomacy, "It is always a pleasure to be invited." It is tough not bringing up the 'please' Keith had mentioned. A childish urge on my part, but it would be fun to see if she would react. Perhaps another day.

Dr. Chatzas sniffs and shifts her gaze to the book.

"The British empire spanned over three hundred years. During that time archaeological finds from the four corners of the earth were brought here. Even though the empire is gone, there is a backlog of archaeological research to be done. This was found in one of the chambers below the museum. Unfortunately, there were no records found with it. We have no history of the book, where or how it was found"

"It is very impressive," a male voice with an American accent can be heard from behind Dr. Chatzas. Dr. Chatzas, Keith, and I turn to see a man in his sixties, with all white hair, of average height and wearing a tailored grey suit walk through the doorway. The man carries a cane with a large polished brass sphere at the top.

The sphere is out of place, too large to fit in the man's hand while walking. Instead, he holds the cane by the shaft using his right hand, just under the sphere.

Why have a walking stick you cannot hold properly?

Dr. Chatzas response is as quick as it is icy, "Who are you, and how did you get in here? This area is for museum personnel only." She glares at the man with open hostility, her hand reflexively reaching for the cell phone at her waist. I am guessing with the intention of calling security.

"My name is Karl Lark, and I heard about this find in the announcement," he replies. He appears unconcerned and smiles at Dr. Chatzas, seemingly immune to her hostility.

"What announcement?"

"There was no announcement? For such an important find? Why not?"

Mr. Lark's face now showing a feigned attempt at innocence. I am unsure if his weird reply is genuine or a poor attempt at humor.

There is an awkward silence, with the four of us staring at each other. During this brief pause, I am aware of two men silently emerging from the shadows behind Mr. Lark, coming to stand one on each side and slightly behind him.

Both men wear grey suits that look really good on them, probably also tailored. One man stands over six-feet tall and has military short, blonde hair. The other man is just less than six feet tall. He has handsome features and short black hair. I am not into guys, but even I can tell the black-haired guy would be considered a good-looking man. Both men are of athletic build.

They look relaxed, competent, and vigilant, all at the same time. My guess is they are Mr. Lark's personal security.

Dr. Chatzas is now holding her phone in her hand, with a finger hovering over the call button. "And how did you get in here?"

"I have been a generous supporter of the museum for several years. As you know, such support has its privileges, including access to my areas of interest, and this book interests me."

"We've never met at any of the events our patrons attend."

"Indeed. That explains the *anonymous* part of my

support."

Mr. Lark has her boxed in. She could pursue this with security, but if he really is a generous anonymous donor, then she would have a problem. In the end, his mere presence wins the discussion. How else could he have come to be here if he is not who he says he is?

A tense, long pause ensues, which I end by extending my hand to Mr. Lark, "My name is Thomas Davies. I am here in a consulting capacity. This gentleman here," I point at Keith, "Is Keith Higgebotham, resident archaeologist. It is our pleasure to meet you."

Keith nods while looking at Dr. Chatzas for a clue on what to do. Both of us are waiting to see how this man's sudden and unusual appearance plays out.

Mr. Lark shakes my hand, looks me in the eyes, and then nods his head to me. "It is a pleasure, Mr. Davies."

During our exchange, Dr. Chatzas apparently decides to accept Mr. Lark's presence. Extending her right hand, "I am Dr. Chatzas, curator of the ancient Middle Eastern collection of the museum. I hope you understand my response was only out of concern about the safety and security of the museum. How can I assist you?"

The phone disappears from her hand and back to her waist. I had to give it to her. As soon as money is involved, she switches gears pretty fast. I also love her non-apology apology.

The room is also starting to feel claustrophobic. Six people in such a small space makes it a bit crowded.

Both bodyguards remain within arm's length of Mr. Lark. They exude a quiet professionalism. I have other clients who have bodyguards. Most of them are either former law enforcement or really big, thuggish looking guys. Mr. Lark's bodyguards more remind me of who you would see guarding foreign dignitaries. Silent and competent looking.

Before Mr. Lark is able to reply to Dr. Chatzas' offer, four more men show up at the door to the room. All are big, burly guys, above average height and wearing full-body coveralls. Once they see the room full of people, they stop and exchange confused looks with each other. They seem genuinely surprised at finding this many people crowded into this little room.

The new arrivals all have a patch on their coveralls that says, "Executive Transport". All four men are of similar height and weight, facial features and dark curly hair. The impression being they are related, maybe brothers or cousins? Their mannerisms are oddly out of place. The way they stand and look at each other.

The third long pause of the morning plays out as we all stare at each other.

One of the four men nods to the others, and two of them rush Mr. Lark's bodyguards. The two remaining men unzip their coveralls and begin reaching inside.

The attack on the bodyguards does not go as the attackers would have liked. The dark-haired bodyguard sidesteps and lunges forward while sweeping his arm upwards, hooking the neck of his attacker. The man flips over backwards, going down hard on the concrete floor, flat on his back.

The blonde bodyguard grapples with his attacker and swings completely around him, building up momentum. He then flings his opponent onto the two others, just as they are removing pistols from inside their coveralls.

One of the guns inadvertently discharges with a flash of light and thunderous report. In the small room it is deafening, and my hearing is almost gone. The sound of Keith and Dr. Chatzas' screaming is faint even though they are standing right next to me. I remain frozen in place, silent, shocked by what I am witnessing.

In the middle of all this mayhem stands Karl Lark, next to the table, looking unconcerned, leaning on his walking stick.

A second gunshot resounds, the flash strobing the room with orange light.

One attacker is flat on his back, and the other is in a pile on top of the other two. Mr. Lark's bodyguards draw their own pistols from under their jackets with remarkable speed and dexterity.

The attacker flat on his back sees this, rolls over onto his feet and sprints out the door. The second attacker who bowled over his colleagues, pushes down on the two men with pistols underneath him to get to his feet and follow on the heels of his compatriot running out the door.

The remaining two men struggle to recover from being bowled over by one of their own. Having been further pushed down did not help their recovery.

Perhaps realizing getting to their feet will take too long, they stop trying to get up and shift on the ground while trying to bring their guns to bear on the bodyguards.

It is too little too late. They never get the chance to fire. Each bodyguard picks a target and fires a pair of shots into the semi-prone men in coveralls, ending the encounter. The boom sound of the bodyguards' weapons contrasting with the crack-sound from the coverall men's weapons.

I see blood and look away. Not even morbid curiosity could get me to look back.

This is when I notice Keith slumped against a far wall. One of the shots from the men in coveralls had hit him in the chest by accident. He is pale and unmoving. I had always found Keith unpleasant, but I would have never wished something like this on him.

What just happened? Who are these men? This is a museum, not a battlefield. My hearing returns with a rushing noise.

"...Both of the armed men are dead," I turn to see the blonde bodyguard talking.

Karl Lark says, "And the archaeologist, Mr. Held?"

The blonde bodyguard, apparently his last name is Held, walks over to Keith and puts his fingers to Keith's neck. "Dead."

My legs start to wobble, and I find myself supporting my weight by leaning against the table. *What just happened?*

Mr. Lark nods towards Dr. Chatzas, "Dr. Chatzas, this is all most unfortunate. However, I must avoid any legal entanglements. I will take my leave now." He turns and briskly strides from the room.

Mr. Lark calls to me as he is leaving, "Mr. Davies, please accompany me to my car."

The dark-haired bodyguard is next to me, indicating I should follow.

"Mr. Daugherty, please assist Mr. Davies if necessary. It is time to go." The impression is my leaving with Mr. Lark is not optional.

The blonde man falls in next to Mr. Lark as they walk out of the room, with me stumbling along behind them, my ability to walk recovering quickly. Mr. Held strides ahead, and half-way to the lift, I find myself alongside Mr. Lark. The hall just as dark and quiet as when I had arrived. The bodyguards still have their guns out.

"What just happened?"

"Perhaps that is not the best question to ask. You just witnessed what happened. Perhaps you should start by asking why it happened."

The lift car must have been close by because the doors open shortly after pushing the button to summon it. The four of us crowd in, and Mr. Held pushes a button. After the doors close, the bodyguards return their pistols under their jackets. The ride up is quiet. My ability to put thoughts together is not working well, and I remain in shock from the violence that played out just moments ago.

We exit onto a different floor than the one I had arrived on. A side exit is conveniently located nearby, and we walk through it to leave the museum. Navigating a short path to nearby VIP parking, Mr. Lark offers to give me a ride home. I numbly nod in acceptance, giving him my address.

Soon we are in a large, grey Mercedes sedan, driving in the general direction of my flat.

My ability to process thoughts returns in the car. "Shouldn't we be waiting for the police to give our statements? Couldn't we be charged with fleeing the scene of a crime?"

Mr. Lark waves a hand indicating this is not an issue, "Dr. Chatzas will not be calling the police." Mr. Lark is apparently unconcerned with the multiple felonies committed minutes ago.

Now that he mentions it, I realize the phone she pulled out in a blink of an eye when Karl Lark showed up stayed in her pocket after the shooting.

"How did you know about the book?"

"I make regular donations to Mr. Higgebotham's vacation fund, and he kept me apprised of things of interest. His death is unfortunate. I will now need to cultivate another source of information.

"He informed me today was the only day the book would be in a predictable location and relatively easy to get to, so I decided to visit. Apparently, I was not the only one with similar plans."

"Who were those other guys? Why were they there? And why did they have guns?" My thoughts racing with the questions.

"Slow down, Mr. Davies. You are getting over-excited. I am fairly sure they were there to take the book." Mr. Lark is as unflappably calm now as he has been through this whole experience.

"Is that why you were there? To take the book?" My questions come out harsh and demanding. My emotional state is showing in unconstructive ways.

"Taking the book was unnecessary. I just wanted to see the book and look at its pages. Once I have viewed it, there is no need for the original."

"The interruption of your visit kept that from happening."

"Not at all, it only took a moment for me to flip through seven pages. I did that during the exchange of gunfire.

"You see, Thomas, I have an eidetic memory. All I need to do is view each page for a brief second, and it is recorded forever."

"Why the violence? Archeology is a peaceful science. That book is thousands of years old. Whatever is in it will only be of interest to archeologists."

"Don't be so naïve. Modern archeology is a form of control. To join, one must spend years toiling away for little to no pay. Year after year, proving oneself to the orthodoxy. Any brilliance or initiative is weeded out when unapproved questions are asked."

"Should you graduate to an upper-level of the priesthood of archaeology, you are almost entirely dependent on museums and universities for your livelihood. Even a minor deviation from the defined narrative will see you cast out. And what living can an archaeologist earn for themselves outside of archaeology?

"The question you should be asking, Thomas, is why such control has been instituted over the study of the past?"

Mr. Lark's statements reveal monumental cynicism.

It is also all true.

"Here is your door, Mr. Davies. May I call on you in a few days? I may have more to discuss."

I just stare at him. He wants to see me again?

My reply is more of a mumble, "Certainly, please call ahead if possible. Here is my card." I fish a business card from my pocket and hand it to him.

"Thomas, a bit of advice before you go. Perhaps, you are considering contacting the authorities. My suggestion is you wait to see if they contact you first."

I nod and exit the vehicle. While walking up the steps to my front door, the sound of the Mercedes leaving is behind me.

Entering my flat, I close and lock the door behind me. Two thoughts are in my head. What really just happened? Why was this Karl Lark coming back?

# CHAPTER TWO

In the two days after the events at the museum, I have a hard time concentrating or sleeping. The waiting to hear a knock at the door, expecting to find the police there, is like an itch between my shoulder blades I can't reach. After checking the internet, over and over, looking for something about a shooting at the museum, I finally force myself to stop looking.

There is nothing to see. Apparently, what I witnessed was not brought to the attention of the authorities or the media.

Lunchtime arrives, and I finish what passes for the lunch of a perpetual bachelor.

Not that it is a goal of mine to be single. I do date women, just less often than I would like. My work tends to get in the way of romantic attachments.

On more than one occasion, I got caught up in a project and forgot about a lunch or dinner date, sometimes, even forgetting to stay in touch regularly. Members of the opposite sex find that particularly offensive, and it would become a black mark on the relationship. No amount of apologizing would make up for my becoming sidetracked.

The business I am in is actually great for meeting someone of the opposite sex. The libraries, universities, book stores, and book events I often frequent are a great way to connect with women. My average looks and non-threatening nature make women feel comfortable approaching me, and apparently, I am easy to talk to, at least that is what I have been told. My work is endlessly fascinating to women who enjoy books and reading. This would lead to dating, and a few times the relationships became serious. Then work would get in the way, and it was all downhill from there.

My lunch is warm beer and a can of soup. No influence of the feminine there.

The doorbell rings.

Looking up from my desk to the door, who can it be? No one is expected, nor should I be receiving a delivery. The memory of what just happened at the museum triggers a moment of panic, wondering if the police are finally here

Or worse, it could be Karl Lark.

The doorbell rings again. This time twice in short succession. Someone is impatient.

Pushing up from my chair, I am almost to the door when the bell triple rings. I unbolt the door and open it. The sky is overcast and dim outside, even though it is midday. Everything outside is still wet from the rain this morning.

Standing not a foot past the door opening is a short man. Barely maybe five-feet-four inches tall, if that. And dark, very dark, a dark brown-black complexion, with a little olive color mixed in. Probably Middle Eastern in origin? He is dressed in an all-black suit, with a bright red tie. Thick, jet-black hair is pulled back into a ponytail.

Everything about this man is unexpected, and I find myself staring into the stranger's too large eyes. They are unique, with the pigment of his eye color being a dark shade of amber, tinted with a hint of purple.

After a short pause, with me still staring at him, the man speaks, "I am Amal Halluk." No hand is extended. "May I enter your home and discuss business with you?" Amal's voice is low in timbre and accented. I have travelled Europe extensively and visited most regions of the world in service of my clients, yet I cannot place Amal's accent.

Something here is disturbing in a subconscious way, an almost imperceptible itch. Like something is happening that should not be happening.

My reply sounds mechanical in my ears. "Please enter," I regret saying those words the instant after, but to say anything else would have been rude.

Stepping back away from the door, I watch the

stranger, Amal, enter my home. My flat consists of a great room with doors on two walls leading to smaller rooms. Those doors lead to my bedroom, the loo, and a small kitchen. Amal walks to the center of the great room and turns in a slow circle, taking it all in.

Closing the door and bolting it, I walk slowly towards the man. As I draw close, in spite of the anxiety increasing with each step, I extend my right hand, "Thomas Davies at your service." Amal looks at me and then down at my extended hand, as if thinking about whether to shake it or not. His hand finally rises up and clasps mine. His skin is uncomfortably hot, and he shakes my hand in one quick motion and withdraws.

My original feeling of being disturbed has grown to full-on anxiety I feel in the core of my being. Struggling to stay calm and not overreact consumes my focus. This situation, Amal Halluk, it feels wrong.

My voice almost cracks, "How may I help you, Mr. Halluk?" This brings a brief smile to Amal's face.

"I have recently learned of you and your successes in locating items of age and value. This interests me. I may make use of your services, but I need to know more. Tell me of your recent successes."

Amal is blunt to say the least. This bluntness, showing up unannounced, demanding entry, and now asking about my business, gives me pause.

"Please be seated, and we can discuss your interests further", is what I say versus what I think: *Please leave.* Amal reviews the seating options in turn and picks an overstuffed, tufted, leather chair.

"Before we begin, may I extend the hospitality of tea or, perhaps, sparkling water?" At least my manners are catching up with the situation.

The offer of hospitality seems to have a positive impact on him. "Thank you for the consideration, Thomas, but I am pressed for time."

I sit down opposite the man, in an equally overstuffed leather chair. Down to business, then. "I provide a service to locate rare books and documents."

"What about other things?"

I feel my mood lifting. If Amal is looking for art works, I will be able to say this is not my area of expertise, and he would leave. "Unfortunately, I do not locate art works, as that requires a skill set I do not have."

"I did not say art. I meant artifacts and trinkets from the ancient past," Amal's expression does not change, but his tone has a hint of mild irritation.

"I do occasionally take a commission to locate difficult to find objects of an archaeological nature." Intrigue now mixing with the anxiety.

"Can you tell me about any recent successes in finding an object?"

"Client confidentiality prevents my sharing details about a specific search. I have had success recently in locating something very old and unique for a client. The search took nine months but will result in the client being able to acquire what he was looking for." That is as far as I can go regarding a past success without giving away too many details.

"What was the nature of the object? I wish to know more. I cannot make a decision to hire your services with so little understanding of your abilities."

This conversation is not as professional as I would have preferred, and I must be careful. "My most recent accomplishment was in locating the owner of an object that was several thousand years old. Only an old photograph from the 1920's showed that the object existed. It took significant effort to assemble its history from that photo to its current owner. I then facilitated communications between the current owner and my client. A delicate bit of work, but it ended well." I try to give my most reassuring smile. For me, "ending well" meant everyone got what they wanted, including a healthy commission for myself.

Amal smiles back, this time a full smile showing his teeth. The teeth bright white and narrower than they should have been. When framed in his dark face, including his too large eyes, the overall visage is that of a predator, "Perhaps you are competent. My decision in visiting you is proving productive. You will be contacted when your services are needed. I must leave now."

Amal stands, regarding me for a moment. I also stand, only now realizing that he knows where I live, but I had not given him my proper contact information. Pulling one of my business cards from my pocket, I extend it to him, "Mr. Halluk, my card should you wish to contact me." He looks at the card extended to him between two of my fingers. His left hand reaches out to take the card.

We walk to the door without speaking further, and he stands waiting for me to unbolt and open it. Amal Halluk walks through and out without saying another word. Then down the stairs leading up to my door, turns right and walks away.

Standing in my doorway watching him leave, I can feel my anxiety decrease proportionally to the further away Amal is. Stepping back inside, I close and bolt the door again. The unpleasantness of the dark man's visit sends a shiver through me.

He seemed more interested in what I am working on currently. His brief visit awkward in the extreme, like he wanted to ask his questions and then hurry to get out.

Shrugging, I decide to move on and get back to work.

This is one of the few times in my career I genuinely hope someone never becomes a client.

CHAPTER THREE

It is Friday morning, just two days after the unpleasant visit from Amal Halluk. I rise from bed at my usual time and begin work immediately. Feeling particularly invigorated at this early hour, I dive into my projects. A lead on one of the original 15th century copies of the *Liber Juratus* lifts my mood. It is not *the* original of course, but a first-generation transcription copied from the original. This version does not have a digital copy online, and I was hoping to convince the owner to make and share one or more digital photos of the book's cover and several pages. Then, comparing this to online copies of the other versions I have already located, I am hoping to learn more about the contents of the original. All of this is to support an ongoing project for a repeat client.

As the morning progresses, I notice a chill in the air. Uncommon in the flat for a summer morning. Almost like something inside is radiating cold. The air itself is not cold; it just feels like the walls and ceiling around the corner my desk sits in are cold.

When living in merry, old England, you get used to the cold and damp, and I know the best way to deal with a chill in the air during the summer. I open the windows to let the warm summer air in and return to my desk. The radiating cold is still there, but the warm air coming from outside is pushing it back, and my comfort level improves. My attention returns to my work.

The call to the contact number for the owner of the privately owned book of interest has a positive outcome. The owner is willing to share a digital scan of his copy in exchange for my sharing any history found during the search. After giving my assurances such an arrangement is acceptable, provided my client does not object. All in all, a satisfying outcome.

While I bask in my good fortune, my cell phone on the desk starts ringing. The number displayed is unfamiliar. This is not all that unusual. I receive calls every day from numbers I do not recognize. Probably more than half of my contact with other human beings comes from phone calls. I pick up the phone, "Thomas Davies speaking."

"Hello, Thomas!" a cheery voice answers back. A moment passes before I realize it is Karl Lark.

I am not sure what to say. Just a few days ago, three

men had died violently, and it had apparently been covered up. Mr. Lark was a central part of that event. Why would he be calling me now?

Gathering my courage, "Mr. Lark, how may I help you?"

"I found myself between tasks and thought of you. If you feel up to it, I will stop by your residence. I feel we have some unfinished business."

What kind of unfinished business? I am feeling out of my depth with this. Is Mr. Lark some sort of organized crime figure? And Karl Lark is such an odd name, is that even his real name? Is this unplanned visit just an excuse to snuff out a witness to a homicide?

All of these thoughts race through my mind in an instant. My last thought: if he had wanted me dead, it would have happened at the museum.

One of the downsides of working alone from home are the long periods of time without social contact. I am an introvert and value my time alone as much as any other introvert. But too much time alone makes me occasionally chatty, either in person or on the phone. And now, despite my trepidation, the realization I would probably enjoy talking to Mr. Lark drives my next actions. Perhaps I might even get an explanation about what happened at the museum?

"When today would you be stopping by?"

"In twenty minutes if it is not too inconvenient."

This week has been all about murder, mayhem, and people dropping by unexpectedly.

"Certainly, please ring the bell when you arrive," is

my reply, followed by my hanging up. This gives me too few minutes to prepare. I rush to the bathroom to run a comb through my hair, followed by clearing my desk of the evidence of my lunch. Then to picking up and organizing a few things. Passing a mirror reminds me there is no time to address the three days of stubble on my face.

The doorbell rings.

Stopping, I take a deep breath and look around. Seeing nothing particularly offensive, I make my way to the door and open it. A smiling Mr. Lark is standing there in a grey suit, identical to the one I last saw him in at the museum. His right hand holds the same peculiar cane. The same two bodyguards flank him, also dressed in the same grey suits. I recall him addressing them as Mr. Held and Mr. Daugherty, and I am sure the same guns they used at the museum are under their suit jackets.

Mr. Lark keeps smiling a broad, friendly smile.

"May I enter your home?"

I freeze for a second. Isn't that what Amal Halluk asked just two days ago?

"Please come in," I stand back while the three men enter. Then, I close and bolt the door behind them.

Mr. Lark walks to the center of the great room and looks around. The similarities to the visit just two days ago are almost to the point of déjà vu.

Mr. Held quickly moves to a corner to one side of the door, and Mr. Daugherty takes the other side. The way the three men had entered, dominated the space, and positioned themselves is intimidating.

"Would you like to sit? May I get you some tea or sparkling water?" No sooner have I spoken, and the repeat of the situation impacts me. Talk about déjà vu.

"No thank you on the refreshments. And yes, let's sit and talk."

"To what do I owe the pleasure of your visit?"

"I am interested in the services you provide. I have a private library that needs organizing and several acquisitions I would like to make. Can you help me?"

Relief washes over me. No mention of the carnage at the museum, and he is apparently not here to end my existence. I decide not to be the first to mention our previous shared experience.

"I do provide search services to locate older, sometimes quite rare, texts and documents."

Karl nods, his gaze locked onto mine, "How did you come to be in such a business?"

"It sort of just happened. Originally, I went to university for cryptography, but I could not keep up with the maths. My love of old books then took me in a different direction. An Italian firm specializing in protecting and rejuvenating old books and documents hired me. I worked there for several years, finishing university along the way."

"Ah, I see. This is how you became involved with older books?"

"Yes, in addition to my restoration work, I became involved with numerous university and private libraries. Soon, I was spending as much time generating business as I was restoring."

"This place was a sort of nexus in the old books world?"

"Yes, it provided a common place for everyone in the book business to meet. This progressed into becoming a neutral third party, communicating between the different enthusiasts."

Mr. Lark continues to watch me intently, obviously enjoying the story.

"This business of moving information between customers was not part of my employer's business model. They recognized the value of it, though, and encouraged me to pursue it on my own as a business. Of course, they expect a discount from me on services rendered and to promote them to my clients when possible. In the end, it worked out."

"Fascinating, how very entrepreneurial. My takeaway from your story is I could hire you to find books for me? I was not aware such a service existed before meeting you. What about cataloging and organizing my library?"

"Yes, you can hire me to find additions to your collection and I have done such work organizing private libraries. Private libraries sometimes also need a third-party valuation. This is typically for insurance purposes." I am enjoying where this discussion is going. There may be a real possibility Mr. Lark could hire me to organize his private library. The thought of what could be there almost makes me giddy. Like a child's anticipation of a soon-to-be Christmas.

"How long have you been doing this?"

"Including my time with my previous employer, over ten years."

"I believe we will discuss terms on your organizing my collection. You would need to see it first?"

"That would not be necessary. My fees are based on the amount of time applied to the project. I would begin at your convenience."

Mr. Lark sits back and looks around the great room again, and then back to me. "If the offer for sparkling water still stands, I will have it."

"Certainly, and your companions?" I say, while nodding to one of the bodyguards. Both of them had been standing in their respective corners, quietly keeping a watchful eye.

Mr. Lark waves a hand, "They are here for my security. Based on the events from a few days ago, you can see why. They have no need for refreshment. Please ignore their presence."

I nod and head for the kitchen to fetch water and glasses.

Mr. Lark's voice carries over from the other room, "I see you opened your windows to let in the summer air."

"Not so much to let the summer in as to fight the cold inside. The flat had a colder than usual draft today," I make this comment and then regret having done so. It is more personal and does not contribute anything of value to the client. This is what happens when I do not get out enough; I get chatty.

He does not seem to mind and continues the discussion, "A cold draft in the middle of summer?

Sometimes, older buildings have those."

"Yes, the flat can be drafty, especially in the winter, with the large fireplace. It is not usually an issue in the summer, though. I had to open the windows to warm things up. It must have been unusually cold last night." Hopefully that ends the line of discussion. I do not want to bore Mr. Lark with domestic issues.

Mr. Lark is quiet while I gather up a tray, water, and glasses. When I walk back out into the great room, I stop in the kitchen doorway. Mr. Lark is sitting up in his chair, holding his cane vertically with his hand just below the brass sphere headpiece. His eyes are closed, like he is meditating.

After a moment Mr. Lark's eyes snap open, and he exclaims one word, "Ciorii!"

What the hell is ciorii, and why is my guest yelling?

In a blur of motion both bodyguards produce handguns from under their suit coats. Mr. Lark stands up and reaches inside his suit coat. But instead of pulling out a pistol, he withdraws his hand with something clenched in it.

A clicking noise starts in the corner to my left, where my desk is. Looking over, it becomes obvious the clicking noise is coming from above my desk. Following the sound, I look up at the ceiling corner. Something is there now, and the clicking increases in volume. An oval-shaped, greyish blur shifts into sight. Like something from an out-of-focus photograph.

Out of the corner of my eye, I see Mr. Lark and the bodyguards moving towards my desk. The body guards grip their pistols in two hands, but instead of pointing them upwards at the mass manifesting, they are instead pointing them level into the corner.

Mr. Lark snaps, "Thomas, get behind us."

I do not move, and instead look back on the blur in the ceiling corner. A feeling of cold dread spreads through me, and my feet refuse to obey Mr. Lark's command. Something is wrong here, so very wrong.

The grey blur is wrong, and the more focused whatever it is becomes, the more wrong it looks. The grey blur becomes *something*. It is folded up, impossibly long and thin arms over similarly long thin legs pressed up against its body. Shades of grey, almost black, are its colors. There was a reflective, slimy sheen to it. A head, too long and narrow to be human, with huge solid black eyes staring right at me. The thing obviously the source of the clicking noises.

Right about the time I am able to clearly make out the features of whatever the monster thing is, Mr. Lark's right hand extends in an underhand toss of something small and white, like a stone or marble. Its flight path horizontal from his hand to the desk. But instead of landing on the desk, the white stone changes course, accelerating upwards towards the thing in the corner, and strikes the creature in what I can only guess is its abdomen. The instant the stone makes contact, the *thing* comes completely into focus and falls from the ceiling corner, straight onto the top of my desk.

The appearance of the creature shocks me to the core. Still standing in the kitchen doorway, I can feel my mouth hanging open. *What is happening?*

Then, for the second time this week, my hearing is blotted out by the thunder of gunfire inside an enclosed space. Both body guards open fire, the flash of their gunfire strobing the inside of the flat. I jump in surprise, dropping the tray with the glasses and water to the floor.

The thing on the desktop convulses and thrashes. Being not more than ten feet away, I can clearly see the effect of the gunfire. Fluids spray across the walls behind the creature. The part of the monster's body where the white stone impacted shines with a bright, white light. The creature's whole body is moving around, except for that one bright point of light. It appears to be holding the thing in place.

Mr. Lark now produces a handgun from inside his suit coat. A large semiautomatic looking like something out of a WWII movie. He then joins his henchmen in shooting the creature.

Their shooting is controlled, each shot carefully aimed. Even so, the rate of their fire is a manic staccato. Each man in turn has their pistol slides lock open, indicating the need to reload. This is done with skill, so quickly and smoothly that if you blinked, you would have missed it. Once a fresh magazine is inserted, they release the weapon's slide forward and continued blazing away at the creature. The cordite smell of weapons fire fills the flat.

The initial effect on the monster are sprays of ichor from bullet impacts. As the shooting continues, chunks are blown free. The wall behind my desk now looking like something out of a slaughter house.

Each man must have reloaded three times when Mr. Lark does the unexpected. He drops his handgun onto a leather chair and pulls a foot-long white spike from inside his suit coat. Without hesitation, he sprints towards the creature with dexterity uncommon in a man of his apparent age. He stabs the creature convulsing on top of my desk with the white spike, at the exact point where the white light is shining.

The creature goes stiff for a second, and there is a faint, high-pitched scream I can hear even through my gunfire-induced deafness. The thing then flops down on the desk, going completely limp. Its impossibly long arms and legs dangle over the edges of the desk, all the way down to the floor.

Every surface near the creature is a mess. Splatters of whatever passes for the thing's blood are everywhere. Chunks of its flesh, blown free by the concentrated gunfire, lay about the desk. Mr. Lark calmly withdraws the spike, produces a handkerchief from a pocket, and wipes it clean. He then casually drops the soiled handkerchief to the floor, and the white spike disappears back inside his suit coat.

The dead creature on the desk begins giving off a vapor, like it is being cooked.

The three men do not pause to observe their handiwork. Instead, they bend down and begin picking up spent magazines. Mr. Lark retrieves the gun he dropped, reloads it, followed by returning it to the holster under his suit coat.

The sensory overload begins to fade as I take in the warzone that is my flat. Spent brass casings are scattered about, lying on the floor, on the leather furniture, on the tables, everywhere.

My hearing returns in a rush. At most, a minute has passed since the gunfire started, and I do what any person exposed to sudden, close-proximity violence against a hideous monster would do.

I bend over and vomit.

As I retch, my body starts to shake, while my vision fades into grey. My hand goes to the door frame, as I am barely able to stay on my feet. While bent over, I see the dropped tray at my feet, shattered glass spread out around me. The unappetizing process plays out as I cover the tray and broken glass with the contents of my stomach.

When I finish being sick, my vision and control of my legs return to full ability. Standing upright, I find all three men standing in a semi-circle, facing me. The body guards have holstered their weapons, and their neutral passive expressions have returned. Mr. Lark is smiling at me in a way eerily similar to the day of our first meeting.

He says, "No time to explain; time to leave."

He then turns and walks towards the front door. Mr. Held grabs my right arm and coaxes me towards the door while Mr. Daugherty strides past everyone to unbolt and open it.

Once we are all outside, Mr. Daugherty closes and locks the door behind us. In my semi-shocked state, I watch and wonder, *Where did he get my keys?*

The Mercedes that had taken me home earlier this week is driving up the street to meet us, decelerating quickly to a stop. Mr. Lark sits in the front passenger seat, and the two bodyguards crush me between them in the back seat. No sooner do the doors close, and the car accelerates away quickly.

Should I object to being taken? Is this a rescue or a kidnapping? From my position sandwiched between two armed men, I am fairly sure my opinion does not count for much, and I will be going wherever they take me.

The driver is a big man, burly, barrel-chested, very muscular, and attired in the same grey suit as the others. He speaks as soon as we are seated and driving away, "Is there pursuit?"

Mr. Lark says, "No, drive normally and conform to local laws." From my center position, I can see Mr. Lark's face. He is leaning back with his eyes closed, like he had been while sitting in my flat, just before that monster thing appeared.

The Mercedes' windows are heavily tinted, and anyone standing next to the car would only see vague outlines of the people inside. The modern world is a strange place. One moment, there is a war zone in your home, and the next, you are quietly driving down the streets of London.

Mr. Lark says, "Is the transfer point clear and ready?"

The driver responds, "Yes, everything is ready. With current traffic, our ETA is less than 15 minutes."

A few minutes of silent driving passes, and Mr. Lark says, "Police are notified and responding to multiple calls of loud noises, possibly gunfire, in the area of Thomas' flat."

How can he know this? Mr. Lark is just sitting in the front seat.

Minutes of silence pass before he speaks again from his closed-eye reverie, "Nothing on police channels describing a vehicle or a specific address. The building has thick brick walls, and there was no one immediately outside. If the police drive through, they will not see anything, and there are no witnesses."

We navigate through London's back streets. Still dazed from recent events and not really paying attention to where we are, or how we got there. Focus eventually returns to my thoughts, and I start paying attention to the urban setting outside. Our final destination is an old industrial zone, one of many scattered around London.

How cliché, they are taking me somewhere isolated within the city. The Mercedes turns into a large warehouse and goes in, through an open truck door. As we enter the building, the door rolls down shut behind us. I do not need to look to know. The extinguishing of light coming through the back window informs me our entry point has just closed.

We continue on for, perhaps, 200 meters through the middle of the industrial building, with dark, silent machines on both sides gliding past. There are no lights inside the building, only the Mercedes' headlights illuminate the path ahead. An overhead door opening looms out of the darkness. We slow down to wait and then enter, leaving just enough room for the car to drive through.

Our destination is a well-lit, large open square space. It is clean and bright white, with no windows or doors. Once the car is completely in the room, it stops. Everyone opens their respective car doors, and get out.

Mr. Held encourages me to exit the vehicle with a tug of my arm. When I stand up, he guides me towards the center of the room. Feeling like I am on automatic pilot, cold and distant, I put up no resistance.

None of this makes sense. They are not planning on killing me. They could have done that with one bullet back in my flat. Or, for that matter, back at the museum. Why bring me to this room in an old building? I look around for clues as to what could possibly be going on.

The center of the room is dominated by a circle, perhaps three or four meters in diameter, its perimeter made up of evenly spaced black stones. Each cylindrical stone is maybe a foot in diameter and three feet tall. Reflexively I count them, nine in total.

Just inside the circle of stones is another circle made of copper bar, lying on the floor and unbroken in its circumference. Was this some kind of ritual setup? What is this? Sacrifice a librarian day?

Mr. Lark walks past one of the stones, steps over the copper bar, and stops in the approximate center of the circle. Mr. Held coaxes me into the circle to stand next to Mr. Lark. We are then joined by the other bodyguards.

Five men standing next to each other in the middle of the room, surrounded by a miniature Stone Henge, and all acting like this is perfectly normal. The surreal nature of the situation ads to the confusion I feel.

Without warning, everything goes black. Not like when the lights are turned off, and the light fades out quickly. This blackness is instant, no overhead lights providing a brief afterglow, just black. A moment of pitch-back and silence that feels like forever.

Light returns just as instantaneously, but different and dimmer. And it is freezing cold. My breath makes a cloud when I exhale. We are now standing in another, much larger, ring of stones. These stones are also black and cylindrical, but taller. The concrete floor of the bright, white room has been replaced with smooth black rock. Mr. Lark and his body guards appear unfazed by the instantaneous change in scenery.

A wave of cold nausea rolls over me and I would have fallen if Mr. Held did not have a hold of me.

Mr. Lark barks, "Put him in the cell and wrap him up to keep him warm before he goes into shock." He then walks away, heading out of the circle. Two of the bodyguards each grab an arm and half-drag me in a different direction from where Mr. Lark is headed.

Just before crossing between the stone circle pillars, a copper or bronze metal circle recessed in the smooth, stone floor catches my eye.

On the other side of the pillars, outside the circle, is a building. Hexagonal, and the size of a small house. One of its six walls faces the circle, and the walls and domed ceiling are solid black in color, with a circular opening mounting a bank vault-style, plug door hinged next to it.

Walking into the vault requires a step over a threshold that comes up from the floor almost to knee height. In stepping over it, I can see the wall is perhaps a foot thick.

I trip over the threshold. Fortunately, Mr. Held catches me and then virtually carries me the rest of the way into the room.

The floor is the same black material as the walls and the domed ceiling overhead and differ in appearance from the polished, smooth stone outside. There is a cot with a big cocoon sleeping bag in a military olive drab color laid out. Next to the cot is a drinks cooler. Atop the cooler, a small electric camping lantern. It is the only light in the room, and the light it generates is seemingly sucked up by the black material of the floor, walls, and ceiling. Standing in the middle of the room feels like floating in an endless black sky.

The bodyguards leave me standing on my own in the center of the room, while one of them unzips and opens the sleeping bag. Mr. Held picks up the lamp and places it on the on the floor. He then opens the cooler. Pulling out a bottle of water, he unscrews its cap and hands it to me, "Drink." The first words I've heard him say today, other than "reloading" back at the flat.

Using both hands, I take the bottle in unsteady hands and take a drink. Surprised by my thirst, I drink half the bottle before pausing. Mr. Held takes the bottle when I am done, caps it and puts it back in the cooler. "Get in the sleeping bag," he says, pointing to the open bag. I do not object. I am starting to shiver, the cold taking the feeling from my hands.

Climbing in, Mr. Daugherty zips me in until only part of my face is exposed. Mr. Held points to the cooler, "There is more water and some crackers in the cooler. Don't turn out the light. If you do, it will be completely black inside this room. There is no other light". "Over against the wall is a small chemical toilet." He now points towards a dim white object against the wall.

With that said, both men turn back to the doorway and walk out. I can vaguely make out the vault door closing in the weak light, followed by a great booming sound. Then a metal-against-metal grinding noise. The excitement of the last half-hour slowly fades away, as I feel the comfortable, spreading warmth of the sleeping bag. My eyes close, and I remember no more.

CHAPTER FOUR

The need to relieve myself awakens me. This is followed by a few moments of semi-conscious confusion as to why my body is wrapped like I am in a cocoon, and the air on my face is freezing cold. Recollection of recent events surges, *Karl Lark, my flat, a monster*. I am in a frozen vault, with no way out.

Turning my head, I take comfort from the light of the battery-powered lantern on top of the cooler a few feet away. Feeling around inside the sleeping bag, I find the bag's zipper. Releasing myself from the warm sleeping bag confirms what my face had been telling me. It is really cold, likely well below freezing. My breath forms a cloud in front of me when I exhale.

Lifting myself from the cot, I stumble to the box

against the wall in the direction Mr. Held had pointed to earlier, finding a compact camping toilet with a traditional lid on top.

Afterwards, I inspect my prison from the inside of what I decide to call a vault. The six interior walls form a uniform, symmetrical hexagon. The lamp barely illuminates the room, and the domed ceiling above is almost lost in the darkness. Touching the walls reveals they are metallic and burning cold to the touch. The impression is of cold radiating from the walls, intense and palpable.

The floor is the same black metal. Copper or bronze rings thick as my thumb are recessed into the floor in concentric circles, with maybe a single strides distance between each ring. They start in the center of the room, with the first circle wide enough for a single person to stand within. The same copper inlay repeatedly rings the walls, starting a similar distance from the floor and repeating up the walls. If this continues to the ceiling, I cannot tell in the darkness.

The floor and wall surfaces, quite smooth in most areas, are covered in scratches and dents in places, left by whatever had been kept in here in the past. The defacement of the walls goes up as far as the light allows me to see, well above my ability to reach. Sometime in the past, something very large and very strong, had been kept in this vault. And it had wanted out.

Walking back to the cot, I rummage through the cooler, finding bottles of water and a box of crackers with common brand names. After closing the cooler, I inspect the lamp. It is a battery-powered LED type, similar to what could be found in any sporting goods store. Returning the lamp to the top of the cooler, the dire nature of my situation begins to register.

Is there even enough air in here? I do not see any vents?

Walking up to the vault door, I yell, "Hello? Hello? I am awake, is there anyone out there?" There is no reply. Recalling the walls are a foot thick, my guess is it is unlikely anyone can hear me.

After making a few laps inside the vault's perimeter, the realization the heat generated by exercising is overwhelmed by the bitter cold sets in. Once I start to shiver, I crawl back into the sleeping bag, feeling warmth return to my body.

I am not tired, and by not having a watch, there is no way to tell how long I had been asleep. The vault is dead silent, with nothing to indicate the passage of time. There is nothing else to do but just lay here in the cold and the dark, thinking about what had just happened. Trapped inside the sleeping bag due to the cold; trapped inside a vault worthy of a Greek God. Sort of like the imprisonment version of a Russian nesting doll.

With time and lack of distractions, I consider my predicament. Obviously, Karl Lark had rescued me from some... *thing*. Why it appeared above my desk, back in my flat, is beyond me. Mr. Lark called it a ciorii, whatever that meant. I have read a lot of mythology in my life and do not remember any mythological monster called a 'ciorii' referenced in any book.

And why the magic trick back at the warehouse? Turning out the lights and moving me to a freezer? And why am I in a vault? The rescue turned into kidnapping when I was locked away against my will.

Mr. Lark and his team were avoiding the police when they left my flat. Is he part of some intelligence service like MI-6? It would explain his ability to discharge weapons and kill people in the city without any apparent repercussions.

My reasoning produces no answers, just more questions. I do not believe Mr. Lark intends to harm me. He could have just shot me after they finished off the monster and left. Perhaps, I am locked away for my protection, but protection from what? I am in the book business, a librarian. Not the sort of business a person is likely to acquire mortal enemies in, much less monsters demonstrating supernatural abilities. None of my clients had ever expressed the kind of dissatisfaction that could result in gunfire.

After what could have been minutes or even hours, my having no way to tell, the grinding metal noise of the door reverberates inside the chamber. While waiting, I position myself in the sleeping bag, so I can watch the door. The grinding noise stops, and the vault door opens silently.

Mr. Lark stands outside, still in his grey suit, and carrying his copper or brass, sphere-headed cane. He is not smiling his peculiar smile this time, instead a mask of concentration looks right at me as he enters into the vault, carefully stepping over the doorway's ridiculously high threshold.

The few times I have seen the man, he was always smiling, before, during, and even after the gunfire. My guess is it is worse that he is not smiling.

Behind him is Mr. Held, dressed in what looked like an all-black tactical uniform and carrying a small chair. He maneuvers around Mr. Lark and places the chair facing me, perhaps four feet from my horizontal form. Mr. Lark takes a seat while Mr. Held exits out the doorway. The vault door swings closed, apparently locking us both in with that grinding noise again.

Mr. Lark sits, silently looking at me. After several seconds, I take the initiative and speak first, "Perhaps thanks are in order for the rescue?"

Mr. Lark's expression remains unchanged, his voice flat in reply, "It was not a rescue."

"If not, then what is going on here?" My voice lacks conviction, now realizing my earlier line of reasoning is likely incorrect.

"The thing in your flat was a ciorii. When they first establish themselves in hiding, they absorb thermal energy from the surrounding environment. In layman's terms, they essentially radiate cold. The reason for my visit was genuinely about hiring your services. When you related the feeling of coldness on a warm summer's day, I had a hunch. I then investigated my hunch."

"A hunch, all that came from a hunch?"

Mr. Lark frowns, "When you operate within the spaces my organization does, your survival depends on a serious amount of paranoia and listening to your instincts. While you were getting the water in the kitchen, I consulted my *oculus*."

"*Oculus?*"

Now, Mr. Lark smiles, "I am sure you wondered about my oddly-shaped cane. The headpiece is obviously too large for a person's hand to grip. It is a device of my own creation. It allows me to see… things. Also, my attempt at explaining your situation is going to take a long time if you keep interrupting me".

After a pause, he resumes, "Ciorii are used as assassins, kidnappers or watchers. My hunch was correct, and a ciorii was present. I still do not know which of those three roles brought it to your flat. As soon as I could see that a ciorii was indeed present, action was taken."

I decide to risk another interruption, "I see, sort of. You acted to protect yourself, but why take me with you? The thing was dead."

Mr. Lark takes the interruption in stride, "My organization prides itself on complete anonymity. I had just met you a few days prior, and during my second time meeting you, I find a ciorii in your home. That leads to two possibilities: you knew it was there, or you did not. Based on your *reactions*, it was obvious you did not know it was there. Someone sent it to watch you, not me, but whom?

"I bear you no ill will, Mr. Davies. My concern is for my privacy, and if it were somehow compromised. The monster needed to be destroyed before it could report back, and I needed to remove you before its master came for you."

Mr. Lark lets this sink in for a few seconds before continuing. "Have you ever heard of a daemon's true name?"

Wow, talk about a subject change. What the hell kind of question is that? I want to know why some assassin kidnapper monster was hiding in my flat? Did Karl Lark bring this madness down on me by accident or on purpose?

"Yes, Mr. Lark, I have read enough fiction to understand the concept of a daemon's true name," My reply displaying more sarcasm than the sensitivity of my situation really allows for.

Karl nods, apparently unoffended, "Ciorii exist in the wild, I guess you could say. They can be bound into service by possession of its true name. From a more technical viewpoint, it could be seen as a password to program its actions. With the proper knowledge, you can take ownership of such a creature. It will follow instructions, even complex ones. Not only could I see the ciorii in your flat, but I could see it was following instructions and had a purpose. It belonged to someone."

His explanation makes it sound like that thing was intelligent and someone had put it in my flat on purpose. He was also making it sound like ciorii are daemons.

Mr. Lark's facial expression shifts dark, looking almost angry. "I must now apologize to you for two things. The first is locking you in this chamber. It was necessary to put you someplace safe and out of reach from anything. I needed time to consider all angles of these unusual events. My second apology is for the mistake I made in getting involved.

"I do not believe the ciorii was there due to our meeting. It was not looking for me. There really was no reason for me to become involved. The ciorii was sent in response to something else. Have you had any recent visitors that left an impression on you?"

If I was hearing him correctly, Mr. Lark just said he would have left me in the ciorii's clutches if he had known better. As for weird visitors, other than Karl Lark, there was Amal Halluk.

I did not see any reason to protect someone who put a monster in my home. "A man named Amal Halluk visited me two days before you came to my flat." I then went on to describe Amal Halluk in detail.

Mr. Lark smiles, "As I suspected. The man you are describing most likely sent the ciorii. Why is another question? Such a being would not normally get personally involved. Perhaps he was looking for something and did not find it? Then, he sent the ciorii to watch you? I would speculate this is related to the events at the museum.

"Your description of Amal sounds like he is a Djinn, probably of low rank. Djinn do not normally leave their estates to visit humans. They have bound human servants interact with the outside world.

"Whatever that book at the museum contains, it must be very valuable or dangerous for a Djinn to become personally involved. Perhaps, it is a matter of honor? Regardless, Amal Halluk decided to watch you very closely."

Mr. Lark sits thinking for a bit, in the profound silence in the vault.

"This brings me again to my second apology. My organization is very private. By bringing you here, I have created an untenable situation. Everyone you have met in my service is permanently bound to me. I can't just return you to your flat. As they say in the movies, you know too much."

I feel real fear bordering on terror. *Oh God, is he going to kill me?*

"The world I operate in is dangerous. Without secrecy, I would come into conflict with other organizations and entities that I would prefer do not know of my existence. No one from the outside world is ever allowed where you are now.

"You cannot make any promise of secrecy that would make me feel secure in releasing you. You may believe you can keep a secret, but I assure you, should someone want to extract what you know against your will, they could.

"I could offer you a role in my organization. Unfortunately, that is complicated by the fact that when I recruit, it is for people that fill roles that need filling, and you do not meet any of the criteria for joining."

My feeling of terror is now approaching panic. This is the end. Zipped up in a sleeping bag, not four feet away from someone I am positive is about to murder me. There is nothing I can do. Even if I was standing, with my hands free, I am fairly certain Mr. Lark would not be challenged 'taking care' of me.

"I put a lot of thought into what to do with you. Your ability to locate things related to my organization's sphere of operations could be useful. After significant weighing of the possibilities, I have come to the conclusion you may be able to make a meaningful contribution. If things do not work out, I will dispose of you later."

Who says things like that?

"Please understand, Thomas, when I make an offer to join, it is a one-way street. You join, or your life is ended."

I was having a hard time organizing my thoughts. Is he saying what I think he is saying, "Is that a job offer?"

Mr. Lark's face changes, becoming a mask of controlled anger, his eyes shining with cold light. Not an actual light, but his eyes are devoid of emotion or empathy. "There are no jobs here, Mr. Davies. When you join, you are telling me you have no reservations, that you will make every effort to achieve the goals of the organization. There is no going back, no reluctance, no attempts to escape. You will not be an employee, and this is not a democracy. You will serve my will. Anything less, and I will kill you. Joining is forever."

The emotion subsides, and Mr. Lark sits back in his chair, "I only make this offer once. You can take a few minutes before you answer."

A few minutes? He is offering a few minutes for such a decision? This would be comical if the stakes were not so high. As I see it, there is really no choice here. I had no one who would miss me other than my parents, whom I see only once or twice a year.

Regardless, everything I have seen during my brief time with Karl Lark points towards my joining his organization being the first step in an adventure. I had never really been interested in adventures before, but now, instead of fear, I feel.. intrigued? What wonders would I see? There is only one way to find out. And whatever Mr. Lark has in mind is preferable to a prompt death.

"I will join your organization," The words are said with a conviction I do not feel. My former life starting to slip away, even as I said them. Would I ever get to return to my flat? Whatever Mr. Lark has in mind is the only future I have now.

Mr. Lark looks at me for a long time before replying, "I accept your service, Thomas Davies. We will discuss your role more when we get to our destination."

"May I ask questions?"

"I always welcome constructive questions, and I answer them if it is something you should know. Now, we need to travel to a more hospitable location to begin your integration into my organization. We can talk along the way. Get yourself out of that bag."

No sooner had Mr. Lark spoken, and the grinding noise of the door unlocking echoes through the chamber, followed by it swinging open.

Extricating myself from the sleeping bag, I stand up and immediately start shivering from the cold. Fortunately, Mr. Held comes through the door and hands me a great coat.

The coat hangs all the way to my ankles and is well-insulated. A pair of gloves is in one of the pockets. I button up the coat and put on the gloves. The well-choreographed routine gives the impression I am not the first person to undergo the interview process. Every action taken is being executed like clockwork.

Mr. Held says, "We are ready to travel."

That Cheshire cat grin manifests on Mr. Lark's face as he ushers me out of the vault, "Come, Thomas, it is time to show you a bigger world."

CHAPTER FIVE

Things had been pretty hazy when I arrived at… wherever this is. Walking out the vault door, the dark outlines of the other five identical, black iron vaults, their hexagonal shapes, themselves forming a hexagon shape are around the Stonehenge-like circle of stone pillars I had arrived in.

There are three identical roads leading away from the vaults in three different directions. The roads appear to be at precise angles to each other and perfectly straight for as far as I am able to see.

Past the flat space of the stone pillar circle and the vaults, what passes for ground appears to be rough, very uneven, grey stone. The elevation of the grey stone landscape shows no pattern, rising and falling with small peaks and deep pits everywhere. The changes manifesting in both steep angles and gradual ramps. Attempting travel by foot across the open grey stone spaces would be tough going. Only the three roads offer a path of reasonable movement away from the vaults.

Mr. Lark walks to one of the three roads. Mr. Held is the only other person present. I join Mr. Lark in walking side by side, down the center of the road.

The road is broad, perhaps ten-meters across, and made from perfectly flat, fitted black stone. An easy surface to walk on, Karl Lark sets a brisk pace. Still wearing my 'around the flat' loafers, the surface is a bit hard for my footwear, but at least it is consistent and smooth.

As if anticipating my question, Mr. Lark states, "Our destination is a thirty-minute walk".

Mr. Held trails us by a respectful distance, looking his usual alert self.

Observing our surroundings as we walk, it becomes obvious we are not in London. It is as dark as a moonless night and there are no stars overhead. The air has a gloom to it, like a fog, that limits visual distance. Buildings and other structures can be seen spaced some distance away from the road. Constructed of the same black stone as the road, starkly contrasting, with the grey of the sterile landscape. No plants, grass, or trees, everything in sight is as barren as the surface of the moon.

The distance and gloom compete to fade the view of the buildings. Their placement is seemingly random, almost non-sensical. A few have paths, narrow and similarly paved, running to the road. Other buildings jut out from the moonscape plane in isolation, with no apparent connection to anything around them. Small, single-story structures make up the majority, with the occasional monolithic structure thrusting up, out of sight into the sky.

Following one such outline upwards, I search the sky for the stars. In the vague, fading distance high above, I make out something floating overhead. Concentrating, I now see more than one something is up there. Perhaps a dozen diamond-shaped blimps can be made out. The surface of the blimps is uneven and bumpy. Their color is difficult to determine from this distance, perhaps a light grey or pink. Long, thin ropes hang down from the blimps.

Except these ropes are moving and snapping.

What are those things, because I don't think those are ropes? Those shapes floating so far up must be some sort of living creature. They are entrancing to observe, and I am having a hard time looking away.

Mr. Lark takes notice of my staring and snaps, "Don't look at them, or for that matter, do not look up at all. They know when they are being observed, and it draws them to you."

With some mental effort, I shift my gaze and focus on the road ahead. "I was looking for the stars. What are those things up there?"

Mr. Lark waits a moment and then responds, "There are no stars up there. This place is a pocket dimension. We are someplace other than Earth.

"The normal rules do not apply here, and you must be careful. For right now, you must understand this is not the world of man. Your mind is unguarded, and you are radiating your emotions and thoughts to everything around here. If you were not in our company, you would be quickly swept up by *something*. It would be a meeting from which you would not survive."

The dread I had felt earlier, when I thought Mr. Lark was going to kill me, returns. It is a cold twisting in my chest.

Mr. Lark continues, "The place we arrived is called the Compass. It is the front door, so to speak, and the only way into this place. The space between the Compass and our destination is left wild. Any unwelcome visitors who find their way here will need to contend with the many uncivilized and dangerous denizens between the Compass and our destination, the Citadel, if they wish to disturb me here."

Nervously looking about, I ask, "Why are we not being disturbed now?"

"I have reached an accommodation with the things in residence along this road. It is an imperfect agreement, but if we travel in pairs, walk with a purpose and keep our wits about us, we will be unmolested."

My gaze is pulled to the right. The movement of my head involuntary. Next to a building, not close, but not too far, stands a man shape. At first it blurry and inconsistent, its image quickly comes into focus, *a clown?* What is a clown doing here?

Mr. Lark speaks again, his tone harsh, "Eyes ahead, Thomas." His voice breaks the spell, and I am able to look back in the direction we are walking. "What did you see?"

"A clown, like in a circus or at a children's birthday party," an involuntary shiver goes down my back. "Is there someone, or something, out there trying to look like a clown?"

"There is no human person out there. What you saw was one of the wild residents of this place. These things do not necessarily see us the way we see each other. It looks like a clown, because it thinks that is what we look like to each other. It is trying to look human to get you to move closer to it."

"So, this place is filled with predators?"

"While it seems like that, what with everything here apparently trying to kill you, in fact, there are no predators or prey here. The things in this place are old, old beyond ancient. They were tools, fantastically sophisticated instruments and machines. Used for the creation of things beyond the ability of most to understand.

"When whatever created them was done with them, they were just left here. It is similar to when you are driving in the country past a farmer's field and see an abandoned piece of rusty farm equipment in the corner of the field. Its usefulness ended, left to rot.

"The things here, the ciorii, and others, are left over from a long time ago. Left to their own devices, some attempt to find a purpose for themselves. Most are attached to a single location, following whatever their last instructions were.

"They have differing levels of self-awareness. Many have come to resent the freedom of humans. Others just want something to do, perhaps an equivalent to children playing. Their playing with someone is almost always fatal. The concept of living creatures and mortality are not part of their being. Where possible, it is best to give them a wide berth."

"So, they are Machines, like androids? Can they be commanded?"

"Your insight is impressive. These things were built long before English was a language. With careful research, some trial and error, and controlled conditions, it is possible for a human to gain imperfect control of some of the Lesser Created."

"Lesser Created?" These words beg the question, if these nightmares are lesser creations, what is a Greater Created?

"If there are Lesser Created, are there Greater Created?"

"Yes, there are Lesser Created, and there are Greater Created. They are all immortal and virtually impossible to permanently destroy. The Lesser Created are the faeries and goblins of myth, along with the ciorii and others. The Greater Created exist are not something to seek out or discuss in the open like this.

"Perhaps, calling them Created is a dry and overly technical term, but I wish to define them in a way that is separate from the emotions of mythology. Enough questions for now. We are almost at our destination".

We walk in silence for a few more minutes. Straight ahead, looming in the distance, a structure seems to rise from the plane as we get closer. Much wider than any of the buildings witnessed in this place so far, it appears to be our destination.

I turn to Mr. Lark, but he speaks before I ask the question, "Yes, Thomas, this is our destination. I call it the Citadel.

The road ends at giant double doors, dull steel in color, the same width as the road and four times the height of a man. The doors are set in jet-black walls so high they extend upwards out of sight. I wonder how they work, as no handle or lock are evident.

On each side of the door is something twice the height of a man, perhaps statues, but blurred. At first, I thought the lack of focus was due to the distance, but as we walk closer, the blurry nature of the figures does not change. Their appearance is that of giant men with four arms and two legs. Their body, arms and legs thickly built and what, I guess, is their heads are sunken into the top of their chests with no neck evident.

"Mr. Lark, what are those?"

"They are ushabti repurposed to guard the doors to the Citadel. The name ushabti is ancient Eqyptian, but these Created existed long before the pyramids were even conceived of. In the ancient past, they were employed for tasks on a massive scale. They are an example of a Lesser Created that I have repurposed to a task of my choosing. In this case, they are guards of the only entrance to the Citadel."

When we are not more than twenty paces from the doors, they swing open outwards, apparently without any signal. Bright light stabs out from the interior, causing me to raise a hand and shield my eyes.

As we enter, Mr. Lark announces, "Thomas, welcome to the Citadel."

CHAPTER SIX

Neither Mr. Lark nor Mr. Held pause as we enter the Citadel. Our small group purposefully walking through the doorway, into the well-lit open space beyond. Once inside, the doors silently swing shut behind us.

The first thing I notice is how brightly lit this place is, the gloom outside did not follow us in.

From inside, I follow the walls to the ceiling high overhead. If I was to guess, I would say at least ten stories tall. While the exterior walls had been void black, inside they are snow white.

Overhead, a domed roof arches further upward from the walls. Mounted at even, symmetrical spacings just below the ceiling, are coffin-sized huge glass or crystal cylinders, each is hollow and transparent. Inside is a glowing stream of gas, emitting light, bright but not overpowering. Everything inside the domed space is illuminated, and the overall effect is that of a brightly lit sports stadium.

The space under the dome could have been a half a kilometer across. Inside the domed structure are other buildings, all different in appearance. Some are cylindrical, and others are rectangular. Some small, like a yard shed, while others are multi-story structures that extend upwards to meet the domed ceiling. Everything is of stone construction. The air, light, and apparent lack of plant or animal life…this place feels sterile.

The organization of the building demonstrates no discernable pattern. No urban planning commission or sane architect was involved. The dimensions are wrong, too. From my experience, architects and artists use the golden ratio. Objects constructed following this guideline will be pleasing to the human eye.

Whoever built this place had never heard of the golden ratio.

An unfamiliar man is standing in the middle of the open space. Tall, over six-feet, and wearing the same black tactical uniform as Mr. Held. He has an athletic build and based on the grey in his short cropped dark hair, is in his early forties. A large, holstered handgun at his hip, he has that same alert watchfulness the other men accompanying Mr. Lark exude.

While I stand in one place and gawk at my surroundings, Mr. Lark walks up to the waiting man, and they exchange words in a low voice, preventing me from overhearing. Mr. Held wanders away at a casual pace, his immediate duties apparently complete. The change in his body language noticeable. Whatever this place is, we must be safe, as the hypervigilance displayed on the walk here is gone.

Mr. Lark waves me over to join him and make introductions, "This is Illych. Think of him as the headman of this place. He will give you a tour and settle you in. I strongly suggest you take his instruction seriously."

Illych smiles and extends his right hand, "Pleasure to meet you, Thomas." His accent marks him as another American. His handshake is very firm.

"Thank you, and likewise."

"A Brit? Tank is going to love this," Illych is grinning now.

"What Tank?"

"Not what, who, and you will meet him shortly. Big bear of a guy, you can't miss him. You already met Held and Mike," Illych continued.

"I understand Held is the gentleman who Mr. Lark addressed as Mr. Held. Who is Mike?"

"Everyone here, other than Mr. Lark, is ex-US military. We do not necessarily address each other by our given first name. My first name actually is Illych. Mike Daugherty is the dark-haired gentleman whom you have already met."

Mr. Lark interrupts, "He has not been introduced to the others, I trust you will take care the details and help

Thomas settle in."

Without another word, Mr. Lark turns and starts toward the main gate doors. They swing open again, without any apparent command. He passes through them, and they silently close behind him.

Illych says, "Mr. Lark explained the unusual circumstances of your induction to the team. By the look on your face, I can tell you are a little more than concerned. You can relax. This is not the military or the mafia. It's a job, and a good one, just not one you can quit."

He pauses, and waits for me to ask a question, but when I do not, he continues, "First things first, let's get you situated. We run on a twenty-four-hour time cycle here, based on United States east coast time, making it now three in the afternoon. There is time to get you a room and a shower before dinner."

"Dinner?" I stutter, "A shower?"

"Yes, and a real bed."

Illych pauses again to watch me, "I will warn you ahead of time. Some of the work here is ugly and dangerous. But overall, this is a rewarding place to be. If you are not careful, you will start to like it here. I know I do."

Illych leads me away from the open space by the doors. We walk past several buildings, and I catch glimpses of other people moving about their business. I recognize them as Held, Mike, and the muscular driver of the car, whom I guess is Tank.

Illych walks through an open doorway, into a

building serving as living quarters. Inside are desks, chairs, couches and other furniture spaced out around the room. There is even a sitting area with overstuffed couches and chairs. Along one wall are book shelves filled with books. Everything is neat, clean, and organized.

Doors along two walls open into single rooms, and inside the rooms are neatly made beds. Illych walks over to one of the doors and points inside while saying, "This is your room." The room has a bookshelf, desk and chair, a large chest at the foot of the bed, a small dresser, and a single bed. I would not say it is austere, as much as efficient. Perhaps, with time, it will grow on me.

"Let's get you to the showers and then some clean clothes." I follow him back out of the living quarters. Next door is a small, circular building, which Illych directs me to enter and shows me a set of private showers on an elevated platform. Hoses run to and from the shower setups out through a window like opening in the wall.

Noticing my interest in the hoses running outside, Illych comments, "There is all the hot water you want. This place does not have a natural water supply or a water treatment plant, though. Everything is brought in, and when something is used up, it must be taken out. You will learn more over the next few days. Go ahead and clean up. Personal hygiene stuff is in that cabinet over there. I am going to find some clean clothes for you. Expect me be back in maybe a half hour."

I grab one of everything. The shower operates

normally, and I go about cleaning up and feel better for it.

Illych walks in afterwards and hands me a green cloth bag. Inside is a pair of black combat boots and a full set of clothes, all in black.

"Put them on."

I look around for something that might give some privacy for dressing.

Illych shakes his head, "No need to worry about someone walking in on you, it's just us guys here." He then stands in the doorway, looking out while I dress. The boots and clothes are well-made, and everything fits and is comfortable.

As we walk back to the living quarters together, Illych has more to say, "This is how it works. We are typically on duty for Mr. Lark for 90 days and then off for a 30-day vacation. Time on and time off is the same for everyone. We are all here together for the same 90 days, and then this place is empty for 30 days.

"During the 30-day vacation, you can go anywhere in the world and do pretty much anything you want. We do get a paycheck, and it is more than enough for anything you want during your time off. All that is required is you don't draw attention to yourself, don't talk about what we do here, and when it's time to go back to work, show up healthy and rested."

Illych let that sink in for a bit as we arrive back at the living quarters. "During the 90 days, we do whatever task is given to us by Mr. Lark. Additionally, we train and maintain this place. I am working on the scheduling for your duties.

"You are the only person at the Citadel who is not ex-military. Every morning at 6am we all gather for calisthenics, weight training, and a run around the perimeter. Then, we split up for whatever our assigned chores are. Breakfast is at 8am. Lunch is at noon. Dinner is 6pm."

An image of us eating from cans pops into my head.

"How do the meals work?"

"Everything is brought in. We usually have three to four days of what are essentially catered meals on hand. The Citadel is not a place to leave organic matter lying around. Everything organic that comes in must go back out."

"How many of, I guess, us are there here?"

There is Held, Tank, Mike, you and me, for a total of five residents of the Citadel. Don't worry about being stuck here all the time. We spend most of our time in the real world. The Citadel is just a base of operations and a place to keep supplies."

"Can you give me an idea of what we do for Mr. Lark? He did not clue me in on much during the brief job interview," I ask.

"There aren't a lot of secrets here, Thomas. You can ask anything you want. You can tell anybody here anything. The exception is Mr. Lark. He will tell you what you need to know. You can ask him questions, but more likely than not, he will ignore you. As for what we do: we move things and/or people from place to place, sometimes we retrieve objects. We may provide security for short periods of time in some strange places. Never a dull moment," Illych smiles as he rattles off the services the organization provides.

I thought about what he just said, "Like smuggling?"

"It is one of the organization's sources of income. If someone or some people have enough money, you can arrange with Mr. Lark to move anything, from anywhere to anywhere. Hazards at the origination or destination are irrelevant. Customs and legal requirements ignored. All, I believe, for a very impressive fee." Illych does not speak like a man trapped here by Mr. Lark.

Since Illych is in a talkative mood, I decide to ask more questions. "How did I get here from London?"

"Mr. Lark has something called the *'ouiblet.'* It allows movement from point to point, anywhere in the world, pretty much instantaneously. I don't know how it works, and he never explained it. Mr. Lark controls it, but he also gives out what he calls a *'dongle'* that allows limited use of the *ouiblet.*

"Travelling between the stone circles is preferred. If the trip has both sides being an unprepared site, the experience can be pretty rough." Illych looks at his watch, a confusingly oversized contraption. "I have some things to do before dinner. Feel free to wander around. Stay out of any buildings you have not already been in. And here," he reaches into his left trousers pocket and pulls out the twin to the oversized watch on his own left wrist. "Put this on. It tells the local time here. You are from Europe, so you already understand 1800 is 6pm. Dinner time is at 1800. Wander around, and you will find the cafeteria. See you then." After handing me the watch, Illych walks away.

The watch is big, bulky, and about the size of a pack of cigarettes. The band is a synthetic material with the usual buckle and eye arrangement for fastening it to my wrist.

Studying its face reveals an unusual approach to displaying the time. The left of the face has thin, glowing, green vertical lines in rows. Based on, what I believe is, the current local time, the number of vertical lines arranged in four rows of six lines for hours. Circling these in a pattern similar to a starburst is an arrangement of amber lines representing minutes. On the right side of the watch face was a faint, amber light that pulses in second intervals. Looking at this Brobdingnagian creation on my wrist, I wonder why Illych did not give me something a little more normal.

I wander the Citadel for the next hour. Everything is well-lit by the big lights overhead. The place smells sterile and dry, almost metallic. There are no sounds, except the tap of my feet on the floor. The lights overhead do not even buzz. It is not just quiet; it is dead silent.

After taking note of the cafeteria as I pass it, I circle the entire complex. Then I begin weaving around in between the buildings, occasionally catching a glimpse of my fellow residents.

It is a big space for only five people. Returning to the cafeteria, my nose leads me for the last part. Whatever is for dinner appears to be a vast improvement to what I would have had back at my flat. Inside is a large table with comfortable looking chairs pulled up to it. The cooking area is separated by a wall from the rest of the cafeteria. Between the wall and the tables are glass cabinets with heat lamps in them. Everything is clean and neatly organized. The clash of pots and pans in the cooking area, as well as occasional human voices talking to each other, lets me know I am not alone.

I take a seat and wait. The terror of all the earlier events, combined with an hour of walking around has left me tired and hungry.

Depending on who shows up for dinner, I plan on asking questions, if the opportunity presents itself. Regardless, I am starving, and the smell of good food is almost too much.

At ten to six, Held and Illych walk in together. They see me and sit across from me at the table.

Illych says, "Did you walk around and check the place out?"

"I did, big place for five guys."

"We use a lot more of it than you might think."

The doors to the kitchen open, and Mike and Tank begin bringing out pans and trays of hot and cold food. There is a variety of meats and vegetable dishes. Everything looks fresh and inviting.

Serving is buffet-style, with no apparent order of who goes first. After filling a plate, I find myself sitting in the middle of the four other men.

Tank is talking with Held, "A ciorii in his home? That is nasty business. Did Mr. Lark let on why?"

Held replies, "Mr. Lark shared as much as he usually does. It was a short firefight, and Mr. Lark used Truestone to hold it in place until we destroyed it."

Tank looks at me, "What did you do that brought that nightmare to your home?"

I say, "I am not sure, but Mr. Lark thinks it had to do with a Djinn visiting me a few days earlier."

Tank whistles, "A Djinn? Whatever you did to get that things attention, don't do it again. Nothing involving Djinn ends well."

"Whatever it was I did, I've no plans to repeat it."

I lift my hand, showing the watch, "Ilych, why is this watch so large? I would be willing to accept something less… bulky."

Illych replies, "That's a watch and an alarm. One of the most dangerous weapons we can encounter is an EPS. That watch runs on light only. No batteries or electronics. Electronics have limited uses here at the Citadel.

"EPS effects are not instantaneous. They take about sixty seconds to get to the level where a person loses the ability to move. That watch will alarm the instant an EPS starts to take effect. It gives you time to react."

"Wouldn't I notice the effects when it starts?"

"I'm not a scientist. All I can tell you is what Mr. Lark has explained in the past. Every sense in the human body uses electricity to communicate to the brain. An EPS affects how electricity works. Right about the time you realize what's going on, it's too late and you can't move."

Tank says, "Kinda disturbing isn't it?" Held chuckles after Tank's comment.

I still do not fully understand the purpose of the watch, but it must be important if Illych requires it.

The rest of dinner is informative. Apparently, off-color joke telling is part of the meal ritual. They are a serious group that enjoys their downtime, and I am able to talk to everyone before dinner ends. Illych tells me I can walk around, go to bed, whatever, my choice. Nothing else is planned for the evening.

With a full belly and feeling exhausted, I retire to my room. Taking my boots off, I choose to sleep in my clothes. My last thoughts are that tomorrow cannot not be stranger than this long day has been.

■　　■　　■　　■　　■

I am awoken the next morning by a knock on the door. It is Held collecting me for morning calisthenics. In his hands is clothing appropriate for me to exercise in. Quickly dressing, I join the others, only surviving thirty minutes of stretching and calisthenics before my huffing and puffing gets me sent to the showers.

After breakfast, Illych takes me on a guided tour of the Citadel, filling in the blanks I missed on my self-guided tour the previous day.

After lunch, he takes me to the main doors. They open right when we arrive, and Mr. Lark walks in through them. Behind him is Mike, operating a powered cart hauling a number of wooden boxes.

Mr. Lark walks towards me, "Thomas, you won't be

able to return to your flat, so I took the liberty of having your personal effects boxed up and brought here, mostly books or meaningful personal property.

"Unfortunately, your cell phone and computer cannot be brought here. I have also arranged for the sale of your flat. The proceeds will be put in an account at a bank of your choosing."

After the events of the previous day, I had thought nothing more shocking could occur. I was wrong. The sale of my flat, my home, without my involvement, felt like something cold stabbing me in the chest. And how can someone else legally sell your home without your permission?

My emotions must have been visible, because Mr. Lark says, "With enough money, anything is possible, Thomas. Accept the situation, and appreciate that I have made an effort to protect your interests."

It is true. In the last week, Mr. Lark had saved me from the gunmen at the museum, the predations of a monster, and even refrained from killing me for being in the wrong place at the wrong time. Perhaps, it is best to look at it as a glass half-full situation.

Life is not fair, but this is a lot of unfairness in a short period of time.

Karl Lark continues, "Thomas, I have something for you to work on. I am going to give you another day to get situated, and then I will send instructions." Without so much as a goodbye, Mr. Lark turns to leave, walking alone out the Citadel doors.

CHAPTER SEVEN

Illych directs Mike to deliver my things to one of the buildings in the Citadel. This is to be the library, per Mr. Lark's instructions. The next day, shelves, desks, chairs, and all the things needed to setup the library arrive. From the way everything showed up and the level of organization, it is obvious Mr. Lark runs a tight ship. The setup is done quickly, competently and without complaint. I even got to help.

During lunch, I notice a white board in the cafeteria with the number 63 written on it. I ask Illych what it is, and he explains the white board displays how many days since their last break. Day 90 is the last day before they are off. Nodding, I realize day 61 was the day I arrived.

In a serious tone, he asks me to wait around after lunch, and I can tell from his body language that whatever it is, I probably won't like it. After the cafeteria cleanup is complete and only the two of us remain, he finally shares, "Thomas, you have been here long enough, it's time for you to see the Doctor."

I thought I had met everyone at the Citadel, "There is a doctor here?"

Illych grimaces a bit, "We have a doctor here. You haven't met it, because it is not human."

It? I feel that all too familiar feeling of cold dread that I am beginning to associate with everything Karl Lark. What nightmare am I about to be subjected to now?

Illych continues, "There is one of the Lesser Created within the bounds of the Citadel. It's in the infirmary, which wasn't part of our tour the other day. It's kept locked up; the Doctor isn't allowed out."

"I feel fine. Why should I see this doctor?"

"This isn't about illness or even having a physical taken. You are the only person here who has not had a crown installed yet. Your thoughts and emotions are being broadcast, and the Created can detect those better than hearing or seeing you. The Doctor is going to install a weave of something like fine copper wires in your scalp to prevent your broadcasting." Illych is obviously not comfortable with the subject.

"Maybe I am being overly melodramatic, but some creature is going to cut my head open and install something?" It comes out angrier than was perhaps prudent.

"The procedure is painless and there's no scarring or even recovery time for that matter. The Doctor is a Lesser Created, similar to what most call a goblin from mythology. Mr. Lark domesticated it to provide medical care. The thing can fix gunshot wounds, amputations, anything. The best part is you're unconscious during the procedure, and everything is healed when you're done. No stiches or bandages, and better yet, no recovery time."

"Regardless, the procedure is not optional. It's for your safety, as well as everyone around you. We'll go to the infirmary now." Illych spoke these words with absolute conviction. He expects to be obeyed.

Resigning myself to what is probably going to be another horrifying experience, we walk together in silence to one of the small buildings I had seen in my tour around the Citadel. Illych removes a key from his pocket and unlocks the door. Inside, is a small, for the want of a better description, waiting room. A gurney and some chairs along the walls. Opposite the entry door is another door. Next to that door at eye level is a shelf with a number of colored stones small enough to fit in the palm of your hand.

Once inside the waiting room, Illych explains, "This is how it works. The Doctor performs operations based on the stone chosen. A person who needs a crown installed takes the blue stone. A wounded person takes the red stone, etcetera. Then you lay down on the gurney. Once you are horizontal with one of the stones in your hand, you will instantly fall asleep. The Doctor comes out and wheels you into the next room. When the Doctor is done, he wheels you back out."

Illych pauses and then continues, "Never walk into the other room. It is not safe. The Doctor only works a certain way. Do you understand, Thomas? Never enter that room."

I nod. Yes, I will never enter the creepy monster lair.

"Now pick up the blue stone and lay down on the gurney".

Shrugging, I grab the blue stone from the shelf. It is cool to the touch and fits the palm of my hand comfortably. I then shuffle over to the gurney and lay down, closing my eyes, and wait.

Perhaps ten seconds have passed, and I open my eyes wondering when I will fall asleep or if this will be painful.

Illych is still standing by the entry door, but for some reason, he is now smiling. "That wasn't so bad, was it?"

I don't see what's so funny, "When does it start?"

Illych chuckles, "It's over. The Doctor came out to get you fifteen minutes ago. It just rolled you back out. You were unconscious the instant your head hit the pillow. I know it feels like it never even happened. It was like that for me my first time, too. Very convenient when you pile someone wounded and in pain on the gurney. Just put the red stone in their hand, and they're out."

It is only then that I notice the stone is gone from my hand. Getting up from the gurney, I feel around my head. Nothing seems different. There are no surgical openings or stitches. Nothing is tender to the touch. I still need to look at myself in the mirror, but from what I can tell, nothing has changed.

Illych comments, "The Doctor works fast and returns the patient in ready-for-duty condition. I don't know how Mr. Lark set this up, but as long as you're still alive when you make it to that gurney, you'll be as good as new in no time."

We leave the infirmary, and Illych tells me nothing else is planned for the rest of the day. Left to my own devices, I decide to organize the library and unpack the rest of my things. There is a comfort to be around things familiar, something that is mine. This takes the rest of my day.

■　　■　　■　　■　　■

On day 64, just after calisthenics, I watch Held and Tank gear up and head out to the Compass. They return with the cart stacked high with wooden crates.

Everything on the cart is delivered to the library. The shipment comes with instructions and an envelope with my name on it. The expectation is for me to organize and catalog the contents of the boxes, with the understanding there is more to come.

After everything is unloaded into the library, and feeling like a child receiving gifts, I begin unpacking the crate's precious contents. Carefully placed inside are books, tomes, codices, and folios from across the centuries. More time is need to confirm, but my initial opinion is everything is original. Midway into the experience, I open the envelope with my name on it. Inside are handwritten instructions from Mr. Lark:

Thomas,

Please review and analyze what I have sent you. They were acquired in a bulk purchase of old papers, documents and books. Most of it may be garbage, but there are drawings with a mark on them that is rare and not commonly known. The drawings came from the collection of a French diplomat posted to Romania in the early 1900's. His name is written in the corner of each of the drawings.

Apparently, Romania was not exciting from a diplomatic view, and he became involved in the study of Transylvania, looking for evidence of the supernatural. These drawings were in his Romanian collection with no explanation as to what they are or where they came from. I look forward to what your expertise develops from this.

Karl Lark

I now have a project to work on. It starts with the several oddly shaped parchment drawings mentioned in Mr. Lark's letter, along with two modern books. They share a common subject: the myths and mysteries of a haunted forest in Romania.

I have never heard of Hoia-Baciu forest. Apparently, Hoia forest, as it was commonly called, is claimed to be the "most haunted forest in the world." It is more likely such claims are rooted in an attempt to increase tourism, rather than reality. However, considering my recent experiences, anything is possible. Since Mr. Lark took the time to bring all this to my attention, I will give my best effort in reporting on them.

Spending the rest of the day, well into the night, and then all the next day studying the books and drawings, I begin to hand draw copies of the drawings as a way of better familiarizing myself with them. As I have done many times in the past, I immerse myself in study. Hours and then days slip away, and I feel insight beginning to form.

My investigations finally bring fruit, and now I have something to report. Gathering my thoughts about my conclusions, I leave the library and search for Illych, finding him not far away, walking past on an errand.

"They're maps! What Mr. Lark sent me; I believe they're maps of Hoia forest!" So excited, I just blurt it out. Illych, obviously concentrating on some mental task, is startled by my sudden outburst, causing him to stop and look at me.

Frowning, he says, "Thomas, Mr. Lark didn't clue me in on what was delivered to you. So, I have no idea what you are talking about".

"I thought you're in charge here and Mr. Lark would have told you what I am doing?"

Illych looks annoyed, "That's not how it works. I believe Mr. Lark considers me the most senior person here. That level of experience means he comes to me with things more than the others, but he's never formally put me in charge. As to your role here, all I've been told is to support you. Within reason."

"Understood. There was a letter from Mr. Lark asking me to review some old drawings and to come back to him with comments. That's what I have been working on in the library. Now I think I have something. How do I contact Mr. Lark?"

Illych looks interested, "I can do that. I have a way to contact Mr. Lark from here. What did you find?"

Taking a moment to breathe and calm myself, my excitement subsiding below histrionic. Also realizing others may not find this discovery as stimulating. "I was copying the drawings as part of studying them. I then realized that three of the drawings had similar markings in certain locations. If I matched up those markings and redrew what was inside them, combining all three in one drawing, they appear to form a map of Hoia forest in Romania.

"There are places marked out in the compiled map. I matched what I drew to a map in one of the modern history books of Hoia forest. Some things have changed, but I am fairly sure it is a valid map."

Illych nods, "Getting a message to Mr. Lark is easy enough. Just so you understand, we're here at his convenience. He may respond or he may not."

There is no problem accepting either of those possibilities. There is plenty for me to study in the library. In the end, it is just an old map with markings on it. None of my research indicates what the points on the map are. A map with details having no direct interpretation as to their value is probably not a priority.

■　　■　　■　　■　　■

A reply from Mr. Lark is not long in coming. Later that afternoon, a team returns from the Compass with letters for both Illych and me.

The letter to me is short:

Thomas,

Excellent work. I suspected those drawings might have additional meaning. I observed them with the oculus, and I could tell they had been touched by something.

I have directed Illych to form a two-man team to accompany you to Hoia forest. Visit each of the locations that the map indicates as unique. The team will have an oculus, and its operator will let you know what he finds with it. Do not engage any locals or leave anything behind. Write up a report upon your return and give it to Illych to send to me.

Karl Lark

Surprisingly, Mr. Lark is sending me to the places on the map. I will actually be going to a strange forest in Romania. During my studies, it never occurred to me that Mr. Lark would have me go in the field. What if there were ciorii, or something like ciorii, in that forest? Or worse than a ciorii? Is that even possible?

This line of thinking brings me to the edge of the beginnings of a panic attack. I love books and reading about strange places, but I have never pictured myself an explorer. Right about the time I am getting to hyperventilation stage, there is a knock at the library door. Unable to stand, I squeak out, "Come in".

Illych pokes his head in the door. "Everything ok?"

Speaking is a challenge right now, but I manage to squeak out, "Feeling a little tense about going to Romania is all. Give me a few moments."

Illych waits patiently for a few minutes, watching me visibly decompress. When my emotional state drops below critical, he says, "Mr. Lark sent me a letter also. It gives instructions to put together a two-person team to accompany you to this forest in Romania. Observe and return only.

"I am sending Held and Mike with you. It's too late today and Romania is seven hours ahead of us in time, so plan on going late tomorrow. This will give you plenty of time to prepare for a walk in the woods."

Nodding in acceptance "We start getting ready after the morning exercise?" If there is one thing I learned in the last few days, these ex-military guys love to exercise.

Illych smiles, "No workout tomorrow for you, Held, or Mike. You'll be getting plenty of exercise on your hike in the woods."

Illych leaves, and I am alone again in the library. The rest of the evening is uneventful, but I do not sleep well that night, waking up several times feeling anxious about the next day's trip.

In the morning, I shuffle my way to the cafeteria for breakfast. Americans are not partial to tea and there is none to be had at the Citadel. My caffeinated options are coffee or nothing. The upside is the coffee is fantastic and available in the cafeteria anytime of the day. I pour myself the first of, what I am sure will be several, to get my day started.

Held and Tank are also in the cafeteria when I arrive. Taking my coffee, I do the sociable thing and sit by them. The residents of the Citadel are a relatively friendly group that enjoy mealtime camaraderie. This morning is no different.

Tank's extroverted behavior is overpowering and

almost too much for my comfort level. Not having the stories or experiences to draw from that power the mealtime conversations, I gravitate towards sitting at the edge of the group when they are all together.

Today is not a typical day though, I am feeling inquisitive, "Held, how long have you been here with Karl Lark?"

Held does not answer right away, and I wonder if the question is impertinent, "Bad question?"

"No, not a bad question. Everyone here has a story that leads them to this place. None of them are pleasant stories. Tank here's is especially horrifying. I've been in the service of Mr. Lark for just over three years. Ilych has been here the longest at eight years. He remembers the early days, even before the Citadel."

Held continues, "I know your story, Thomas, so it's only fair if you know mine. It started when I was wounded in combat while I was a Green Beret. Head wound, major loss of vision in my left eye and permanent brain damage that basically left me angry all the time."

What Held is saying makes no sense. The man at the table is a mild-mannered guy. I see no facial scars or any evidence of such an injury.

"I was given a medical discharge. I started getting into trouble right away. Fist fights, couldn't hold a job, my family disowned me. I refused to take the meds for my condition, or visit a VA hospital. Homeless, and drifting from one shelter to the next, after being kicked out of each one in turn for fighting. I was in a bad way that was going to end with me in prison or dead. Then Karl Lark picks me up saying he had work for me." Held looks wistful as he says this.

"Illych was already with Mr. Lark then, and they drove me out of the city I was in at the time to an isolated park."

He says, "They had picked up fast food for me, and at that point in my life, hot food and a full belly did not happen often. More than enough to make me willing to go anywhere with them. Once we were out in the middle of nowhere, we stopped and got out of the car. Illych pulls out a pistol, and Mr. Lark made his pitch." Held is reliving the experience and not enjoying the telling of it.

"I almost told Mr. Lark to shove it, but some little voice in my head I do not remember ever hearing before told me to take the job. This would be my last chance. So, I drank the Kool-Aid and joined, it has been an adventure ever since."

"Wait, what about the head injury? You don't exhibit any symptoms of what you said was going on."

"Mr. Lark and Illych brought me here to the Citadel and took me directly to the infirmary and handed me the red stone. When I awoke, I realized I had full vision in my left eye and full control of my faculties, like before my injury. The doctor fixed me."

I had to ask, "Is Mr. Lark serious about his join or die speech? When he presented it to me, I took him to be dead serious at the time. But since then, I have had my doubts. Mr. Lark seems like a serious person, but I don't get a 'murderer' vibe from him. Not that I have much experience with people being killed."

"Thomas, if you cross Karl Lark or try to renege on your agreement with him, Mr. Lark will kill you on the spot. Have no doubts about it. I had been here a little over a year when a new guy was brought in. He made it to his third cycle and wanted out. Apparently, he missed life in the outside world."

"Mr. Lark told us to get ready for a mission. This guy then decides to spring his rebellion. He started in on Mr. Lark in front of everyone. He had had enough of this organization and demanded to be taken back to the real world. Sprinkle in some profanity, and you will have a pretty good picture of the scene."

Held takes a breath and continues, "Mr. Lark gets this Cheshire cat grin on his face. Almost ear-to-ear, I swear. He moved, and I mean moved and fast, slapping the guy in the chest. It was like the guy went instantly drunk. He tries punching Mr. Lark with a clumsy, slow haymaker with no luck.

"Mr. Lark then grabbed the guy by the back of his collar while still facing him and effortlessly dragged the guy to the gate doors. The doors open as usual, and Mr. Lark hauls the guy out past the guardians, maybe fifty feet down the road, and then pushes him a good distance more down the road.

"He turns and walks back into the Citadel, leaving the new guy out on the road. I was looking through the gate at the lone figure just as Mr. Lark walks back in past the guardians. Something rushes from the side of the road like a flash and disappears out the other side. Just like that, the guy Karl Lark tossed out was gone.

"When Mr. Lark came back in, the Cheshire cat grin is gone, and we continue on the mission as planned. No mention was made of what had just happened. So, believe me when I tell you, don't challenge Mr. Lark. You will not survive his response."

Considering what I had just heard, I say "Thank you for that, it explains a lot." Note to self: quitting is suicide.

Held hesitates for a moment, obviously considering something, and then says, "Thomas, one last thing, I have learned over the last three years that Mr. Lark is not what he looks like. Never underestimate him."

The normally talkative Tank has been silent through all this and makes no comment at the end of Held's story. My guess is asking him about his induction is something to be discussed another time.

Held, Tank and I sit in silence for a while, finishing our breakfast. Mike walks into the cafeteria, fills up a tray, and sits next to us.

"What do you think, Held? Tonight? A walk in the park, or will it all go horribly wrong?"

"Rules of engagement are straight-forward. Observe only. First sign of anything we're out of there."

"You get the *oculus* and the *dongle*?"

"Yes, I did."

My ears perk up at the strange terminology, "*Dongle*? What is a *dongle*?"

Held clues me in, "When we get to the Compass, there will be a *dongle* waiting. It will be a small brass baton, maybe six inches long. You stand in the middle of the Compass and unscrew the two parts from each other and flip them around and screw the previously open ends back together. Everyone in the Compass stone circle, along with their possessions, will be translated to wherever the *dongle* is set for.

"To return to the Compass, you reverse the *dongle* again. You can be anywhere, not just your arrival point, and it will still return you to the Compass. Mr. Lark sets them up and leaves them at the Compass, with a note about where we will arrive."

"Illych explained some of this. This *ouiblet* provides teleportation."

"The *ouiblet* provides something like teleportation. And don't ask me what the word *ouiblet* means, I don't know. It allows the moving of people and things between two points anywhere. It has to be set up first. It's not like in science fiction where they lock onto your location and beam you up. Mr. Lark sets up the *dongle*s to move a person, a group of people, or the contents of a shipping container from one place to another."

"That is unbelievable. I experienced it coming here from London, but I thought it was some sort of magic trick."

Held shrugs, "Perhaps it is magic, I don't know. The batons can be a one-way only version or a returning version which lets you travel to a place and then, when reversed back to the original position, returns you to another location."

"The stone circles with the circular copper bars are setup to make the trip less physically agonizing. If the origination or destination is a stone circle setup by Mr. Lark, the trip is unpleasant and disorienting. Movement from an unprepared origination to an unprepared destination will leave you unable to function for at least a minute afterwards. This is why most movement starts or ends here at the Compass."

"Good to know. When do we leave?" I ask.

"Now," Held says, with Mike nodding his head in agreement.

CHAPTER EIGHT

It turns out to be not exactly now. There are some preparations to be made.

From when we leave the cafeteria after breakfast until we return for dinner, the three of us engage in continuous preparations. Held directs me to get dressed into the black tactical uniform everyone else wears. A bulletproof chest carapace tightly fitted to me, with pockets, straps, and hooks for an assortment of equipment strategically located on it. Filling those locations: high illumination tactical LED flashlights, water bottles, flash bang and smoke grenades, a pair of tasers, and much more.

The armory includes a long hall with ballistic targets at one end. Held selects a customized handgun chambered for 45ACP, six magazines and ammunition. These details are shared when Held subsequently instructs me in the basics of hand gun operation.

For the first time in my life, I fire a handgun, and it is exhilarating. Pulling the trigger for the first time is frightening. After that first shot, though, it became one of the most amazing experiences of my life. Held coaches me past my inexperience with proper safety and weapon handling. The goal, he says, is not to make me into a marksman in one day. It is more so I can reasonably defend myself in a pinch.

The goal, apparently, is to fire the weapon while keeping my eyes open. I think he is mad to ask such a thing. Who could possibly not close their eyes when the cannon in their hands is going off?

But I was able to do it. By the end of the second magazine, my eyes stayed open. The practice had me firing almost a hundred rounds. Held explains how the movies show someone with a handgun picking off long-range targets one-handed, while barely aiming, is crap. By the third magazine, the best I can do is hit a one-foot grouping ten feet away.

It was a lot to absorb in an hour. Held counsels me to keep the weapon in its holster unless absolutely necessary. How I didn't have the training to properly use it in a fire fight, but it wasn't right to leave me defenseless.

Our team reassembles afterwards. The plan is to translate into Hoia forest in the dead of night. The four locations identified on the map made a parallelogram shape within the forest limits. Giving an hour for each point, both walking and observation, will see the team translate out just after dawn.

Held and Mike have space-age looking rifles. They also each carry in a shoulder rig one of the customized pistols matching my own. Their carapace chest armor sporting plenty of spare magazines.

Held and Mike's hands, faces, and necks are painted pitch-black, and they assist me in achieving the same.

The final piece of gear is a padded helmet. They warn me these are not bulletproof, just padded against hitting your head. Dangling on each side are ear inserts. The helmet contains multiple microphones that amplify quiet sounds and diminish loud noises. They would prevent our hearing from being knocked out from gunfire. Very quiet sounds, like someone sneaking up on you, are amplified. Normally a team member goes through special training to be able to interpret the sound distortions properly. Due to time constraints, I will undergo the training some other time, assuming I survive. For now, I was to wing it.

Dinner happens while in full gear. We eat quickly and head out for the Compass. Illych accompanies us, sharing that he plans to remain at the Compass while we are gone.

Just before going out the Citadel doors and onto the road to the Compass, a change happens to my teammates. The small talk is gone, and they exude alertness, weapons at the ready.

With a nod, we walk towards the Citadel doors,

which silently open in anticipation. The four of us step onto the road to the compass, my colleagues setting a quick pace.

During our silent march, I check out my colleagues' gear. They have some extra items I do not. Held and Mike both have a rectangular box, slightly larger than a pack of cigarettes, in a pouch on their chests. Curiosity gets the best of me, and I ask while pointing, "What is in those pouches?" Held answers, "This is a COMDAT. We will be in continuous audio communication with Illych throughout the mission."

Upon arriving at the stone circle, Illych retrieves the *dongle* for the mission from one of the vaults.

"Mr. Lark has already surveilled the arrival point. His note says it is remote and has overhead tree cover. Highly unlikely anything will be nearby at 0200 local time." He then hands Held a *dongle*.

Joining Held and Mike in the center of the stone circle, I wait in anticipation of what comes next. Illych steps outside and says, "Don't break the new guy. Mr. Lark would be disappointed."

Held nods and unscrews the middle of the *dongle*. He flips the outside ends to the inside and screws them together.

There is no warning. The instant the two ends of the *dongle* reconnect, the dimness of the Compass disappears into complete and utter blackness. Then I feel a warm summer breeze. We have arrived in the middle of a group of trees. I look up and see a few stars peeking through the tree canopy overhead

My stomach churns, lasting for perhaps a minute. While this is happening, I do not pay much attention to anything around me.

Mike watches me work through my discomfort, "I feel it too. You never get used to it. But you will get better at anticipating and handling it, though."

After recovering, I look around and realize that in addition to the darkness from the tree cover, the quiet ads to the spooky ambience. There is the occasional insect noise, but the silence is noticeable.

Held is standing still, looking like he is meditating with his eyes closed. I look at Mike and then back to Held.

Mike says, "He is using the *oculus*."

After a long pause, Held's eyes open. "There are no people anywhere in the forest and no electronic observation devices. However, I picked up a significant amount of background hash."

Even in the dark, Mike can see the question on my face. "Hash is like background noise or static. It means at least one of the Created has been here recently. It may have just popped its head out and left, or it could be walking around."

Held says, "I did not see anything walking around, but there has definitely been some activity in this forest."

The fact that he doesn't currently see anything does nothing to reduce my anxiety. It just means that whenever whatever it is decides to come after us, it will be more of a surprise.

"Let's get our bearings. That way is north," Held

says, pointing one way through the trees.

The map I took from one of the books shows a boulder field in that direction.

"The *oculus* is telling me it is over there. Let's go there first and confirm. With that as a reference point, we can move to the first point on the map," Held says this while beginning to walk in a northerly direction.

As we start walking, I see Mike and Held insert the ear pieces from their microphone helmets. I do the same. The effect is startling. I could hear the sound of our boots on the soft ground almost as loud as if we were on gravel. The sound of my colleagues' breathing is noticeable. They are right; sneaking up on someone wearing one of these helmets would be impossible.

It is tough going, with uneven ground, tree roots, and stones to trip on if you are not careful. Held and Mike occasionally slow down and let me catch up, careful to never let me drift too far behind them.

Between the darkness and the silence, the forest gives off a feeling of us not being welcome with increasing anxiety, confusing my thoughts.

"Do you feel it?" Held whispers to Mike and me, "The anxiety." Mike nods, as do I. I whisper back, "I thought it was just me."

"Something has the mental 'go away' sign out," Mike answers. "The crown the Doctor installed is keeping most of it out. We feel it faintly. An unprotected person would most likely run away."

Perhaps a minute later we reach the edge of the boulder field. Held whispers, "Stop here. We aren't going into that field.".

Mike says, "What do you see?"

"Hard to say, but it looks like a flip-trap. It also looks like the source of the anxiety effects."

"That's an odd combination: stay out or I will keep you?" Mike says while scanning his eyes over the little bit of boulder field visible in the dark.

Held shakes his head, "More like: *'stay out'* and if you *do not listen and come in anyway, you won't leave after seeing what's here.*"

"Now that we have our bearings, let's move to the closest objective. Should be that way," Held points away from the boulder field.

The walking is easier in this new direction. And there is a bonus, as the feeling of anxiety decreases the further from the boulder field we travel. Motivated by this to move faster, soon the sensation is gone.

The first point on the map is a large stone sphere half buried in a hill. Parts have been chipped off and a large crack is visible. Held reports the *oculus* shows nothing of interest. My teammates agree to allow me to turn on an LED torch. Using the light to inspect closely, I find nothing that can't be explained by time and erosion.

"I don't see anything of interest here. Perhaps we should move to the next point on the map?"

Held and Mike have taken up positions on opposite sides of the sphere. They focus their eyes away from the light in my hands, so as not to disturb their night vision. Held shrugs at my comment and says, "Let's move on to the next feature on the map, then."

The three of us head into a more dense and overgrown part of the forest. The trees are closer together and strangely shaped. Some of them have ninety-degree angles in their trunks that is most unnatural to view. They are not tall at all, no more than twenty to thirty feet to their tops. The closeness of the overhead leaf canopy and the trees with respect to each other, combined with the dark and almost complete silence, is claustrophobic, like being trapped in a cave.

My colleagues silently observe the strangeness of this part of Hoia forest. On the walk to the field of boulders and the first map point, they hold their weapons with one hand and pointed down, partially supported by their gear harness. Since entering this dense part of the forest, both men are weapons at the ready. Walking slower than before, and spacing themselves away from each other. Held in front and Mike to the rear of our three-man column.

Fortunately, the ground under the trees is fairly even, with almost no undergrowth to contend with. Despite the easy going, the travel time to the next map point is almost an hour. Held stops us at regular intervals and concentrates on the *oculus*, significantly slowing our progress.

We find the second point on the map easily enough. A collection of oddly shaped stones strewn about. Some parts of the stones appear whole and weather-worn, while others look to have been broken before exposure to the elements. Held and Mike again relent to my using the torch.

Taking a notebook out of my pack, I start taking notes and making sketches. Photographs would be quicker, but I like my amateur archeology hands-on.

Unlike the stone sphere, there is more to be observed at this collection of stones. After making a rough sketch of their positions, shapes, and sizes, I become aware there is a central stone, and the other stones radiate outward from it.

The separate pieces appear to have been a single, somewhat square-shaped stone structure that had fallen apart, or more likely, was blown apart in all directions. There is no way to figure out the original structure in the dark, even with the torch. Still, I am fairly sure it was originally man-made due to the flat surfaces exhibited on some of the stones.

Regardless, I have reached the limit of what can be recorded under the circumstances. I am also not seeing a good reason to study any further what is essentially a rockpile. There is nothing here.

Indicating to Mike and Held we can move on, we do so. The path to our next destination stays in the same dense area of the forest, and the next point is an easy walk. The feature we are seeking turns out to be a clearing or meadow. I read about this clearing in the modern books provided by Mr. Lark describing Hoia Forest. It is a curious circular meadow in the middle of the forest. Trees don't grow here, just grass. Over the years, locals had claimed to see strange things appear in this place. Balls of light and difficult to explain phenomena manifesting. Disappearances are also associated with the meadow, which probably explains how this forest is completely devoid of any human presence on a warm summer night, despite being close to a population center.

As we near the edge of the clearing, Held lifts his left hand with a closed fist. I know this means to stop and do so. Mike pauses for a moment, and then when Held waves his fingers, he hustles to Held.

"What do you see?"

"There has been hash on the *oculus* since we arrived, and I think the source is up ahead. I did not see anything ahead until the last fifty feet. Something is in the clearing, and the *oculus* is having a hard time making it out. Now that we are closer, I can tell something is moving," Held's voice is calm and low as he explains the situation.

Mike says, "Our instructions are clear. Let's retreat about a hundred meters and use the *dongle* to bug out to the Compass."

"Agreed."

Both men keep their weapons pointed towards the clearing and begin slowly backing away. I follow their lead and begin walking away also.

We had not retreated four steps when there is a rustling sound coming from the edge of the clearing nearest us. In the silent night air, the soft sound is amplified by our earpieces into a crashing noise that cannot be missed. Held and Mike freeze in place. I don't need to consciously stop moving, having already frozen from fear. It is beyond my imagining what could cause two experienced, armed soldiers to be so cautious.

Held and Mike focus on the origin of the sound and point their weapons in that direction. They had been standing next to each other and now begin to very slowly put some space between themselves.

The rustling stops for a few seconds and then starts again. It is definitely getting closer. The dark inside the forest edge preventing us from being able to see what it is. I think to myself: *We are probably getting tense over some forest rodent.*

Held is concentrating on the *oculus* while he and Mike continue to space themselves out and move away from the clearing.

Held barks out, "Faerie! Only thirty feet away! It has seen us!" Both men begin walking backward quickly while keeping between me and whatever a faerie is.

From a frighteningly close distance, a high keening cry cuts through the still night air. I can't see where or what is the source.

Mike sees it first and opens fire. Scarcely had the first shot been fired, and then Held opens fire. I see it last. A three-foot tall, gangly creature runs straight at Held with unnatural quickness. They get off two or three shots before the faerie tackles Held. Whatever the thing is made of, it is strong and heavy, because Held is knocked right off his feet.

Mike is forced to stop shooting due to the closeness of the thing to Held. Letting his weapon dangle from his harness, he draws a handgun from a holster on his belt.

In an instant, the faerie beats Held unconscious, grabs him by his left foot, and starts dragging him away, almost as fast as it had attacked. Mike tries to keep up while carefully taking shots. The faerie and Held disappear into the darkness and out of sight into the clearing.

Mike and I are now standing a few feet into the clearing. Mike pauses, swaps a fresh magazine into his pistol, holsters it, and takes up his carbine while saying, "Let's go get Held!"

I am speechless; everything is happening so fast. To my astonishment, I find my handgun in my right hand. When did I draw that? Looking closely, I realize the safety is still on and decide it won't work like that, so I give the little lever a flick.

Mike reloads his carbine and charges into the clearing, following the trail of bent grass left by the faerie dragging Held. Mike is almost jogging in pursuit while keeping his carbine pointed straight ahead.

A small glowing sphere, about a foot in diameter, appears ahead. "It is opening a portal!" The light from the glowing sphere lights up the clearing, showing Mike and me we are only a few paces from the faerie. The creature is facing the sphere and making guttural sounds while waving its spindly arms in an undecipherable pattern.

Mike opens fire at the short creature, even with Held lying flat on the ground nearby. Mike's shots are in quick succession, but not fully automatic. The faerie's body jerks from the impacts, interrupting whatever it is doing.

The shooting continues, slowing the faerie's efforts.

When Mike is forced to reload, the faerie has enough time to complete the opening of the portal. It grabs Held's ankle again and sprints towards the sphere. The faerie and Held just disappear. Mike pulls something from his belt and tosses it to me. It is a small, white pebble or stone. "We are following it through the portal. When we get within ten feet of the Faerie, throw that at it. It's Truestone and will paralyze it for at least fifteen seconds. Hopefully, I can then put it down more permanently." Mike turns to the glowing sphere and runs towards it. I find myself following close behind Mike while gripping the stone tightly.

He runs into the sphere and disappears, same as the faerie. Less than two strides behind him, my last thought before everything changes: *Is this going to hurt?*

I did not close my eyes when entering the portal, and I witnessed the shift from a glowing sphere in a meadow to a dimly lit cave. The portal delivers us to an open space with a relatively flat floor in the middle of what, for a lack of a better description, could be called a cavern.

The faerie is a mere handful of strides ahead of us, still dragging the unconscious Held by his ankle. It turns and takes note of our following it. The thing's mouth open, emitting that high keening cry, reverberating from the chamber walls as a horrifying cacophony.

Mike switches his carbine to full auto and empties

the weapon into the Faerie at close range. The noise would have been deafening in the enclosed space if it were not for the earpieces. Mike must have hit more than he missed because the Faerie is moving away slowly, stumbling as it goes. I sprint towards the creature. Feeling close enough, I throw the white stone at it.

Everything is happening so fast, and I cannot believe I am moving, much less actively participating.

My lifelong avoidance of all things sport-related is on display for all to see in my throwing of the Truestone. The stone is going to miss the Faerie to its left by several feet.

In the end, it does not matter, the stone self-corrects its trajectory, accelerating across the short distance to the faerie, striking it mid-chest. The effect is surprising as it flops onto the floor, convulsing in a fashion eerily similar to the ciorii back at my apartment.

Mike reloads while this is happening and unloads another full magazine at point-blank range on full auto. He then produces a white spike from a sheath mounted on his chest armor and promptly stabs the monster where the light from the Truestone is gleaming. The faerie shrieks again and goes limp.

Mike reloads again and attaches a high-powered LED torch to the carbine and starts sweeping it around the cavern. While doing this, he walks to Held's motionless form on the floor.

After two full rotations sweeping the cavern walls and ceiling, he kneels next to Held. Using a low power penlight, he pulls up Held's left eyelid and flashes it with the light. Then he puts his ear to his mouth, followed by fingers to his neck.

"He's alive."

Mike removes the *dongle* from Held's pocket and puts it in his own pocket. He then begins lightly shaking Held, "Wake up, can you hear me?" After a minute of this, Held's eyes open, and he looks around.

Mike smiles, "Still with us?"

Held groans, "I have a splitting headache." He tries to sit up and stops while making a very un-manly whimper noise. He relaxes back down saying, "Cracked or broken ribs. Give me a minute, and I should be able to stand up."

Mike looks at me. "The portal is closed by now, but the *dongle* will take us back to the Compass, anyway. Since nothing is trying to kill us, my guess is there was only the one faerie living here. Let's take a couple of minutes to look around, and then we're out of here."

I pull out my torch and look around. I had gotten a look while Mike was checking around earlier, but now I can really inspect my surroundings. The floor, walls, and ceiling were all worn, rough grey stone. The cavern is bigger than your typical single-family home. Fortunately, nothing is moving either. Curiously, there are what looks like snow drifts lying about the cavern, in no apparent pattern. But the air temperature is warm, not much different than what it was back in the forest, so snow shouldn't be here. I walk to the closest snow drift to figure it out.

It is not snow; they are bones, artfully stacked and woven into piles reminiscent of snow drifts or foam-covered ocean waves. Looking more closely, I see most of the bones appear to be animal, but there also are human skulls woven into the bone sculpture. The ghoulish artwork is repulsive. Nonetheless, it is skillfully done.

Looking about the cavern reveals an even dozen such bone works. That is a lot of dead animals and dead people.

I call out to Mike, "These are piles of bones, animal and human. The bones have been woven together almost like artwork. It took a lot of victims and a lot of time to do this."

Mike is helping Held to his feet and replies, "These things have nothing but time. Look around some more. Sometimes these things collect artifacts."

Unsheathing a knife from my belt, I poke through the first bone drift, finding bits of cloth from what looks like clothing woven into the drift. Finally, I just give the bone weave a kick to get at whatever is underneath it. Like the hood of a car being flipped open, the sheath of woven bones hinges up and over, exposing a trash pile.

Underneath is more deteriorated clothing. Some of it appears to be quite old. The only object with apparent usefulness is an old broadsword. The blade rusty and pitted, but possibly still serviceable.

Looking at the other bone constructs, an idea forms. I walk to the next bone drift, kicking the woven top away, just like the first one, and find the situation similar. This one contains clothing, for the most part, and a carved wooden walking stick. Walking quickly to each drift in turn, and kicking away the bone shroud covering reveals a piled center containing different objects. In addition to the sword, I discover two large wooden bowls overflowing with silver and gold coins and a few gold rings mixed in. In one of the piles is a leather case I did not want to take the time to open here.

The inspection of the bone-covered piles ends with the sword, the two wooden bowls and their contents, and the leather case, in the center of the cavern, near the now smoking and sublimating body of the deceased faerie. Mike looks at the pile of loot, "That's enough. We need to get Held to the Doctor, so let's boogie." Between the three of us, we pack everything in our rucksacks. Mike then pulled the *dongle* from his pocket, and with Held still leaning against him, he unscrews it, flipping the now separate pieces, and screws them together. Watching this, I brace for what I know comes next. Everything goes black, and we are back in the gloom and cold of the stone circle at the Compass.

Shivering in the sudden cold, I tough out my nausea. Mike and Held look relieved, and I kind of feel the same way. The stress of the last hours begins to bleed away, and I find myself glad to be home? I guess it is one of those "the Devil you know" things.

How things have changed in less than two weeks. The first time I arrived at the Compass, I was disoriented and wanted to go home. Now, I had just come back from a haunted forest in Romania after being attacked by something out of a fairy-tale horror story and am glad to be back at this place.

Perhaps this is a side effect of the environment? Can too much time in a pocket dimension cause mental illness?

Held shuffles over to one of the stone pillars that makes up the perimeter of the circle and leans against it. Mike leaves the circle and disappears into one of the surrounding vaults, reappearing with Illych who inspects Held closely with an *oculus*.

"He can travel. Looks like a concussion or skull fracture, and bruised and broken ribs. He needs to get to the Doctor. Mike, you're in front. Thomas, you walk next to him. Everyone, weapons out. We don't want anything along the way thinking our injured comrade is an opportunity."

Held keeps a good pace in spite of his injuries. We are back at the Citadel and inside the doors in no more than thirty minutes. During the walk back, I realize there are no urges to look up or to the sides of the road. The crown thing that the Doctor put in my head apparently works.

As the Citadel main doors close behind us, Held sinks to his knees and put his hands, palms down, on the ground. Illych and Mike each grab him under an arm, lift him up, and carry him off towards the infirmary.

Standing alone in the open area near the doors, the weight of my pack reminds me what I am carrying. Inside is the leather case from the faerie cavern. Carrying the pack, I follow after the others on the way to the infirmary.

I enter just as Illych puts the red stone in one of Held's hands. Held's body goes still and appears to be sleeping. Mike and Illych step back towards the entry door almost to the point of pressing their backs to the wall. The infirmary's inner door opens, and a creature not more than four-and-a-half-feet tall walks into the infirmary waiting area. It is gangly with thin arms and legs. An oblong head with large pointy ears and large solid black eyes. The goblin's steam shovel mouth is wide, with jagged teeth peeking out from between its thin lips at odd angles. Its greenish skin contrasts with the ill-fitting, faded, red coveralls it wears. The overall effect is of a homeless child, except, of course, for the green skin and scary looking head and eyes.

The Doctor makes no indication it is aware of our presence. It walks to the far side of the gurney; its movements automaton-like. Grasping the gurney push handle, it maneuvers it slowly into the open doorway leading inside.

The unnaturalness of the Doctor is repellent. Only an act of will keeps me from bolting from this place.

Once the Doctor and Held disappear inside the blackness of its lair, the inner door appears to close on its own.

"That is the Doctor? It is almost as scary as the ciorii I saw back at my flat." To think that thing rolled me into that back room and did whatever to me.

Illych nods, "That's the Doctor. Creepiest thing I've been around more than once, but it has saved all of our lives at one point or another."

"How long will Held be in there?"

Mike says, "Not long, maybe fifteen minutes."

On the floor is the pile of gear Illych and Mike stripped from Held before putting him on the gurney. Illych grabs the pack, and Mike picks up the carbine, carapace body armor, and gear harness.

Illych indicates for me to grab some of the pile, "Let's get these back to the armory and get everything cleaned up."

This is an opportunity for an important Citadel lesson: no matter how tired or hungry you are, the first thing you do upon returning from a mission is clean weapons, unload magazines, and get everything back into a ready state. Illych even put Held's *oculus* in a rack with several more of the same devices.

An hour of cleaning, inspecting, and putting everything away adds to my exhaustion. The three of us trudge to the cafeteria. The last couple of weeks of calisthenics have boosted my physical endurance, but functioning while sleep-deprived has never been one of my skill sets.

In spite of their excellent physical condition and military experience, the lack of sleep can be seen on Illych's and Mike's faces.

At the cafeteria, we find Held waiting for us. While we were cleaning and inventorying our gear, he was brewing some of that excellent coffee I had come to appreciate. He had also brought out a plate of sandwiches. And not cheap vending machine sandwiches. The bread smells fresh, the sliced meat is excellent, as are the lettuce and tomatoes. We grab plates and mugs, fill them, and take our places at the table near Held to eat our sandwiches and sip our coffee.

No one says anything at first, then Mike goes first, "You're looking pretty spry for a guy who recently almost had his head caved in."

"I feel great, just hungry. I woke up in the waiting room and figured you guys were busy putting everything away, so I came here and started work on the really important stuff."

Held asks about the loot we had brought back. Illych explains everything is in the armory until Mr. Lark has time to look at it.

"That reminds me, I need to report in to Mr. Lark. There was no time at the Compass," Illych excuses himself, stands up, takes his coffee and sandwich, and leaves.

Looking at Held, I ask, "Is it always this exciting going on a mission?"

Held shakes his head, "That's the thing. It's never like this. Faeries are as rare as chicken's teeth to begin with. Finding one out in the open like that never happens. They're typically tied to geographical locations. They live in caverns like the one we saw. But the connection from the real world to their lair happens only once in a while. Once every seven years is common for some reason. Some connections are random but still spaced out by years."

"The chances of stumbling into a faerie circle while

the faerie is active is pretty small. Looking at the piles of bones, though, I would say that one gets out a lot more often than one day every seven years."

Mike interrupts, "What about the aggression level? And how did it know we were there? We all have crowns blocking our thoughts and emotions. We were all wearing solid black, and we were not making noise. And it should not have seen us because we had not entered the clearing."

Part of what he said grabs my attention, "Wait, there is a practical reason for everyone wearing all black? I thought it was a military thing. What does wearing black have to do with faeries?"

Held fills me in, "The Created have more senses than humans do. We use mostly sight and hearing. The Created can sense our thoughts and emotions, and they can do it through solid walls. So, they tend to rely on sensing those thoughts and emotions when looking for humans trespassing. Since black is really just the lack of light, it works well when combined with the crown. A Faerie is focused on looking for the thing the crown blocks, combined with not seeing reflected light, and there is a reasonable chance you can walk past one even when it is looking right at you."

Mike adds more, "Faeries are tied to a geographical location and can't go far from their faerie hole. This leads to locals identifying a faerie circle over generations of supernatural experiences. I would think that clearing is this faerie's circle. But when it attacked Held, we were still in the treeline."

Held nods, "No wonder the locals stay out of that forest. I thought it was odd that a forest with population centers so close did not have some teenagers out drinking on a summer night, or a young couple sneaking out for a tryst in the woods. When I scanned with the *oculus*, there was nobody else there."

I ask, "Will Mr. Lark tell us more?"

Held replies, "Sometimes he does, sometimes not. We'll see if he comes to visit over this."

CHAPTER NINE

The day after returning from Hoia forest is, thankfully, uneventful. After Illych declines my request to look at the contents of the leather case, at least until after Mr. Lark has a chance to scan them with the *oculus*, I resume my efforts in the library.

Perhaps wishful thinking on my part, but the expectation Mr. Lark will arrive at any moment helps keep me awake through what is a long day. Instead, the time passes slowly, with no Mr. Lark to be seen. At dinner, I take note of the *Day 70* on the white board in the cafeteria and turn in early. My being awake for more than twenty-four hours was an unpleasant experience, definitely something I will try to avoid in the future.

Calisthenics the next day is more challenging than in

the past. Held pushes me harder. Apparently, he came to the conclusion my role now includes field work, and I need to be in better shape. If I am going to participate in more things like the Hoia forest mission, running faster and further will be important. Especially if I am being chased by a monster from ancient mythology.

Afterwards, sweaty and physically drained, I stumble into the showers. At breakfast, I check with Illych, and there is still no word from Mr. Lark. He then informs me the whole team is going for weapons practice today, and I am included. We are to suit up and meet at the main doors at nine this morning.

I make sure to be at the open space by the main doors promptly on time. All four of my fellow Citadel residents arrive at about the same time, and all of them dressed in identical black tactical dress. The mono-chromatic garb does not appeal to my sense of aesthetic, but after learning of the practical value of the color choice, I'm not going to complain.

One of the electric carts is loaded with black ballistic cases to take to wherever we are going.

Everyone is armed, and Illych hands me one of the customized pistols in a holster to belt on. This is followed by numerous loaded magazines, a knife, a super high output tactical torch, plus one of those space age looking carbines hanging from a chest harness. The others get grenades. Illych says I am not ready for those, and I agree.

To the uninitiated, the amount of firepower on display is impressive. It is also noticeable how comfortable everyone is with their weapons and the amount of gear they are carrying. Everything is carried as an extension of their body.

Illych points at Held and then points at me. Held nods and waves me over to the cart. He then instructs me to draw my pistol from its holster a few times. Something in the motion causes him to adjust its position on my belt.

This pistol is the same model as the one I had fired before in preparation for the Hoia forest jaunt. Held produces a second pistol, but the holster for this one is a shoulder rig for connecting to the harness just below my left armpit.

I have to ask, "Why two pistols? I can only shoot one at a time."

"Sometimes there is not enough time to pull a spare magazine out and reload. If you are in that situation, you drop the empty weapon and draw the second pistol."

The other men are inspecting each other's gear. Weapons were being loaded. Handguns holstered with one in the pipe, hammers in the cocked position with safeties on.

Held shows me the best locations to connect the many magazine pouches on my carapace and belt. A scary-looking serrated knife, hanging upside down on my chest over my heart, completes my weapons load out.

The other men have more accessories than I am carrying, including those sleeves for the white spikes and COMDATs on their chest.

Illych looks our way, "Held?"

Held gives a thumbs up.

The doors open and all five of us, plus the cart, head for the Compass. The walk is uneventful, but by the time we make it to the Compass, the weight of what I am wearing has me sweating despite the cold. In contrast, the others look to be enjoying themselves.

The cart is driven to the center of the stone circle, and everyone surrounds it with practiced ease. I keep near Held.

Illych pulls out a *dongle* and activates it. My vision flashes black, and then we are standing on gravel, with a blue sky overhead. The temperature is a little warmer than the Compass, but still quite chilly. The translation nausea now has its way with me, but I handle it better. Experience, I guess. My colleagues might be right, you do sort of get used to it after a while.

We are in a valley with tall mountains on all sides. The valley walls are sheer cliffs going up hundreds of feet. Patches of hardy grass cling to the rocks and gravel, but there are no trees. A wide-open space with blue skies overhead. With my first breath, I realize we are at a high elevation. The air is thinner here.

Having lived in continental Europe, I am familiar with a mountain setting. This pocket valley appears to have no way in or out that does not involve some extreme climbing.

Looking at Held with an obvious question on my face, he says, "This is our shooting range. This valley is in the middle of the Rocky Mountains and is completely isolated. There are no people within a hundred miles. It is only accessible by translating or helicopter."

The men begin unloading the cart and unpacking boxes and cases. In addition to what each of us has strapped on or carries in, there is a collection of heavier weapons, accessories, and ammunition.

Illych references a binder with sheets of paper in it and starts giving instructions. Held nods in Illych's direction while looking at me, "We don't come out here to shoot for fun, although we will get to do some of that. Every man has to qualify with every weapon we brought. That includes you. Expect to have a sore shoulder by the end of the day."

Held was not kidding. By the time we pack up to leave twelve hours later, I have fired handguns, rifles, a submachinegun, and a 40mm grenade launcher. My shoulder really hurts, but honestly, it was so much *fun*.

Illych has me sit out the fire team maneuvers where they practice with live ammunition, where one is shooting while the other reloads.

Illych tests each man on his reload times. Illych is also tested, with each team member getting a turn at being his evaluator.

Everything is packed back on the cart as night falls, and we translate back to the Compass.

The walk back to the Citadel is not the festive event it was this morning. Now I am exhausted, having been standing, shooting and walking for over twelve hours.

Keeping my eyes focused straight ahead, I just keep putting one foot in front of the other. Somehow, I am able to match the group's pace, or perhaps they see my exhaustion and slow down out of consideration for the new guy.

Regardless, we make it back through the doors together.

Standing inside, on the far edge of the open space just inside the doors, is Mr. Lark. He is wearing the same all black tactical gear with his peculiar walking stick in his right hand. I now know the walking stick is a ruse, just so Mr. Lark can carry an *oculus* around without drawing too much intention. Or perhaps, considering his obvious eccentricity, less attention.

Mr. Lark looks at Illych and it is obvious who he intends to talk to. Illych calls out to the team, "Take everything to the armory, clean up and re-inventory, then call it a night."

Illych walks over to Mr. Lark, and they begin speaking together in a low voice. I trudge along next to Held to the armory. Earlier today, when we were getting ready to leave, there had been talking and some kidding around. Now everyone is silent. Tired men finishing up their responsibilities with an hour of work ahead of us.

Slowly, with precise competence, the cleanup and put away of all the equipment is completed. Everyone stays in the armory until the last task is done. Then we all file out and head for the barracks. I go straight to my room and fall to sleep almost the second my head hits the pillow.

Woken from deep sleep by loud knocking on my door, I look at what I had started calling my science fiction watch. It had been less than an hour since the sweet embrace of sleep had taken me. My head feeling like it is full of fog, I yell out, "What?" Hearing my own voice, I realize how angry I sound. Screw it, I am not apologizing. After all, who wakes someone up after they just fell asleep?

The door opens. It is Illych. A sardonic grin forming as he recognizes my condition, "Remember, Thomas, it's all about the pain and suffering."

After a moment of him standing there, grinning at my misery, "Mr. Lark sent me. You're to meet him at the library."

"Right now?" I blink my eyes while trying to put thoughts together. This sleep deprivation thing sucks.

Illych snorts, "Right now." He turns and walks away, leaving the door open. I exit and began a slow, stumbling walk to the library.

I find Mr. Lark sitting in a chair waiting for me. The lights are on, and the leather case we found in the faerie hole is lying on my desk. Mr. Lark has opened it and pulled out its contents. A large, thin, leather-bound book is in Mr. Lark's hands. Another, smaller, leather-bound book and two square-shaped leather purses lay on the desk.

Mr. Lark is casually paging through the tome in his hands. The leather pouches had been untied and left half-opened, revealing numerous gold and silver coins. A tidy sum of glittering treasure.

Mr. Lark looks up from his book, "You look a little tired, Thomas. Unfortunately, my schedule will not allow this meeting to happen during more civilized hours."

I sit down and stare off into space. My voice comes out mechanical from the exhaustion, "I need to take notes while we talk. I do not know how much of this I will recall in the morning."

He nods, "Everything has been checked by my *oculus*. The gold and silver coins are real and very old. The smaller book appears to be a diary. The large book is what really interests me. I do not recognize the language it is written in. That is unusual in itself.

"You are now tasked with researching these documents. If more resources are required, please inform Illych. One each of the silver and gold coins will be left for your reference. The bulk of this I am taking for the operational fund. As before, when you reach any conclusions, have Illych contact me."

Mr. Lark pauses, and I ask, "How soon do you want me to start?" hoping sleeping first is an option.

Mr. Lark smiles an artificially friendly smile, "After a good night's sleep, Thomas."

There is another pause, then he continues, "Illych mentioned you seem to be adapting to life at the Citadel."

Yay for me. I am guessing that comment passes as my two-week employment review. It is still better than *your work sucks, so I will kill you now.*

Mr. Lark is watching me after his statement. For the briefest moment, I wonder if he can read minds. Wouldn't that be terrifying.

He says, "I have completed translating the Sumerian

writing from the incident at the museum. The book is an inventory of ancient artifacts, and I recognized some of the items listed, others I do not. I believe Amal Halluk is after this cache. What I do not have yet is its location. We may be going on a fact-finding mission soon."

"Illych has made you aware of the upcoming thirty days of time off. As you are new, it is unlikely you have determined what to do during your vacation. With less than twenty days to go, I've taken the liberty of setting something up for you. You will have a suite of rooms in an excellent hotel in San Francisco. Identification papers, cash, and a credit card have all been arranged. Feel free to explore and vacation in whatever manner suits you."

"You will not contact anyone from your previous life. Stay out of trouble, if possible, and remember to relax and enjoy yourself."

I nod. It is too much to process while mostly asleep.

He finishes the meeting by pointing at the large book and saying, "Work on this. If you do not reach any conclusions before the break, have Illych update me on the current status of the investigation. I have to leave now. You should go back to bed before you pass out."

Mr. Lark stands, and without even a good bye, walks out of the room. That is the last thing I remember before waking up the next morning, still in my chair in the library.

■　　■　　■　　■　　■

The soreness from the previous day's activities is made all the worse by the awkward sleeping position.

Looking at my watch, I realize I had missed calisthenics and I feel really bad about it.

Standing up, I stretch and head for the cafeteria to find everyone already there. The good news: yesterday's activities keeping us up late overrode the need to exercise this morning.

Sitting next to Mike, I take in the conversation at the table. It is pretty animated this morning, as Mr. Lark's visit last night brought mission instructions for the team. They are getting ready for a transport and smuggling operation.

I ask, "Mike, what is a transport mission?"

"Part of what we do is to provide security for the transportation of whatever Mr. Lark wants protected."

Held adds, "Mr. Lark sets up transport of people or property from one location to another. My guess is he works with some pretty shady brokers to set it up. The kind of high-risk activity where borders, customs, and law enforcement will try to prevent it."

This has me wide awake now, "Karl Lark is a smuggler?" Somehow, I find that disappointing. All the organization, sophistication, and intelligence, only to find out he is a smuggler.

Held says, "We don't transport stolen watches or cigarettes without a tax stamp on them. Only high value items or people. And only for those who are willing to pay an extraordinary amount of money. I don't know what Mr. Lark charges, but keeping all of us on the payroll requires significant funding."

"What about keeping the translating thing secret?"

Mike answers, "With the *oculus*, we know when someone is looking, and with some creative switching of containers, it's possible to get things out of just about anywhere, without anyone being the wiser."

Illych says, "Most of the time we don't know what's in the containers. We're just there to keep everyone honest. That all being said, this means, for a couple of days, it will be just you alone here at the Citadel. I understand Mr. Lark gave you the stuff from Hoia forest to study."

"You are leaving me here alone? Just me, surrounded by who knows what just outside the walls? That does not sound... safe."

"You'll be fine. The Citadel is well-protected. Don't go out the gates, stay inside. Before we depart, there's some work to do. You will accompany Mike and Tank when they go harvest Truestone this morning. It shouldn't take more than few hours. After we're done with breakfast, the three of you can organize your efforts."

Breakfast ends shortly thereafter. Mike, Tank, and I walk to the armory to get ready.

"Where are we going?"

Tank says, "There is a Truestone generator in the wild spaces near the Citadel. We'll take a walk, pick up the Truestone, and get back here."

The gearing up at the armory is quick, and we exit well-armed and equipped, similar to Hoia forest. Not as heavy as yesterday, though, a kindness, as I am still tired.

We stride out through the gates of the Citadel. Tank sets a quick pace, and I have to jog a bit to catch up at times.

"Does this happen often? Harvesting Truestone?"

Mike replies, "There are four Truestone generators we harvest regularly. This one is the closest."

"So, is it like a brick, or block, or something?" I am curious about what we were going to get. I am also concerned that as the junior member of the team, I will end up carrying a heavy block of something back.

"You have seen Truestone. The white pebbles you can hold in your hand. We're going to pick one up."

That satisfies me for now. I am not concerned about a pebble size. Our path is down the road back to the Compass, not cross-country. After arriving at the Compass, we take one of the other roads leading away. It is constructed the same as the road to the Citadel, surrounded by the same rough, grey stone terrain.

Mike and Tank demonstrate alertness on the walk from the Citadel to the Compass. Now, on this new road, they take it to another level. Carbines are at the ready.

After no more than a half-hour, we reach a path leading away from the road. Narrower and as laser straight and flat as the road we took to this place.

The path leads to an oval-shaped building several stories tall. The entrance is on a long side of the oval. High up on the building are huge, irregular curved openings to its interior. The structure has an odd, impossible to explain, unnatural look to it.

Without pause, we take the path to the building ending at a doorway with no door. The doorway is tall, ten feet or more. A giant would have been able to comfortably walk through.

Tank and Mike do not slow down as we approach the gaping doorway with nothing but blackness beyond.

"Looks dark in there? What if something has taken up residence inside?"

Tank replies, "No worries, the Created in this place avoid a Truestone generator. Not sure why, but they do."

That said, we enter the dark interior of the structure.

The entire interior of the building is open. You can't tell from the outside, but it has no roof with the exterior walls forming an oval-shaped bowl. Faint dark green streaks luminesce from within the black stone walls. The streaks resembling veins or arteries from a living thing, pulsing to some impossible-to-determine beat.

In the middle of the building is a plinth about waist high, with a pencil thin metal rod extending up perhaps a foot. Lying on the surface of the plinth, very close to the rod, is a single white pebble not much larger than a marble.

Tank walks up and palms the Truestone, dropping it into a pouch on his belt.

Curiosity prompting me, "What was the original use of Truestone?"

Mike shrugs, "Not sure. We use it to temporarily disable a Lesser Created. I am sure it had some other use, but I have never seen one, and Mr. Lark has never clued us in."

Tank says, "Without the Truestone, we wouldn't be able to operate in these spaces the way we do. The Lesser Created make hard targets, even with modern weapons. Their bodies are made from tougher stuff than ours, and they are stronger and faster than any human. Even when compared to a complete stud like myself." This last part brings a chuckle from Mike.

"What was the spike Mr. Lark used to finish off the ciorii back at my flat? How does that work?"

Mike answers. "That is the White Fang. Again, none of us know what it originally was for. When a Created is stabbed in the right place, it disconnects their spirit, or something, from their physical body. After that, they begin to evaporate.

"The Truestone temporarily paralyzes them and tells us where to penetrate their hide with the White Fang. We use gunfire to open them up, so the fang can do its work."

That explains a lot about what I had seen back in my flat.

With the Truestone in hand, it is time to head back with Tank leading the way.

Mike shares more on the walk back to the Compass, "The problem with Truestone, is it's rare. And when you find a generator like we just saw, it only makes a single piece once in a great while."

"That entire building is the generator?"

Mike nods, "As far as I know, that whole building is there to make that one little pebble every year and a half.

The Truestone grows on the end of that metal rod. Once it is fully developed, it falls off the rod and lays next to it, ready for someone to pick it up."

The three of us walk in silence for the remainder of our return to the Compass. Arriving unmolested. We quickly switch to the other road, and we are on the way to the Citadel.

"Mike, if you do not mind me asking, how did you end up with Mr. Lark?"

"Honestly, I don't know."

He is apparently not going to follow up his statement with any more information, so I have to ask, "Did you magically appear?"

Tank laughs at that, and Mike shakes his head, "No, I really don't know how I came to be here. I woke up in the infirmary here at the Citadel. My last memory prior to that was being an Army Ranger in Iraq. Apparently, I was wounded during a mission and ended up in a coma for almost two years. That's how Mr. Lark found me, in a VA hospital, as a vegetable.

"He decided to sneak me away here and handed me off to the Doctor. I was fixed up in no time. The explosion destroyed the memories close to the time it happened, so I don't know the specifics. Mr. Lark gave me a second chance on life."

I looked over at Tank and start to open my mouth.

Tank growls at me, "None of your business pal." His pace picks up as he puts a little distance between Mike and me.

I look at Mike with the obvious question on my face.

"It is not you, Thomas. Tank doesn't talk about what happened to him. I know what it was, but it is not my place to tell you."

I can accept that, and we continue in silence for the remaining distance to the Citadel.

Upon arriving, the main doors open to a scene of activity. Illych and Held were busy while we were gone. The electric cart is in the entry area near the main doors, piled high with gear for their next mission.

Tank takes the Truestone Mike had been carrying. He then heads off to put them wherever they are stored.

Illych and Held break for lunch. Mike and I join them, followed shortly by Tank. Lunch is quick, and immediately afterwards, the others head for the Compass with the cart.

I find myself alone and left to my own devices. The Citadel has always been a quiet place, but after the team leaves, it is as silent as a tomb.

CHAPTER TEN

Over the next few days, I take advantage of the solitude and lack of disturbances to settle into my research. Starting with the small book from the leather case, The Journal of Captain John Nesbit, whose ship moved cargo between European ports on the Atlantic Ocean.

Perhaps three-quarters of the book's pages are filled with handwritten entries in old English. The mostly legible writing details Captain Nesbit's observations of the mundane on his ship. Mixed in are more interesting commentaries regarding his voyages, cargoes, and some adult reminiscing about women he spent time with while in port. It gives insight into the career of a 1600's ship captain, but there is nothing Mr. Lark will be interested in.

The last entries present an abrupt change. Dated in June of 1674, Captain Nesbit's ship was sailing in open-ocean with fair weather and blue skies, navigating around the west side of Ireland. The trouble begins when it found itself unexpectedly, and without warning, in a fog bank.

The wind pushed them further in, and the captain maintained the ship's heading in hopes of exiting out the other side. From deep in the fog came animalistic groans and barking. The ominous sounds growing closer.

Then, as suddenly as the fog had enveloped them, it was gone, and along with it the disturbing noises. The lookout spied an island straight ahead and called it out. Captain Nesbit was surprised by this, as his maps showed no islands in this part of the ocean.

For reasons he cannot explain in his journal, he chose to sail closer to the island. The wind was light, but they were still able to navigate. The captain ordered the crew to check the depth and found it sufficient to continue sailing closer. The lookout calls out there is a great stone pier jutting out from the island. With skill and care, they were able to dock safely.

Captain Nesbit emphasized in his journal how such adventurousness was uncharacteristic of him. He had not been chartered as an explorer and the hold was full with cargo he was responsible for. Yet he felt compelled to dock, and neither the first officer, nor anyone in the crew, objected. Something was drawing them to the island.

He debarked and walked onto the island alone, leaving orders to wait for one day, and if he had not returned by then, to depart and finish their assignment.

He commented on the collection of buildings clustered near the pier. Passing through them as he walks the road from the pier, heading straight through and into the island.

The road was made of massive stonework. Each slab as far across as a man is tall. The surfaces worn with an ancient appearance he had seen in old Roman structures. Overgrowth threatening to drown out the meager remaining signs of civilization.

He continued through the forest beyond, keeping to the road. The trees around him are towering monstrosities as tall, or taller, than a cathedral's spire. Other than a few birds and the spotting of a few disturbingly large rabbits, his silent journey is without incident.

His wandering ended at open gates, set in a circular wall surrounding a keep. Outside the wall on all sides, trees of great age soar high overhead.

Compelled to enter the gate, he finds the green space inside the walls well-tended. The keep is in good condition as well. Captain Nesbit walked to the keep door intending to see what was inside. As he approached, the door opened, and a manservant came out to greet him and invite him inside

The captain then wrote of meeting a 'wizard' of great stature. They feasted together, and the Magus asked to the captain to deliver something to a far-away place, a task for which he would be paid a king's ransom in advance.

Captain Nesbit agreed and took a leather case containing two leather bags and a leather-bound tome. The bags separately contained gold and silver coins.

The task was to deliver a leather-bound tome to the far side of the European continent. A map on the first page showing where to deliver the book. The coins, his payment.

I blink, this is unexpected. Putting down the journal, I grab the folio and flip it open to find a map accurately showing all of Europe, including the Ottoman Empire, all the way to the near east. A curiously shaped mark showing the destination where Captain Nesbit was to make his delivery. Not far from the Caspian Sea, in modern era Russian Federation territory.

The final entries are of the captain's return to his ship, the subsequent delivery of the cargo, followed by his resigning his commission, and his journey to deliver the tome.

Captain Nesbit made notes of the places where he stopped on his trek across Europe. The last entry was his explanation of a detour through a forest in Romania to avoid trouble on the road.

I consider what I had just read. The tome was supposed to be delivered back in the late 1600's. Around three hundred and fifty years ago. This warrants further investigation, and fortunately, my personal library includes a few texts on ancient myths and legends. One describes oceanic myths, and I read the section on *phantom islands*. Finding a list with a short description for each.

To the west of Ireland was supposedly an island called Hy-Brasil, and it even shows up on maps of the area for hundreds of years. Modern satellite imaging eventually proving it did not exist, and Hy-Brasil faded into legend. Based on the writings in the journal, Captain Nesbit might dispute that legend as true.

It appears I have something to report to Mr. Lark but no way to report it. Notifying anyone will have to wait until my colleagues return to the Citadel.

The next few days are spent in the futility of trying to figure out the pages of handwritten text in the larger book. The quality of the writing is excellent, but the language is unknown to me.

■   ■   ■   ■   ■

A few solitary days later, I am sitting in the cafeteria, taking my lunch, when the team returns. I find myself counting the men coming through the door until I reach four. No one looks worse for their time away and apparently no visits to the Doctor are needed.

Illych waves, "Good to see you survived."

Tank walks past Illych, slaps my back and joins the rest in getting food, returning to sit down around me. I find myself between Mike and Held.

Observing my colleagues' appetite, "There was no food where you were?"

Mike pauses between bites, "It was all camping

survival crap. That gets old quick."

"And the mission?"

Mike puts his fork down, "Yah, it was good. Some wealthy Asian family stashed a pile of money in Canada and were planning to secretly emigrate when the government found out. Apparently, the people in charge frown on taking your ill-gotten gains and making a run for it."

"We're talking an extended family of some thirty people all have their passports confiscated and travel bans put on them. Government agents watching constantly. There's no way they're getting out."

"Ok, how did they find Mr. Lark? Is there an ad in a paper somewhere?"

Illych shakes his head, "That's not how it works. Mr. Lark works with brokers who connect him with these opportunities."

Mike continues, "Anyway, through backdoor channels, the family patriarch learned of these brokers who could arrange for the family's escape. Even in their difficult situation, money was not the issue. The family is fabulously wealthy. The real challenge: how to get the whole family out, simultaneously, all thirty members. Anyone left behind would be jailed as punishment."

Mike pauses, and then, "So, how do you think we did it?"

"I am sure it involves translating. Maybe one-at-a-time?"

"Nope. We rent an empty industrial building in the city the family lives in. The whole extended family was brought there in ones or twos. Using an *oculus* to locate the government minders, who are then distracted or misdirected, preventing any interference in getting the family assembled in one place.

"We anesthetized the whole lot of them. And then we put them in these boxes that were essentially coffins. After everyone is unconscious and boxed, we loaded them up in a shipping container. Once they and us are inside, the *ouiblet* then translates the container away."

"All thirty of them just let you knock them out and stick them in what looks like coffins?"

"A few of them freaked out, but Mr. Lark reminded them the final payment doesn't post until they're in-flight to Canada."

Mike starts eating again, and Held takes over the story, "The family was kept under for twelve hours. It was a lot of work. We were busy monitoring the health of thirty unconscious people."

My expression must have looked like a question.

Held says, "Why twelve hours? That was the estimated trip time if it happened in the more traditional way. A truck drive from the meeting point to the nearest airport, plus a flight to a small, southeast Asian island, with extra time for incidentals, would take twelve hours. Plausible deniability would require the family stay under to make the situation believable."

"In reality, the cargo container, with all five of us inside, had been translated straight to the island. Then everyone waited for the clock to run out on the twelve hours, at which time the family members were awoken and shown to rooms with showers, clean clothes, and a meal.

"Afterwards, a chartered commercial jet arrived to take them to Canada. A Canadian attorney who specializes in high-net-worth immigration was already on-board. First class treatment all the way to Vancouver, Canada.

"They leave, we loaded everything, including ourselves, back into the cargo container and translate away with no one the wiser".

Mike says, "It was too bad we had to leave right away. The weather was perfect, and it looked like the island had good beaches."

"Wow, that was more complicated than I expected. I would never have thought Mr. Lark would be involved in something like that."

Illych nods, "It was time-consuming but otherwise uneventful. If everything is planned correctly and everyone stays on task, it just goes by the numbers."

"And if it does not go by the numbers?"

Illych smirks, "The team is made up of combat arms senior NCO's who have all seen more than one firefight, and we carry a ton of firepower. If things go sideways, the other side is going to have their day ruined right quick."

"Is that why it took so long? You were gone for a better part of a week for a mission that took less than a day."

"Thomas, organizing and coordinating such an effort takes days to pull off."

Explanations complete, and everyone finished with their meal, the team leaves to cleanup and put everything away.

Later on, I go looking for Illych and share what I learned while they were gone. He then gets a message off to Mr. Lark.

Now, I wait...

■　　　■　　　■　　　■　　　■

My work is solitary in nature, and I was always comfortable with that. However, when the team was absent from the Citadel on their mission, my solitary limits were reached. When I lived in London, I occasionally went out into the world to be around people.

Perhaps it is an over-reaction, but now I find myself seeking out conversation with my colleagues. Mealtimes are perfect for this while also giving me the opportunity to listen to their stories. They are very different people than I have been around in the past, with little in common to my own life experiences.

On the second day after the teams return from the transport mission, I am doing just that, sitting in the cafeteria at lunch, listening to another adventure story. This one about a sandstorm in Iraq. I sit and listen, not noticing a black-suited Karl Lark entering the cafeteria.

Realization dawns on me when the storyteller stops the telling and is looking at someone behind me.

Curious, I turn to see Mr. Lark.

Mr. Lark smiles his contrived, overly friendly smile and says "Don't let me interrupt, but I need to take Thomas away."

His gaze shifts to looking directly at me, "Let's go to the library."

We leave and silently walk to our destination.

Mr. Lark's smile dominates my thoughts in that short period of silence. Smiling like that must be some sort of compensation for something. He always starts with friendly and smiling. Except for that time in the vault where he was considering killing me. No smiling then.

Perhaps his smiling meant he is interacting with people and there was no need to commit homicide. Good to know. Smiling good, not smiling, very bad. This leads to the further realization that Mr. Lark is very bipolar in his dealings with people. There must be some deeper meaning to this that escapes me at this time.

We enter the library and take seats facing each other. I start first, "Are we discussing the subject of Hy-Brasil?"

Mr. Lark nods, "I received and considered your message. Now we shall discuss what you found."

"Thank you. First, let's discuss the possibility of this being a hoax. I believe the unusual circumstances of the find make a hoax unlikely. This is somewhat speculative on my part. To be more conclusive, we would need to have the books properly analyzed. Unfortunately, the contents of the book would raise questions from anyone hired to determine its authenticity."

Mr. Lark interrupts, "The book is real. The *oculus* confirmed the age of the book."

I nod and continue, "From what Captain Nesbit wrote, it is implied that once he was close to the island, something there, possibly the wizard he wrote about, engineered the whole meeting. The captain mentions a compulsion to dock at the island, his walking alone to the castle, and then telling his crew nothing of what he found.

"The resignation of his commission, followed by the attempt to traverse late seventeenth century Europe on a journey to the Caspian Sea. It all seems uncharacteristic. Why not keep the coins and retire or pay someone else to deliver the letter?"

Mr. Lark makes a motion with his hand indicating he will speak, "I believe the captain was under the influence of a strong mind control from the moment the ship found itself in the fog. This magician appears to have placed a mental binding on the captain to deliver the folio containing the map."

"You believe what is written in the journal, then?"

"The good captain would have most likely succeeded in his task had he not detoured into the path of a half-mad faerie. The whole story raises my curiosity. Anyone that was on that island is now long dead after three hundred and fifty years. But who knows what was left behind? The other possibility is to go to the map's destination and see what is there."

After a pause, he continues, "Perhaps it is best to learn more about the origination before showing up at the destination?"

"You are considering searching for Hy-Brasil, then?"

"No, I am sending you looking for it."

"The journal does not give the location where they found the island. How would I find it?"

"There are enough old maps around showing the general location. It might take effort to search for, but an *oculus* would speed things up considerably."

"What is Hy-Brasil? The captain talked about trees being on the island, so there is sunlight. It can't be a pocket dimension like the Compass or Citadel, can it?"

"Hy-Brasil is part of the real world, just hidden. A sphere centered on the island and extending some distance out from it has been created around it. Sunlight shines down on it like normal. This non-Euclidean warping of space from one side of the sphere to the other side keeps it hidden. It is a way to hide something in plain sight.

"Any material, a living creature or object approaching from one direction just skips over the island to the other side. A ship sailing through the area with an accurate GPS would see their position change instantly by several miles. But if you have the proper key, you transition to the island instead. The transition zone was the fog the captain spoke of."

"Did the captain have a key?"

"I do not think so. Something on the island, probably that same magician, opened the door, and they just sailed in. I, however, have become quite good at making such keys. I will send you to find the place where the island is. Then I will join you and provide the key to open the door. A team will then accompany you to the island. Afterwards, you can report back what you find."

"After what happened at Hoia forest? I think Held was almost killed by that faerie," my voice is a little shrill, caused by the anxiety over another adventure, especially in the middle of the ocean. I know how to swim, but I do not think that will help that far out to sea.

"Thomas, one of the reasons for adding you to the organization was the hunch that you are good at finding things. Since coming here, you have proven me right. Perhaps now is not the time to disappoint me by breaking a winning streak?"

I can think of nothing to say in reply.

"It is settled then. I will talk to Illych. The team will need to setup somewhere on the Eastern seaboard of the United States. Europe would be closer, but the team would not blend in as easily. You will need a ship of some sort. There may be enough time to get everything started before the next scheduled break. Then you go on vacation. And when you come back, off exploring you go. Questions?"

I shake my head and Mr. Lark leaves.

Time to go looking for hidden islands in the middle of the North Atlantic.

■　　■　　■　　■　　■

Illych began preparations immediately. It will be

Illych, Held, Mike, and me going to Hy-Brasil. Mr. Lark assigning Tank to another task that would keep him from joining us.

Illych leaves the Citadel for a few days. He then returns to update us on the mission's setup progress.

He had located a shipyard in Charleston, South Carolina, that would prepare the ship he had purchased. It was an old steel hull, two screw, Vietnam-era boat that requires a lot of work. He had reviewed the plans with the shipbuilders, and the tear-out had already begun.

The four of us were to return to the ship yard and supervise the refit. The plan is to put to sea after returning from the upcoming 30-day leave. We will sail out perhaps fifty miles and then translate the whole boat to the general location of Hy-Brasil.

While the refit progresses, I am tasked with finding the best maps for locating Hy-Brasil.

We leave the Citadel the next morning and translate from the Compass to a hotel suite in Charleston.

My three companions had all packed civilian clothes, whereas I only had my Compass-provided attire. I was to remain in the hotel suite, while the three others left for the shipbuilders.

Illych also left me with additional instructions: to order clothes and a computer for immediate delivery. Illych handed me a large envelope just before the team left. Inside is a California driver's license with my name on it, a black credit card also with my name on it, and five-thousand US dollars in various denominations.

Included in the envelope is a plane ticket for a flight from Charleston to San Francisco and reservations at a hotel in San Francisco for my upcoming leave. In addition to searching for Hy-Brasil, I was to acquire everything I needed for my upcoming vacation in San Francisco.

For the first time in a month, I found myself in the real world, unsupervised. Illych told me to stay in the hotel room until the team returned later that evening. I am not an adventuresome person, but I am surprised I did not have an urge to run out the door.

A visit to a coffee shop would be nice, if for no other reason than to watch the pretty girls walk by. Looking out the window confirms it is a beautiful summer day outside and there are pretty girls in Charleston.

Instead, I call the front desk to get a phone number for the nearest computer store. This will give me internet access, and ordering what I need will be easy. Illych had said money was not an issue and to consider the credit card to have no limit.

I decide I will be going to San Francisco in style.

The computer is delivered to the hotel room door in less than two hours. I went right to work, combining ordering things off the internet with my search for the location of Hy-Brasil.

Everything I need is available online, and by the time my three team mates had returned, I have a general idea of the location of Hy-Brasil.

A nearby print shop makes laminated copies of the maps to be delivered. We need them for our voyage and waterproof seems prudent.

Illych approves of my accomplishments for the day. The suite we had originally translated into, and where I had been all day, was just for me. It is a relief to find out all four of us are in similar, but separate, suites. I had been curious and concerned all day how the four of us would be sleeping in only two beds.

As I still did not have civilian attire, we could not go out for dinner. Room service was ordered instead. We all sat together in my suite and shared a meal.

I ask Illych, "Can we talk here, I mean, about anything?"

Illych nods, "Our rooms were swept for surveillance devices before we even arrived, and I have an *oculus* with me to keep watch. We can speak freely here."

Held says, "Wondering why you didn't want to go outside while we were gone?"

"Yes. I was a little worried I was going to go outside and get into trouble, but I really did not want to. It occurred to me this was a little strange. I have been at the Citadel for almost a month."

"We're all like that. Nobody does anything that endangers our anonymity. My guess is Mr. Lark does something when the crown is installed. A compulsion to not draw attention to ourselves."

"He didn't say anything about that," Has my behavior been modified? Am I still me? What else did Mr. Lark do to me I do not know about?

Mike talks between bites, "It's a little creepy, but it's part of the job. I don't think any of us would appreciate the attention we'd get if someone knew who we are or what we are doing."

Illych speaks next, "I was a Green Beret, and I can imagine just about any intelligence service, or some of the bigger private organizations, would give anything to get their hands on an *oculus* or to learn of the oiublet's capabilities. The compulsion for secrecy protects us from a lot of bad players."

"Did you experience anything like this when you were in the US Military? Green Beret is pretty elite. isn't it?"

"The Green Berets are special forces, and I was involved in missions against conventional opponents. But we also got involved in operations against 'unconventional' problems. Joining Mr. Lark's organization was not as much of a shock as it probably was for you. I had already seen some strange stuff. Working for Mr. Lark, I find, provides better explanations."

Satisfied for now, the conversation becomes more social. The rest of the evening spent in friendly banter and some storytelling. Illych brings it all to a close around nine-thirty, explaining the next day's activities would see the other three going back to the shipbuilder, and I would remain at the hotel

I am alone the next day until the evening. My clothes did arrive, so at least I would be able to leave the hotel room. I even had time to watch some American television. The pay-per-view had some movies I had not seen, and the laminated maps arrived late morning. It felt good to enjoy the simple things in life for a bit.

When the others returned that evening and saw me in civilian attire, it was decided we would go out for dinner. Illych gives me a slip of paper with a phone number on it before we went out.

"This is the emergency call-in number. Memorize it. It changes each time we go on vacation. If you have problems, for instance you are robbed, call it. The cavalry will come to the rescue."

Dinner is at an excellent steakhouse. I had been to the states previously and knew that American steaks are fantastic. The meal did not disappoint. It felt good to be out in the world. Seeing women again, after a month without, was a pleasure I enjoyed throughout the evening. I wasn't the only one gawking. Mike, Illych, and Held were checking out most every woman in the place. Our staring bordered on the scandalous, and it was probably good it all ended by ten o'clock with our return to the hotel.

■　　　■　　　■　　　■　　　■

First thing the next morning, we meet in the hotel lobby. Illych had rented a Cadillac and drives us to the shipbuilder. The scent of the ocean growing in strength as we near our destination. The sun is shining down on beautiful, warm sunny day. Illych parks, and we walk to a dock and out to the boat.

It is bigger than I had expected, with plenty of room for dozens, much less the five of us. Activity around the ship is intense. A crane is lifting what appeared to be the ships engines, removing them for replacement. There are groups of men working all over the ship, with lots of shouting, the sounds of machinery in operation, and the flashes of welding.

A man from the shipbuilding company ushers the team into a small building on the dock, not far from the ship. Details of the planned refit are shared.

The ship is old, and the inside is being gutted, reinforced and rebuilt. All the windows are to be replaced with smaller, bulletproof versions, and many of them will be completely removed, with plates welded flush over the empty holes. A heavy-duty railing is being installed around the complete perimeter of the ship. All new electronic equipment and numerous technical updates are planned

I am not a military man, but even I recognize the ship is being modified to provide a better defense. The perimeter railing forced anyone boarding the ship to lift themselves up and over it to get on the ship. The superstructure cabin now has a single point of entry, a sheltered door opening that could be used for cover and to funnel anyone trying to get in into single file. The steel plate and tube infrastructure being added wasn't necessarily just to stop bullets, but to keep anything from getting in too easily.

The crow's nest on top of the superstructure is an armored pillbox. A hatch in the floor leads down into the pilot house. Anyone in the crow's nest will have a clear line of sight to all points on the deck.

That night, as we are coming back from dinner, the lift door opened at our floor to reveal a grey-suit clad Mr. Lark standing half-way down the hall. He is just standing there, brass sphere-headed cane in hand.

Walking out of the elevator, we collectively approach him.

He says, "We have work to do."

CHAPTER ELEVEN

The team gathers in my hotel room. As we pull our chairs into a circle, Mr. Lark shares what he is here to discuss.

"Not long ago, a visit to the British Museum resulted in a chain of events that led to Thomas joining my organization. The source of the conflict was an ancient Sumerian... -let's call it a "book." It is not a book in the conventional sense, made from paper or clay. This book used thin copper sheets for its pages, and the cover of the book was made from hard stone. This method of construction was chosen for its potential longevity. This book could be left in a damp cave for ten thousand years, and after the dust is brushed off, it would still be legible.

"My source inside the museum tipped me off to the book's existence. Unfortunately, there was another interested party involved, a Djinn named Amal Halluk. Amal infiltrated an armed team into the museum to recover the book. My presence there that afternoon prevented the book falling into his hands. The resulting violence cost me my long-time contact within the museum.

"Investigating after the fact, I was able to determine the shooting at the museum was never reported. This leads me to believe Dr. Chatzas serves Amal and is his inside contact. The fact she was a witness and is still alive reinforces this belief.

"During the brief outbreak of violence, I was able to page through the seven pages of the book and memorize the contents. Later, I translated the text from memory. The book is an inventory of ancient artifacts. Some of the artifacts I recognize, others are unknown to me."

"We would recover this cache of artifacts, if only I had its location. The *ouiblet* makes taking possession a straightforward affair. Unfortunately, the text only lists the artifacts, not the cache's location.

"There is a consideration to be observed in the series of events regarding this book. Why did Amal Halluk want the book itself? Why not just have pictures of the text sent and then translate them? All the subterfuge that occurred seems unnecessary.

"If physical possession of the book was required, then I understand the attempted armed theft of the book. It would perversely legitimize its removal from the museum. There would have been an investigation if it just disappeared. Questions would have been asked, and a certain curator's financials would have been investigated. A patsy would need to have been set up as a cutout. But this level of scrutiny is different than a straightforward theft. Additionally, Dr. Chatzas was using the situation to eliminate an unwanted employee. Or in your case, Thomas, the termination of a long-standing nuisance.

"This has led me to speculate the location of the cache is in the book, perhaps hidden in, or on, the stone box. This would explain the need to take possession of the physical book itself.

"The British museum catacombs are extensive to say the least. Regardless, I attempted an *oculus* scan in order to locate the book, and I found it, still at the museum, in the secure vault on the fifth sub-floor.

"Our immediate concerns are two-fold. We need to break into the museum and steal the book. I know it would be easier to use the *ouiblet*. Unfortunately, there are so many cameras and vault doors that just having the book disappear would draw the attention of entities or organizations I would rather not involve. Their interest would not be in the theft of the book itself but in how security was defeated.

"The second action we will take is the interrogation of Dr. Chatzas. It is important we know if Amal Halluk has inspected the book, and if so, how long ago."

"Interrogate Dr. Chatzas? What does that mean? You're going to torture her?"

Dr. Chatzas is a bad person and had apparently plotted my death during the museum incident, but I can't be part of torturing a person in general, a woman specifically.

"Your chivalry is admirable, Thomas. Especially considering Dr. Chatzas arranged for your murder. However, we do not torture people, at least not in the traditional sense. There are more civilized ways to convince someone to talk. Dr. Chatzas will be kidnapped and taken to a quiet place. Then, after a short period of time, she will volunteer everything we need to know. Afterwards, she will be returned home, none the worse for wear.

"This is going to happen regardless of your outrage. And your willing participation is required.

"Once we have the location of the cache and Dr. Chatzas clues us in on the competition, we will move to collect it.

"These two initial operations must occur soon and in quick sequence. If we grab the book, Amal might try to keep Dr. Chatzas from us. If we grab Dr. Chatzas, Amal may decide to secure the book.

"My guess is Amal has inspected the book and has the location of the cache. He left the book at the museum to prevent any questions about a mysterious disappearance. So now, it is a race against time.

"Illych, does the shipbuilder have everything needed to continue without anyone from my organization being present?"

Illych nods, "Yes."

"Then everyone has fifteen minutes to gather up their things and meet back here. We will translate directly to the Compass and gather the appropriate equipment from the Citadel. Then we will translate to London and execute both operations."

Mr. Lark looks around at the assembled team, "Any questions?"

From what he just said, the team is about to commit a breathtaking array of serious crimes. It is also apparent my thoughts on the matter are irrelevant.

■   ■   ■   ■   ■

It does not take long to prepare after we make it back to the Citadel. Perhaps it should disturb me that the team is able to put together the kit to rob the museum in such a short period of time. Almost like they have done this many times before.

When Mr. Lark explained the mission back in Charleston, I had not seen a role for myself in the museum mission. It appeared they would drop me at the Citadel, just like the Asian mission, to wait around on my own while everyone else left.

I was wrong.

During preparations Mr. Lark shares the details of his complete plan. Not only am I going on the museum mission, but I will also play a key role as the mule carrying the book out. Illych fits me with a large, frame-supported rucksack, similar in appearance to a large pizza-delivery case. Once the Sumerian book is in hand, it will go into my backpack, and I will then carry it out. This will free up everyone else up for security and running interference.

With multiple *oculus* users on the team, it is unlikely museum security will prove much of an obstacle. The final mission profile is fairly straightforward. We will travel to the museum in two vans. One van will be left close to an eastern exit from the museum.

The second van will pick up the driver of the first van and the entire team – including Mr. Lark and me and will park near a west side entrance to the British museum. This will be our escape vehicle. After driving to the other side of the building, we will enter the museum as a group, through an east-side service entrance, during normal business hours.

There are three lifts that provide service to all four sublevels below the museum. On the fourth sublevel is a single lift connecting the fourth and fifth subfloors. The entire fifth subfloor is a special security vault.

The team will meet at the nearest lift and use it to travel to the fourth subfloor, followed by taking the special lift to the fifth subfloor. After the book is heisted, we will return to the fourth subfloor, and the team will ascend to the lobby using a different lift. The team will then walk out through the lobby exit at the western side of the museum, piles into the waiting van, and make good our escape.

Should we be detected at some point in the heist, this bit of subterfuge should obfuscate museum security blocking our escape. Our leaving by a different route than we entered will hopefully buy the team critical seconds.

My participation is advantageous for another reason. If we need to speak to anyone, my native English accent will go a long way in making our presence more convincing. Illych coaches me that if questioned about our presence, to say we are there to repair a compressor on a refrigeration unit. It is an emergency because the museum is afraid an ice core will defrost.

This explanation should be backed up by the coveralls we are wearing, eerily similar to those worn by the thugs on the first day I had met Karl Lark. It also provides a plausible explanation for the tool cases with our gear in them.

Like any modern building, every entrance to the British museum is always locked. The eastern side was chosen for its easily approachable service entrance. The service entrance also has its own small parking lot. Entry to the museum requires a key card and a four-digit code. Mr. Lark assures us he can defeat any locks we might encounter, electronic or otherwise.

By the time Mr. Lark is done explaining the mission, I come to two conclusions. First, Mr. Lark is a very thorough planner. Second, that having an *oculus* makes stealing much too easy. We know ahead of time the complete layout of the building, the location of every lock, every security device, etc.

Seems almost unfair.

The equipment loadout is impressive. We carry tasers under our coveralls, in addition to knives, pistols, small explosive charges, gas masks, and more. The larger pieces of gear are in roller hard cases.

Mr. Lark gives specific instructions to disable and restrain any opposition when convenient, and we each carry multiple zip tie handcuffs for just such an event. However, if the obstacle threatens the mission's success or injury to one of us, we are to use appropriate force to stay on mission.

I think this was Mr. Lark's nice way of saying we were not there to kill people or break things. However, should someone try really hard to get in our way, removing them is sanctioned.

Everyone demonstrates calm competence while getting ready, the team's experience really showing.

Each of us is issued a COMDAT communicator and earpiece, enabling the team to talk and listen as a group.

■　　　■　　　■　　　■　　　■

We translate from the Compass to the stone circle in London. Memories of passing through here on that fateful day, not that many weeks ago, color my feelings about seeing this place again. The last time I was here was close to my last day as my own man.

It is the same sterile, brightly lit, open white space. The grey Mercedes parked off to the side. Also parked in the room are two small panel vans, one white, the other black.

From the mission planning, I know the black one

will be parked waiting on the west side for our getaway. The white one to be abandoned in the service parking area.

I have seen Mr. Lark in his grey suit and in black tactical wear. Now, I see him in a formless set of coveralls, and it is an odd look for him. Less distinguished, maybe even approachable.

Tank jumps into the driver's seat of the white van, and Held drives the black. Both men obviously comfortable with the right-hand approach to driving in the UK.

Tank and Held are both on their best behavior, and the drive to the museum is uneventful. The four of us not driving are sitting in the back of the white van. Mike and Illych doing what all military men do in this kind of situation, checking and rechecking their own and each other's gear. Mr. Lark sits quietly with his eyes closed, apparently observing with the *oculus*. I, however, do not have the penchant for review like the others, nor the same amount of gear on my person. My loadout is missing the more extreme options, like grenades. Just a pair of single-shot tasers, a handgun, and this ridiculous backpack. The van is windowless, so I am left gazing out the front windshield as London passes by. It is a cruddy, grey day outside. The rain being on and off, seeming unable to make up its mind.

Held parks the black getaway van and joins us in the white van.

I expected the tension to rise the closer we are to the museum. Looking at my colleagues, all I see is borderline boredom. Mr. Lark is his usual unreadable self.

As for myself, having survived the Hoia Forest killer faerie, I am feeling confident going into this mission. My anxiety less than I had expected.

Once we arrive and park, I follow the others out of the van towards the door. Six men, looking like some sort of plumber gang.

You can take the soldier out of the army, but you cannot take the army out of the soldier. The four former military men unconsciously line up and start marching across the parking lot, their strides matching. It is so out of place.

Moving closer to Mr. Lark, I point to the marchers, "Should we be marching in?"

Mr. Lark hisses, "Illych, spread out and stop marching!"

The four men, now realizing what they were doing, separate and changeup their pace.

The service door is solid metal with a flange over the lock. Off to the right is a keypad. Mr. Lark approaches it and puts something in his palm up against the side of the keypad. He then types in a series of numbers. The door buzzes and clicks. Mr. Lark pulls the door open.

He sees the question on my face, "Using the *ouiblet* to make the book disappear from the vault would draw unwanted attention. But making a key card disappear just looks like common theft."

Mr. Lark had shown us maps of our path through the museum back at the Citadel. That, and my own years of experience with the place, allows the team to move with confidence to the first lift.

The lift down is not far in from the service entrance, through a wide corridor. We pass a few people on the way, and none take interest in six men in coveralls.

The same key card summons the lift. The doors open to a large, service-style, rectangular platform. We all pile in, with room to spare, and begin our descent into the bowels of the museum.

A question pops into my mind, "Mr. Lark, you are not concerned about getting stuck in the lift?"

Mr. Lark shakes his head, "It would look odd on our way in to take the stairs rather than the convenience of an elevator. On the way out, though, we will be taking the stairs. Because, yes, I am concerned about getting stuck in an elevator."

At the third subfloor, the lift dings and stops. Apparently, someone is getting on. Before the door opens, Illych tells everyone to relax and let me do the talking.

The door opens.

Dr. Chatzas takes a step into the lift.

Her emotionless mask abruptly changes into surprise with no small amount of disdain. Her wide eyes stopping at my face while her mouth forms a silent, *you?*

The spectacle does not last long. Illych produces a taser from inside his coveralls.

Mr. Lark barks, "Take her!"

Illych's arm extends, and he takes two steps towards the shocked Dr. Chatzas. At point-blank range, he aims for her chest and pulls the trigger. A pop sound reverberates inside the confines of the lift, and we all watch the needles and wires erupt towards Dr. Chatzas.

He was aiming for her chest, but the universe decided to intervene for a bit of comedy, as each of the two needles picks a separate breast to impact and stick to. The attached wires hang down at an angle, and for a brief moment, I think of tassels. Then the taser makes a buzzing noise like angry bees as it discharges.

And nothing happens.

Dr. Chatzas looks down at her chest, back up, and then starts to turn away. Held steps up and uses a handheld unit, pressing it to her side and tasering her. His free hand going for her mouth, thankfully dulling her brief scream. Her body goes stiff, then convulses a bit, and she begins falling over. Illych catches her, pulling her further into the lift. Held glances around outside the elevator, and seeing no one, steps back in, and pushes the button to close the door.

After the doors close and our downward descent resumes, Illych lays Dr. Chatzas down gently and proceeds to grab her right breast with his hand. Apparently squeezing and massaging it.

"What the bloody hell, man? You can't just grab her like that!" My outrage is loud and accusatory.

Illych smiles, "Relax, Thomas, I'm not copping a feel. I'm checking why the taser didn't work. Her bra is heavily padded and has a wire running the full length of the bottom of it. The taser needles didn't even get close to skin contact. They shorted out through the wire."

Wow, the busty Dr. Chatzas is less busty than she appears. And it served as a defense against tasers. Who would have thought?

Mike asks, "I thought we were kidnapping her *after* we steal the book?"

Mr. Lark is looking down at Dr. Chatzas prone form, "This is not part of the plan. However, it does save on time. She comes with us, killing two birds with one stone, so to speak. Tank, carry her. Taser everyone we see between here and the next elevator."

The path to the next lift is a short walk down a corridor, then a left turn, followed by another short walk. From prior experience, I know not a lot of people come down to the fourth sublevel. If we are lucky, we will walk all the way to the next lift without meeting someone.

The first corridor is uneventful. The team turns left, and then less than a dozen strides later, five people – three men and two women – walk out into the corridor through an open doorway.

I wish I had a camera. The looks on their faces are priceless. They stop as one, and all five pairs of eyes shift to the bum of the woman draped over Tank's shoulder.

Then their eyes shift to the guns pointed at them.

Mr. Lark inhales deeply and then exhales, "Tank, Mike, Held; take them to a room, bind and gag them, and lock them in. Then proceed to the exit elevator, remain nearby, and hide the best you can. Dealing with this will slow us down. Illych, Thomas, you are with me." He turns and starts walking towards the lift that will take us down.

Illych is close behind Mr. Lark, and I jog to catch up.

The lift to the security vault sublevel is a service-type and twin to the one we had just taken here from the ground floor. As the three of us reach the doors, Mr. Lark raises a fist. Illych freezes in place, and I mimic this unexpected change. Mr. Lark closes his eyes for a few seconds, consulting his *oculus*.

Opening his eyes, he pushes the button to call the lift. The rumbling of the car coming up the shaft can be heard through the sliding doors. After waiting a bit, there is a 'ding' sound, and the lift doors slide open, revealing an empty interior.

The inside of this lift shows considerably less wear and tear than the one we had just been in. My guess is not a lot of people know about the fifth sub-floor. I never heard of it in all the years I had visited the museum, and I doubt it is on the visitor maps.

Upon entering the lift, a security camera catches my eye. Positioned in a ceiling corner, opposite the doors, there is no way to avoid it. Most security cameras today are not much bigger than an eyeball in a small fishbowl. This one is larger, a box with a transparent window. A pencil-like rod extends forward a few inches from the camera. At the end of the rod, a few inches from the lens, is a small box about the size of a person's thumb.

The doors close for our descent, and I point at the obvious camera. Knowing Mr. Lark sees it also does not stop me from asking the obvious question.

"Is that security camera a problem?"

"Not at all, Thomas; and let me answer your question with a question: What do security cameras in elevators see most of the time?"

I had to think about that for a second, "An empty elevator?"

"Precisely. If someone were to insert a loop into the camera feed, the elevator would appear empty all the time. The *ouiblet* allows me to do this perfectly. I believe there was a movie where the thieves snap a Polaroid photo from beside a security camera and then place it in *front* of the camera…so it looks to security like nothing has changed when people enter. What I have done is a little more sophisticated; the results are the same, however."

"What is that thing sticking out from the front of the camera?"

"That is there to prevent what I just described. That little box displays a four-digit number code to the security camera. That four-number code is randomly generated back in the main security room and transmitted here, changing every few seconds. If the camera is spoofed to feedback a looped display, that number will not match the one in the security.

"The loop feedback I engineered still allows the camera to see the changing numbers. The rest of the camera feed shows an empty elevator."

I have never been a technology guy. At least not *modern* technology. I am more into older technology, like fountain pens and vellum. Honestly though, being around Mr. Lark is like participating in a children's science show. Add firefights and other-dimensional creatures, and you have a children's science horror show. Something not likely to get past the censors.

The security camera explanation ends just as we arrive at the fifth subfloor. The duration of this leg of the journey was longer than travelling one floor down. My guess is the fifth subfloor is more than a single level of distance below the fourth subfloor.

The lift doors open to reveal a brightly lit corridor, leading to a traditional-looking, circular, plug-type vault door. Two of the unusual security cameras are mounted to the ceiling at the midpoint of the corridor. One points towards the elevator doors, the other towards the vault door.

Just beyond the threshold of the elevator doors, the entire floor of the corridor all the way to the vault doors is sunken down about two inches.

And filled with water.

I look at Mr. Lark. "My apologies for my never-ending questions, but why is there water on the floor?"

Mr. Lark nods, "The visible light spectrum is subject to manipulation. It can be bent or hidden. Something invisible would not be seen by those security cameras. But the disturbance of the water as something traverses this corridor would be visible. Notice how the walls of the corridor are angled outwards from ceiling to floor? The walls are hardened, polished stainless steel. If you touch them, you will find they have been lightly oiled. It would be almost impossible to leverage against the walls to travel the corridor's length. This corridor is as much a part of the vault's security as that huge steel door ahead is.

"The vault itself is a vacuum-tight steel bubble suspended inside another vacuum-tight steel bubble. The space between them has had all the atmosphere removed, a vacuum. Anyone trying to dig in would trip at least one of the multiple pressure sensors, and an alarm would trigger.

"The only practical way into the vault is through the vault door. Since the entire internal vault chamber is suspended, its weight is also monitored. Even a one-pound change in weight will trigger an alarm. The weight sensors I have already defeated in a way similar to how the security cameras were defeated."

Karl ends his monologue explanation, and after a brief pause, "Illych, the water please."

Illych opens his roller case and produces a roll of fabric from inside. He places it on the threshold of the lift and begins unrolling it into the corridor on top of the water. The fabric instantly expands, absorbing the water. He unrolls it all the way to the vault doors.

I look at Mr. Lark.

He glances my way, "I do not want to be walking around in wet shoes, slipping on everything."

Mr. Lark exits the lift and walks across the impromptu carpet to the vault door. Three combination dials next to the vault door now his focus. Mr. Lark begins turning the dials, sometimes switching back and forth between them, working through a complicated combination.

After a minute of demonstrating his superior manual dexterity, Mr. Lark grabs the handle and pulls it down. There is a loud clunk, and the massive vault plug door swings open, outward into the corridor.

The vault's interior is as big as a good-sized home and well-lit. Aisles are neatly laid out in painted lines. Outside the aisles are squares of uniform size, painted onto the floor. Inside most of the painted squares is a single, unmarked wooden crate. Each crate is identical in appearance to the others. There are no markings anywhere; not on the aisles, the painted squares, or the crates. How do we find what we are looking for when everything is identical and unmarked?

Perhaps that is the point?

As I take in the playing field, so to speak, the absence of video cameras is noticeable.

Mr. Lark beats me to my question. "If there are no cameras, no one can look at what is in here. Nothing is marked, because if someone broke in and did not know which crate they were looking for, they would be delayed in locating their target. Some of the crates are filled with a few sandbags and are here as decoys. Only the vault master knows which crate is which.

"Fortunately, the *oculus* defeats such diversions. Our target is that one," Mr. Lark points to a crate down the right aisle, four crates in.

"Thomas, please retrieve the book while Illych and I observe."

Observe?

"Is it safe?"

"This vault contains no traps or mechanisms, nor anything animated or alive. As to it being safe, I am reasonably sure it is."

That word, *reasonably*, inspires as much confidence as *observe* at this point.

I shrug my shoulders, step into the vault, and pause. No lightning strike; nothing grabs me. Resuming breathing, I continue to the crate Mr. Lark had indicated.

There is a simple latch holding it shut, no lock. I open it and find the stone box inside, resting in a velvet-lined, jewelry-box-style tray.

The stone box book is heavy and clumsy to maneuver into my backpack. Once it is strapped inside, I heft its awkward weight onto my back. Feeling more like a pack mule than anything else, I adjust the shoulder straps. If we have to run for any reason, I will be properly screwed.

Turning to look at Mr. Lark, I nod and start towards the exit. As my leg moves forward, there is a scraping noise. Out of the corner of my eye, movement catches my attention. Fear courses through my body, and I sort of half-stumble, half-sprint, towards the vault door. Not more than a handful of strides later, something hits the back of my legs.

Mr. Lark shouts, "Stop moving. Freeze!".

Despite my fear, and the throbbing of my legs from the impact, I do as instructed. The threat becomes obvious as I look around in panic. The crates each have an extra layer of wood on their sides. When I had started walking back to the door, these extra sides separated from their respective crates and started moving towards me. There are perhaps a dozen total crates in the vault, making a total of forty-eight vertical sides. I am surrounded by a forest of what could be described as wooden playing cards, standing edgewise, vertically upright.

Mr. Lark calls out, "Thomas, they move towards you whenever you move. The ones that hit your legs were from the crate the book was in. The more you move towards the door, the more you will be boxed in."

"The *oculus* did not show this?"

"No, I was looking for guards, mechanisms, or poison gas. Detachable, person-seeking, wooden panels are unexpected. Just do not panic. Give me a moment to think."

I can see him concentrating on the *oculus*.

He then does something I could not have expected.

He steps into the vault. I reflexively brace myself.

And nothing moves.

He continues walking towards me, "When the trap is triggered, the crate sides divide themselves between everyone currently in the vault. Since you were the only one in here, they are all coming after you. Anyone entering after the trap is triggered will not be targeted."

Oh God, he is going to take the backpack with the book and leave me here! Literally boxed in, like some sort of twisted version of Edgar Allen Poe's: *The Cask of Amontillado.*

"You're taking the book and leaving me here?!" My

voice is more high-pitched than normal.

Mr. Lark keeps walking towards me, "I do not leave people behind. Makes it difficult to maintain loyalty. You are a valuable asset, and it would be wasteful to depreciate your value unnecessarily."

None of what he is saying is comforting.

Mr. Lark walks to the upright crate sides just behind me. He places his hands on their top edges and effortlessly lifts them straight up.

"As I suspected, they are connected to you. They move when you move. However, anyone not associated with the trap can pick them up and move them. Give me a moment please."

He picks up and moves all the crate sides within ten feet of me. Strangely enough, when he put them back down, they remain vertically on edge.

"Thomas, please take one step towards the door. One step only."

I do as instructed, and the crate sides – all forty-eight of them – scrape the floor towards me. My step had been maybe two feet, but the crate sides traveled much further than that.

"Yes, the ratio is four-to-one. Thomas, for every foot you move towards the door, these things will move four feet towards you. What a clever trap. Anyone breaking in would literally be boxed up and waiting for the authorities."

Mr. Lark moves several more crate sides. "Illych, assist me."

Illych enters the vault and copies Mr. Lark's

technique for moving the crate sides. I am able to take a few more steps. Then they shift more crate sides. Eventually, I cross the vault door threshold. As I leave the vault, all the crate sides fall over to lay flat on the floor. Illych and Mr. Lark join me on the water absorbing pad in the entry corridor.

Mr. Lark says, "That was educational but time-consuming. This mission has been delayed far too much."

Over the COMDAT, Mr. Lark asks "Held, status?"

"The five we ran into are bound, gagged, and locked in a room. We're approximately twenty feet from the exit elevator, in a room with a locked door and the lights out. Dr. Chatzas regained consciousness and made a nuisance of herself. She's now sedated. I have no unusual security activity to report from the *oculus*."

"Expect us at your location in ten minutes."

Mr. Lark looks at Illych, "We are going to risk the elevator. This run of good luck without security responding to our presence can't last much longer, though."

The squishy sound of our tread on the absorbent mat is disconcerting. It has an organic sound that sends chills up your spine.

The lift car is still waiting, and the doors open immediately when the button is pushed. The three of us enter and begin our ascent to the fourth subfloor.

During the ride up, Mr. Lark is concentrating on his *oculus*. I am fighting a creeping sensation up and down my spine – the anxiety of waiting for the sudden lurch of the lift stopping with us trapped inside.

But it never happens. We arrive at the fourth subfloor and walk undeterred to meet with the rest of the team. As we arrive at the exit lift, Held, Mike, and Tank open a door a little further down the hall.

Dr. Chatzas left arm is draped over Tank's shoulders, and he is half carrying her. She looks like a little doll next to his robust frame. Her expression is blank, and her eyes are almost closed.

Carrying the box book, even this short distance, has me sweating. It is really heavy. Fortunately, Held sees my distress, takes it from me, and places it in a roller case.

"Illych, the distraction, please," Mr. Lark says this while pushing the button to summon the elevator. Illych pulls a small device from inside his coveralls and flips open the top like it is a Zippo lighter. This reveals a red button inside that he presses without hesitation.

I wonder, "Distraction?"

Illych says, "The white van we drove here in just caught on fire and is making some very loud popping noises. Nothing dangerous or lethal. I'd expect the museum to be evacuating by the time we reach the ground floor."

The elevator ride up is filled with anxiety that ends with a 'ding' sound, and the doors open to a scene of chaos in the grand gallery. We nonchalantly exit, turn, and begin our walk towards the main doors. The team instinctively spreading out around Tank to help block line of sight to Dr. Chatzas.

As we integrate ourselves into the exiting crowd, a nearby man turns his head and sees me. He is one of Dr. Chatzas' toadies, although I can't remember his name.

I can see his mind working to recall who I am before he speaks, "Thomas Davies, it has been a while." At least he keeps walking towards the entrance and does not stop to shake my hand.

"It has been. Do you know what all the excitement is about?" This was a fun lie to say.

"Something about a potential terrorist threat, and we are to leave the building. Say, is that Dr. Chatzas? Is she ok?"

"When the alarm went off, it startled her and she fainted," It is a poor explanation, but the best I could come up with. Anyone who knows Dr. Chatzas, knows she is not the fainting type.

The man begins to put distance between us while looking at my coveralls and then the other men in the same coveralls nearby. The expression on his face tells me he knows something is up.

Dr. Chatzas is a tyrant and not someone people are loyal to. I decide to take a risk and leverage the possibility the toadie is not personally concerned what happens to Dr. Chatzas.

"My suggestion is you walk away and forget you saw me here. Nothing good will come from you talking about this."

The man looks at me while a flash of fear crosses his face. He nods and shifts the direction he is walking a little bit. The distance between us grows until he disappears in the crowd.

We emerge outside through the gallery doors and begin a brisk walk across the plaza. The crowd is dissipating now, and with it, the camouflage we had benefited from by being a part of also disappears. Now we were six men in coveralls, suspiciously carrying away a professionally dressed woman.

Fortunately, everyone with the appearance of being a member of law enforcement is running towards the museum. Regardless, London is known for the literal million-plus video cameras installed around the city. We are on video somewhere.

As we approach a bench at the edge of the plaza, Illych says to Mr. Lark. "Let's leave Held, Thomas, and Dr. Chatzas on this bench. The rest of us can get the van and come back for them. Carrying her around will draw negative attention if we continue." Mr. Lark nods his head in agreement.

Illych points to a nearby city bench, "Wait there."

Tank gently sets Dr. Chatzas down in the middle of the bench in a sitting position, and Held and I join her, one of us on each side. We watch silently as the four others walk away towards the parking lot where the van is waiting.

I look around, relieved there is no one nearby. Filling my lungs with a deep breath, I exhale, and the feeling like I had just gotten away with playing hooky from school washes over me. Only now do I realize how tightly wound I was when we were in the museum.

Held is calm as ever. He sits back in the bench

looking casual. His coveralls now unzipped, partway open. To the casual observer, it looks like he is taking a break.

I ask Held, "So was this mission a success?"

"So far, so good. We'll know for sure when it's over."

"What was given to Dr. Chatzas?"

"Injectable tranquilizer. She's still barely conscious. It'll last for a couple of hours. Makes her compliant, easier to transport."

"What will happen when she is interrogated?"

"We'll ask her questions, and she'll answer them."

"And if she does not answer?"

"Then she'll be persuaded to answer."

"Torture?"

"Not in the traditional sense. There won't be any rubber hoses or thumbscrews. That's not Karl Lark's style. There won't be any blood, but Dr. Chatzas will talk, whether she wants to or not."

"So, it will be a gadget that they interrogate her with? Or some monster like the Doctor back at the Citadel? Or that science fiction movie I saw where they put some creature in their ears?"

Held snorts, "I can see where your idea for a gadget comes from. Mr. Lark does have a lot of gadgets. But no, the method isn't science fiction.

"Torture has never been a reliable method for extracting information. Eventually people will say anything to make the pain stop, and it becomes difficult to separate the truth from fiction.

"It's also a poor choice when complex information is

needed. However, aggressive interrogation techniques will help when simple knowledge must be revealed. In Dr. Chatzas' case, all we need to know is who her sponsor is regarding this book. We also need to know if her sponsor has viewed the book up-close.

"The interrogation techniques we use are effective and significantly more humane than old-fashioned, bloody-handed torture. My suggestion to you, Thomas, is to relax and watch. Mr. Lark isn't a warm, friendly guy, but he's also not a bloodthirsty monster."

Not long after Held finishes explaining Dr. Chatzas' soon-to-be fate, the van pulls up by the bench. Held lifts Dr. Chatzas into a standing position and supports her while we walk to the van.

She is hoisted inside and laid down in the back of the van. Tank is driving, and Illych has shotgun. The rest of us sit on the benches in the back of the van with our prisoner at our feet.

The drive back to the warehouse is, fortunately, quiet and uneventful.

At the warehouse, Mike checks Dr. Chatzas' pulse and blood pressure. She is still very much out of it. He then administers another shot that knocks her completely unconscious.

Tank and Held move her onto a stretcher, and the two lift it and walk into the stone circle. The rest of us follow. Mr. Lark works his *ouiblet* magic, and the cold of the Compass stabs us wide awake, quickly followed by the translation nausea.

Dr. Chatzas is carried off to one of the vaults,

different than the one I had spent a night in.

I decide to follow and see what will happen, and no one stops me.

This vault is well-lit and has a large heater in it. The temperature is less than comfortable, but it is not the freezer I had been in. Dr. Chatzas is transferred to a bed on the side of the vault across from the vault door.

A box mounted to the wall has a steel cable protruding out from it. The cable ends in a loop, obviously intended to be attached to someone's arm or leg. Held grabs the cable and fits the loop to one of her ankles. A tight fit, not too tight to cut off circulation, but enough to make sure she is not going to be able to escape from it.

The vault has the same small camping toilet and cooler with water bottles and crackers. After securing Dr. Chatzas and tucking her into a sleeping bag, everyone exits the vault, whereupon it is closed and locked.

Mike updates Mr. Lark, "She'll be unconscious for at least four hours."

Everyone collects up their respective equipment, including the roller case with the goal of the mission contained within it, and we walk as a group back to the Citadel.

CHAPTER TWELVE

Most times walking to or from the Citadel is a relatively quiet experience. Not this time. Everyone is talking.

Mr. Lark walks alongside me, "Thomas, you and I will start work on this book immediately. After the gear is stowed, meet me at the library."

"You said it was an inventory list of artifacts. What kind of artifacts?"

"Human civilization's time on earth goes back much farther than modern history represents it to be. There was a cataclysm around twelve thousand years ago. The destruction was near total, and the human survivors numbered in the thousands.

"Attempts were made to restart their civilization.

Those attempts failed. Other attempts were made to store and preserve artifacts for future generations. This Sumerian text lists a variety of the ancient civilization artifacts. We just need to figure out where this cache is stored."

"What kind of things are in the cache?"

"I recognize the descriptions of some of the items. More than half of them I do not understand. You must understand, Thomas, that this ancient civilization did not operate the way our modern world does. There was no 'planned obsolescence.' Everything was optimized to its function and built to last forever.

"One of the items I call a plasma candle. It is a cylindrical, metallic device used for illumination. When left unattended, it has a small plasma glow. But when a person moves close, the plasma glow expands greatly, providing a bright, white illumination. They consume no fuel and emit no gasses or pollution. From what I can tell, they essentially last forever.

"Another defining characteristic of the ancients is their use of electricity. However, they had nothing to do with low-voltage electricity. An EPS or electromagnetic pulse can wreak havoc on today's modern, low-voltage systems. All the ancient electrical systems are high voltage, thousands of volts and higher."

This was my chance to get answers to something that had been on my mind since my first day at the Citadel.

"Mr. Lark, Illych equipped me with this watch my first day at the Citadel. He said it detects EPS effects.

Now you mention EPS again. What does it stand for?"

"EPS stands for Electron Probability Suppressor. I will explain its function another time."

He pauses and then returns to the original discussion, "Excellent examples of this are the Egyptian light bulbs images found in a few different ruins in Egypt. The pillar supporting the bulb shows distinct rectangular ridges typically seen in high-voltage systems. It is kind of a giveaway.

"The inventory lists some of these lights being included. There is more. We need to find its location, and Dr. Chatzas must clue us in if we have competition."

"But if someone else already has the location, won't they be way ahead of us?"

"Possibly, but if that cache is still undiscovered after all these years, then it is likely in a remote part of the world. Whoever else is looking for it must travel there by conventional means. The *ouiblet* may still get us there ahead of them."

"Mr. Lark, if you don't mind my asking, are you the only person with a *ouiblet*?" That question has been on my mind for a long time, and this seems like a good time to ask.

"I am the only person, or otherwise, in possession of a *ouiblet*. It's a device of my own creation that came about under what I have determined to be unique circumstances. I have never seen evidence of another *ouiblet*, and I have diligently sought such evidence."

Good to know.

"It may take a few days to extract the information we

need from Dr. Chatzas. By then, we must have the location and be prepared to move out."

"Illych, begin general preparations for a long-term expedition with broad contingencies. Mike, when Dr. Chatzas is conscious, start her pharmaceutical regime. Thomas and I will be in the library."

Our conversation ends as I realize it has taken up the entire duration of the walk to the Citadel. We are just now entering through the main gate into its well-lit interior.

There is no pause or break. As we enter, Held passes the roller case with the book in it. I now trudge behind Mr. Lark, pulling the heavy case behind me as we walk straight to the library.

Working together, we lift the book onto a table in the center of the library.

Back at the museum, when Higgebotham had been killed, I did not get much time to inspect this unique find. Now I grab a magnifying lens and a bright lamp. Mr. Lark has his *oculus* in his hand. We open the heavy stone lid and look inside. The copper pages appear unchanged. In spite of my fatigue, I am excited. This is a treasure hunt of epic proportions.

We search every surface, inside and out. I look for differences in the formation of the characters and the grain of the copper for a hidden map or a clue of any kind.

After hours of exhausting searching, I ask Mr. Lark if I can take a break. He pauses and looks at me for a few seconds. "Of course, Thomas, get some food and rest.

We can start again in the morning."

I leave the library and Mr. Lark, sitting with his eyes closed, communing with his *oculus*. I wonder how much time Karl Lark spends sleeping? I have never seen the man tired.

Shuffling my weary body to the cafeteria, hoping there is still something reasonable to eat there. I am surprised to find the rest of the team, all four of them, dining and talking together.

While I was in the Library with Mr. Lark, they put everything away and staged the equipment for whatever our next adventure is going to be.

They then cooked up a veritable feast and are now relaxing and enjoying each other's company.

They even have beer. I am more of a wine guy. But after the day I had just been through, any form of alcohol is acceptable, and the beer is exceptional.

Serving myself food and a bottle of beer from an open tub of ice, I take the empty seat next to Mike.

The conversation is about the recently awoken Dr. Chatzas.

Mike says, "She was *pissed*…not intimidated at all. She screamed at me to release her immediately and that she's part of a powerful organization that'll be looking for her."

"All I could think was, *good luck them finding you here.*"

Held says, "Did her tune change when the injections took affect?"

Mike nods, "Oh yeah, she started shaking and

screaming questions at me about what we had done to her."

I interrupt, "Pharmaceuticals injected?"

Illych looks at me, "I think it's time for you to learn how an interrogation works. First, we lock the subject in the vault you saw. It has a heater that keeps it warm enough to prevent hypothermia but cold enough to be quite uncomfortable.

"The subject is then stripped naked and given a hospital gown and shower sandals to wear."

"Those hospital gowns that open in the back?" Dr. Chatzas wearing nothing but a skimpy hospital gown. I wouldn't mind seeing that at all.

"Yes, and then we inject the subject with a powerful stimulant. This prevents sleep and keeps their minds sharp. Then they're injected with an anxiety-inducing drug. The anxiety level is crippling. People will do anything to make it go away.

"The injections need to be administered every six hours. Now that the first round has been administered, we wait."

"When will she be asked questions?"

"Not yet. We wait at least twenty-four hours and see how the subject is holding up. The anxiety thing – combined with not being able to sleep – works fast on getting the subject to answer questions. We want them fully immersed in the experience before asking questions.

"That's it? No torture?" This is shocking. I have developed respect for these men and have a hard time picturing them torturing anyone, much less a woman.

Now I find out they will not be laying a hand on her. It is all drugs and sleep deprivation.

Illych says, "The record for anyone holding out is four days."

"What about when she gives us what we want?"

He shakes his head, "This is a catch and release. She doesn't know about the *ouiblet* and she hasn't seen anything unusual. When the interrogation is complete, we knock her out and leave her in her own bed at her residence. No muss, no fuss."

Seeing the relief on my face, he continues, "You were worried we were going to butcher her, weren't you? Not necessary, and it's not something any of us would do."

"I am truly sorry for thinking that of you."

Tank says, "No worries, everyone here is an experienced killer with significant body counts, including Karl Lark. You're the exception to that, of course." He is looking at me while smiling a predatory grin.

The rest of dinner is more pleasant, with Tank and Mike singing some wildly inappropriate songs at the end. Finally, Illych points out it is late, and we all go to bed.

I fall asleep quickly and am dreaming I am in that vault with Dr. Chatzas. She is facing away from me, and I am admiring how the hospital dress opens up much more in the back than I would have expected. Then she turns, and we step closer to each other, our lips moving to meet. I can feel the heat of her body.

Then someone taps me on the forehead, waking me.

It is Mr. Lark looking down on my prone form, tapping me with his finger to wake me. He is grinning that grin again.

What now? This is a horrible way to wake someone.

"I tried calling your name, but you were deeply asleep. Please get dressed and meet me in the library. I found the location. And don't fall back asleep."

Working for Mr. Lark is very interesting, but this uncivilized lack of respect for sleep is unreasonable. Dressing in black tactical, I pull on my boots. Considerable will is needed to put each foot in front of the other, but I make it to the library.

"Thomas, I have exciting news! I found the location of the cache. The secret of its hiding place is within the cover of the box. There are microscopic voids etched inside the plane of the cover."

Not being sure about the explanation I follow up, "This is a solid piece of stone. Did they form the stone around the voids?"

"No, there is an ancient tool that can be used to cut, or machine out, a void inside a solid object without piercing the surrounding surface. Very useful for surgery, I would think."

"Do you have one of those gadgets, Mr. Lark?"

"Unfortunately, no, but I am aware of their existence. I eventually set the resolution of the *oculus* small enough to detect them. The voids form a simple map of the continents with a location marked. Next to that map is another more detailed map of the specific location."

"And where are we going?"

"India, the Ellora Temple complex."

"I have never heard of it."

"Very interesting place. It is a huge complex of temples and tunnels. Vast sections are sealed from public view, and there are no complete archaeological studies in the public record. It has numerous examples of stone work that cannot be explained, even if modern technology were used."

"You never took the *ouiblet* there and checked it out before?"

"Thomas, there are thousands and thousands of megalithic sites around the world. It would take a hundred lifetimes to thoroughly inspect a fraction of them with the *oculus*. I explore when there is evidence something might be there. This is also one of the reasons you have been added to the team. To increase the team bandwidth to locate these opportunities."

My voice is robotic from the sleep deprivation, "What's next?"

"You are going back to sleep. I need to setup the *ouiblet* destinations for the Ellora complex. It is daytime right now in India, and we will go at night. Also, Dr. Chatzas remains to be interrogated to determine if there is competition."

"Let's just go. How tough can the competition be? I'll bet the team can handle anything," This is an awfully aggressive comment coming from me, but I am not fully awake either.

"Your enthusiasm is noted. However, our potential

competition is a Djinn. I have no interest in matching wits or strength against such an Adversary. Go to bed, Thomas, we will talk more tomorrow."

Mr. Lark's last statement is sharp in its tone. Must have touched a nerve.

Leaving the library, not even undressing or removing my boots, I return to bed and sweet, sweet sleep. Unfortunately, the dream with Dr. Chatzas does not return,

I am awoken by a knock on my door.

"Thomas?" It is Illych.

"Yes, I am awake."

"Cafeteria in five."

That is not enough time for anything other than to go to the cafeteria straight away. Fortunately, I am already dressed. I stand, stretch, and walk there quickly.

The complete team is gathered, including Mr. Lark. The four military men sit at, or stand near, the one table. Mr. Lark is a distance away, observing them.

Mike is speaking, "Tank and I went to give her the next round of injections. She didn't struggle at all. I could tell the first twelve hours did its work. Instead of giving her the injections, I asked if she was ready to talk. She said she was.

"I stuck to the prepared script. Who was her sponsor that was interested in the Sumerian stone book? She said it was a man whose name was Amal Halluk.

"I asked if he came to the museum personally to view the book. Dr. Chatzas nodded and said we'd missed him at the museum by just a few hours when we kidnapped her.

"The next question was dependent on her having someone come to the museum. Did Amal Halluk find what he was looking for? She nodded again, saying he'd been quite pleased with something he wouldn't explain.

"The last question was how long she'd been on her benefactor's payroll. She said she'd been selling information to Amal Halluk since before she'd become a curator. As her patron, he'd made the arrangements to put her in place years ago."

So that was why the relatively young Dr. Chatzas had been elevated so quickly? She was talented and driven, but her sponsor had removed obstacles and prompted action from key people to get her in place. She is an archaeological spy in the British Museum.

Mr. Lark says, "Excellent, we are less than twenty-four hours behind Amal Halluk, assuming he moves immediately. During the last few hours, I have been using the *ouiblet* to cast an *oculus* to the Ellora complex to take snap shots for me to observe what we are up against.

"The Sumerian map gave a *general* location, not a *specific one*. I found a stasis well deep underground, far below the ground level complex. Translating close to a stasis well is one of the few hazards or protections against the *ouiblet* that I am aware of. We will need to translate some distance away from it and then spelunk our way through the labyrinth of caves to the cache.

"The next challenge will be in disabling the suspensor generating the stasis well. Then we grab everything and translate out. Questions?"

I raise my hand.

"Thomas, you do not need to raise your hand, just ask the question."

"What is a stasis well?"

"That exotic watch you were given your first day here is to provide an alarm in the event of a suspensor event. A suspensor can be used to shut down low-voltage equipment like an automobile, or paralyze a human being. At higher settings it will stop your thought processes, rendering you effectively unconscious. This also explains memory loss described by UFO abductees. Their memories were not erased. They were prevented from being recorded in the first place.

"The next higher setting creates a stasis well. The movement of electrons is so suppressed, hence the term EPS, that nerve function and chemical reactions essentially cease. Anything placed in a stasis well will be frozen in place, never aging or degrading.

"The next higher level stops electron movement sufficiently that the wave of continuous life functions is broken, and living creatures die. Their bodies are undamaged and have no evidence to show why they are dead. This setting can be used to kill people over a large area.

"The cache is inside the stasis well. If we attempt to access it, we will be trapped in the well. This brings us to another consideration for our expedition. Others may have stumbled upon the well in the past. When we deactivate it, we may find more than just the cache waiting."

UFO abductions? Was Mr. Lark saying such things were real? Just when my belief that the level of weird has reached maximum, Mr. Lark reveals there is more.

"Other questions?"

Illych speaks, "The disposition of Dr. Chatzas?"

"I will talk to her briefly, and then she will be returned to her home. Amal Halluk has likely been too busy to miss her. She will be my double agent now, informing myself and Amal Halluk at the same time about future finds.

"If there are no other questions, Thomas and I will take care of Dr. Chatzas. Illych, how long until the team will be ready for spelunking?"

Illych looks at the three other men and then back to Mr. Lark, "One hour."

Mr. Lark nods and looks at me, "Let's go to the Compass and chat with Dr. Chatzas."

We stop at the armory to pick up equipment for the Ellora mission, followed by a brisk walk to the Compass. Mr. Lark is walking so fast we are almost running. For an old man, he has impressive endurance. I am sweating and breathing hard by the time we arrive. Mr. Lark on the other hand, shows no sign of physical exertion.

The Compass is the same cold, gloomy place with its strange alien architecture. Mr. Lark opens the vault, and we step into its brightly lit interior, closing the door behind us.

Sitting on the edge of the cot is Dr. Chatzas. She is pale, and her typically magnificent mane of hair is a terrible mess. Her makeup is smeared, and she is hunched over with her arms hanging down her sides. Her head hanging down, facing the floor. Even from the doorway, she is visibly shivering from the cold while at the same time sweating from the drugs.

She looks exhausted and lost. A pang of sympathy blossoms in my chest. Being around someone who is suffering like this is new to me. In spite of her attempting to have me killed back at the museum, I want to sit next to her and comfort her.

Mr. Lark walks to within a few feet from her and says, "Elizabeth Chatzas, you have answered our questions, and I wish to clarify some details of our relationship going forward."

Hope emerges on her face. I understand, having been in the same place, locked in one of these vaults, waiting to die. She also does not know yet that it is not going to be a clean getaway.

"I doubt your patron is aware of your absence. We will be returning you to your home shortly.

"I will give you a phone number to call when something of interest crosses your path at the museum. Things that you would bring to Amal Halluk's attention, you will notify me first. Do you understand?"

Dr. Chatzas gives a small nod without looking directly at Mr. Lark.

Mr. Lark grabs a small duffel bag from near the vault door. It would have been out of reach for Dr. Chatzas with her foot tethered to the cable. He tosses it onto the cot next to her.

"The clothes you were wearing when you arrived are inside. Please change into them, and then you are going home. Thomas will remove the cable from your ankle now."

He hands me the key, and I remove the tether. I then stand with my back to Dr. Chatzas. She put a warm hand on my shoulder to balance herself while she dresses.

Once dressed, she nods, indicating she is ready to leave.

Mr. Lark addresses her again while holding a business card, "This will be in your bedroom when you wake up, do not lose it."

Dr. Chatzas speaks, her voice more a croak, "When I wake up?"

Mr. Lark's free hand is suddenly a blur as he presses an autoinjector to her neck. Her eyes open wide as she tries to pull away, but it is already over with.

"You will need to be asleep for your trip home. Thomas, support her, and let's get her outside. The drug is fast-acting."

I put her right arm over my shoulders like I had seen the guys do when they carried her in. Mr. Lark reopens the vault door and steps outside. Holding up the now sagging Dr. Chatzas, we shuffle towards the nearest circle pillar.

During the short walk to the center of the stone circle, the freezing cold accentuates the warmth of Elizabeth's body pressed to mine. I have never been this close to her. In spite of my nose telling me she needs a shower, I am enjoying the contact.

By the time we make it to the center of the stone circle, she is completely unconscious, and I have to use both hands to hold her up. Mr. Lark looks at me and pulls a *dongle* from a pocket. With practiced ease, he activates it.

Everything flashes black, and then we are in a woman's bedroom decorated in lace and floral print. A spacious room with the center dominated by a large four-poster bed.

Then the nausea from the translation hits. I spend a minute recovering while trying to not drop Dr. Chatzas.

Mr. Lark, unfazed, stands waiting for me to recover and then says, "Thomas, put her in bed. We need to leave." That said, he closes his eyes, obviously communing with his *oculus*.

I pull back the covers of the bed with one hand and try to carefully place her onto it. I lose my grip, and she falls face-first onto the mattress. Trying to maneuver an unconscious person into bed reminds me of trying to pick up a house cat that does not want to cooperate.

By the time I have her properly positioned and the covers pulled up over her, I am upset with myself over my juvenile enjoyment of the process.

Carrying and maneuvering her unconscious form was strenuous, and I am breathing hard again. When I stand up and face Mr. Lark, his eyes are open, and he is looking at me.

There is a question that I must ask him, and this is as good a time as any. "Why didn't you use an autoinjector on me? Back at my flat after the ciorii was down? You could have knocked me out, and your secrets would have been safe? I could have gone home after the interrogation."

"I do not carry autoinjectors around with me."

I nod. Question asked and answered. For the lack of a single tranquilizing device, I am doomed, while Dr. Chatzas gets to go home.

"I am ready," as I say the words, I dread what is next. I have never translated twice in such a short period of time.

A *dongle* is in Mr. Lark's hand, and with a quick motion, it flashes black again. The cold telling me we are back at the Compass.

My fears are justified. Translating again so soon is worse than the first one. I stumble over to one of the stone pillars and support myself on it until the feeling of nausea subsides. Something that feels this bad can't be good for you.

Mr. Lark starts for the Citadel at the same blistering walking pace as before. I jog through the last of the nausea to catch up.

Once we are inside and the doors close behind us, I rest by bending over with my hands on my knees. In the open space near the main gates are the four others. They are dressed in all black, with bulletproof tactical vests.

Nearby are zippered black bags, lacking any handles. Instead, they have metal rings robustly sewn into the fabric of the bags.

Fifteen minutes of quiet preparation later and we are

headed out through the main gates. The pace to the Compass is more reasonable this time. Thank God for this small mercy; I am carrying thirty pounds of gear on me.

Arriving at the Compass, we immediately cluster together in the stone circle, ready to go.

Time to visit the Ellora caves.

CHAPTER THIRTEEN

From a pouch on his harness, Mr. Lark draws forth a collection of *dongle*s, handing one to each of us. "These are your escape *dongle*s. Use them only if you are in dire straits." I pocket it and brace myself for what is coming next.

He pulls out another *dongle*, "We will be translating into a fairly large chamber," with a quick movement of his hands, the world flashes black for the briefest instance. This is my third translation today, and I have been dreading it since our return to the Compass.

It is as bad as I had expected. Actually worse. Everything turns black and stays that way. Wherever we are, there is no light. Complete, void black. The nausea is distressing enough that I sit down on the floor until the effects pass.

My teammates switch on their torches.

Illych opens one of the black bags and pulls out a handful of what look like hockey pucks. He walks over to the nearest wall. Taking the puck-like device in one hand, he uses his other hand to peel a thin film from one side. He then presses the puck to the wall at shoulder level and gives it a twist. The puck illuminates with a bright, diffuse light.

He notices me looking at what he is doing. "Thomas, this isn't the first time we've been exploring underground. These are LED light devices with a high-capacity battery attached. They'll provide light for more than a week. Be careful with the adhesive, though. It's aggressive, and if you get it accidentally stuck to your skin, the only way to remove it is to take the skin with it."

Mr. Lark says, "We leave one every fifty feet. This chamber is the closest location large enough for the entire team to translate into and still be a safe distance from the stasis well."

Once several of the light pucks are in place and everyone has activated their forearm and weapon-mounted LED torches, I am able to look around the chamber.

Square in shape and hewn from dark, grey bedrock with a ceiling vaulted high overhead. Each of the four corners has an ornately carved pillar rising all the way upwards to the ceiling. There are three entrances to the chamber. Two appear to be finished stone and centered on their respective walls. The third is offset near a pillar and jagged in appearance, appearing to have been hacked into existence.

The air temperature is warm to the point of being almost uncomfortably hot, especially having just come from the cold of the Compass. With all this gear I am carrying, there's going to be a lot of sweating.

Mr. Lark says, "We wait here for a moment. The stasis well prevented proper *oculus* inspection prior to our arrival. Now that we are here, I need a few minutes to look around." He then closes his eyes and stands quietly in place.

Illych's hands move with silent commands, and the others each take an entrance with weapons at the ready.

Illych and I stand by Mr. Lark and wait. Minutes tick by.

Mr. Lark opens his eyes and says, "There are no threats in close proximity. We start through that doorway there," Mr. Lark points at the finished doorway Tank is guarding.

Illych nods, opens another bag, and pulls out some boxes, spools of wire, several disc-shaped objects, and a wire cutter. Over the next five minutes, they place a box and disc at the doorways we will not be travelling through. They then string black wire between the box and disc pairs.

Illych notices me watching intently, "Flash-bang trip wires if something tries to sneak up behind us. Not as effective against the Created, but any living thing has a pretty good chance of setting them off."

Illych points at Mike and makes a hand gesture. Mike stalks to the doorway we will be entering, pauses, and then disappears into the dark opening.

Illych looks at Mr. Lark, "How far?"

"Over a mile to the stasis well, and the path is not straight. We will be taking some turns, and there is a shaft we will need to rappel down."

As point, Mike takes his time, closely observing all the surfaces of the corridor. The team lets him get about twenty feet ahead and then follows. The dark stone does not reflect light, and without a torch to illuminate it, this place would be profoundly dark, the blackest of black. Illych attaches light pucks to the wall at regular intervals, leaving a glowing trail of breadcrumbs as we go.

The corridor is wide enough for two men to comfortably walk side-by-side. Between the heat and the dark, the anxiety of claustrophobia dances on my mood.

The corridor ends in a cylindrical room. There is a circular hole in the center, big enough for a man to slide down feet first. There is an exit, another corridor only big enough for the team to proceed single file.

I walk up to the center hole and shine my light down. It is a smooth stone tube so deep my light is lost before I can see the end.

"Thomas, get away from there," hisses Mr. Lark. Doing as I am told. I step back to the wall.

Mike enters the single-file corridor first. Progress is slow enough that I can illuminate the walls around us and observe they are covered in carved reliefs. Mostly Indo-Aryan people involved in various ceremonies. All of them resembling what I have seen in Hindu religious texts like the Bhagavad Gita.

This corridor ends in a large, circular room dominated by a central Linga. A Hindu religious structure that water is poured over. The water channel runs to a small opening in one of the walls. As I trace my light around the chamber, I observe a number of small openings in the walls at floor level.

Mr. Lark directs the team to a doorway opposite the corridor from which we had just entered. While the team is preparing to enter, I use the delay to look around the room.

The walls are floor-to-chest-height carved reliefs. Few are human. Most are of small lizard creatures with human faces and snake tails I recognize as depicting Nagas.

Nagas are mythological creatures, but considering what I have experienced since meeting Mr. Lark, they may exist. I cannot remember if they are peaceful or not, as visions of Nagas pouring into the room through those holes by the floor, thirsting for my blood, fill my imagination.

Illych snaps his fingers to break my reverie and points to the doorway, indicating it is my turn to enter.

Hurrying to the doorway, I enter. Relieved to be leaving the Naga chamber.

This corridor is all smooth surfaces, no carved reliefs, and slopes downwards at a gentle angle. Looking up, I am shocked by the ceiling rising an unexpected fifty feet or more upwards. The tactical LED torch illuminates the space, but it is creepy knowing there is so much empty space above us.

The downward slope increases and turns leftward, ending in a square room. Almost the entire center of the room is carved into a four-sided funnel, ending in a square hole some twenty feet down. There is only a narrow ledge wide enough for one at a time around the perimeter of the room.

Mr. Lark says, "Here we rappel. This shaft drops down into a chamber shaped like a large bowl. The shaft is perhaps fifty feet, plus another fifty-foot drop to the floor inside the chamber below us."

Tank and Mike move with purpose, dropping their bags and pulling out battery-powered drills with diamond bits. They quickly drill a series of holes into the floor. Into these, they place expanding anchors with steel rings. Bundles of rope are removed from the bags and quickly fed through rings while Mike and Held put on rappelling harnesses.

Illych lights a flare, and with a casual toss, down the shaft it goes, followed shortly by Mike. Quickly disappearing from sight, only a minute passes before his voice in my earpiece says he is down. Held immediately follows. Illych begins fitting me with a harness, "You're next."

"I have never rappelled."

"Relax, we're going to lower you down."

Tank and Illych grab one end of the rope fed through a pair of supporting rings. They tell me to walk backward slowly.

I do as instructed, and I soon find myself dangling inside a shadowy shaft, one hundred feet above what I am sure is a very hard, stone floor. It is over quickly enough. Mike disconnects me, and the rope is pulled back up.

In the time I was being lowered, Mike and Held have been busy illuminating the chamber. A half a dozen puck lights evenly spaced around the room light the place up.

Next are the gear bags, followed by Mr. Lark and Illych. The last one down is Tank. The ropes left in place, presumably for our escape if necessary.

The geometry of this chamber, also made from carved bedrock, is not natural. It follows a general four-walls design with a gently sloping bowl-shaped floor. Nothing is symmetrical, however, and the walls and ceiling display a significant amount of non-uniformity. Each of the walls has an exit doorway, and they are also not symmetrical, lacking symmetry in position, shape, or dimension. Ranging in size from a single-man doorway to the largest being able to accommodate a car driving through it.

Mr. Lark points at the largest doorway as our next pathway.

My head turns towards the man-sized entrance, and I walk over to it. Switching off my torch, I peer into the darkness of the corridor extending away from me.

After my eyes adjust to the darkness, I can make out the faintest green luminescence somewhere in the distance. I can't make out the source, but it is there.

A hand lands on my shoulder, and I jump. It is Mr. Lark.

"Thomas, why are you over here?"

I look over at the team and realize they are all looking at me.

"Something caught my eye, and I took a look."

"Let's stay on task. I am trying to avoid attracting the attention of what might possibly be down here with us. You wandering off does not help."

Wait, there is something down here with us? In this dark?

Mike takes point again and walks through the large doorway.

I hurry to take my place in the center of the team, finding myself shining my light into every nook and cranny we pass. This part of the journey takes us down another stone corridor, wide and tall, crudely hewn from stone.

Moving closer to Mr. Lark, I whisper, "How did they get the materials in the cache down here. Is everything in it small?"

"No, there is another larger, broader path that provides a more direct route. I deemed this path safer, if less direct."

I nod and continue walking.

The corridor begins to show signs of illumination ahead. Shifting from pitch black to dark grey. The path we walk is not proper straight, and soon we see shadowing on the floors and walls from direct lighting up ahead.

After a final subtle turn, the corridor ends in a short, straight section opening into a great domed chamber. It is huge, hundreds of meters across and high. Coffin-sized glass cylinders similar to those back at the Citadel are fixed to the domed ceiling at regular intervals. Their internal brilliance too overwhelming to view directly.

The effect is of clear, white illumination. Everywhere in the chamber is well-lit and visible.

Making what is in the center of the chamber that much more difficult to comprehend. The center third of the chamber is a static, uneven mass of grey and silver, extending upwards as high as it is wide. The mass demonstrating aspects of a mist or cloud to it, as well as reflective, angular shaping in some places.

The incomprehensibility of it makes my eyes hurt, and I force myself to look away.

An alarm cuts through the silence, and everyone in the team, except for Mr. Lark, jerks. A shrill "beep, beep, beep," and it is coming from Illych. Then another beeping joins it, this time from Held. The bulky, unconventional watch given to me my first day also begins beeping.

Mr. Lark shows me how to shut off the alarm, and the others do the same.

"The mass in the center of this chamber is the stasis well. We are close enough that we are being affected. The transmission of information through our nerves, the firing of the neurons in our brains, and the chemical reactions that occur in our bodies have all imperceptibly slowed. We are experiencing what is called 'time dilation' or 'lost time.'"

"As long as we keep as much distance between ourselves and the event horizon indicated by the edge of the mass, we will be ok."

All of us spread out around our entry point, hugging the walls while keeping watch.

Mr. Lark and I now stand near each other. His eyes closed, consulting his *oculus*.

I wait quietly for several minutes until Mr. Lark's expression changes from blank to his happy smile.

"I found it!"

I give him a questioning look.

"The EPS is centered in the stasis well, Thomas. How do we turn it off?"

I think for a moment, not terribly appreciative of Mr. Lark's question, "With a switch?" I am almost joking as I say it. Honestly, I really have no idea.

"Exactly, physical objects can be extended into the stasis well and pulled back. You could even walk into it if you wanted to. From our point of view, you would get slower and slower until you crossed the event horizon. Once inside, you would be frozen in place. But if we tied a rope to you before you went in, we could pull you back out.

"Unfortunately, it is impossible to see beyond the event horizon, photons passing out of the stasis well undergo a multi-dimensional-frequency-dependent-non-linear shift."

"Mr. Lark, that sounded very important, but I have no idea what you just said." I have come to understand that Mr. Lark is a high-order genius, but if he does not filter his communications, no one can understand him.

"Light is composed of photons, which are different than electrons. The EPS affects the probability of electrons moving or changing state, not photons. Light moves freely in and out of the stasis well. Unfortunately, the edge of the stasis well, called the 'event horizon', scrambles the light going in and coming out into an almost random jumble."

Based on the look on my face, he could tell I was still not getting it.

"We can't see what is inside the stasis well, because the light we see going back and forth is scrambled."

I nod my head, "OK, so how do we turn it off?"

"I did not know until just now."

"We came here not knowing if you could turn it off?"

Mr. Lark smirks, "We came here not knowing for sure if it was what I thought it was and not knowing how to turn it off. The *oculus* is impaired with the stasis well so close. I needed to be here, in this chamber, to figure out the secret of turning it off."

After a long pause, I ask, "And?"

Mr. Lark turns and walks along the wall of the dome. The surface of the walls displaying the same rough-hewn stone construction. There are also vertical square columns of smooth, finished stone rising from the floor, recessed into the wall at regular intervals. Each perhaps a foot square and four-feet tall.

"We flip a switch, Mr. Davies." Having said that,

Mr. Lark firmly plants his feet while facing one of the square columns, squares his shoulders, and places both hands on the top of one of the columns. He then pushes with what looks like considerable force for an old man.

The column levers back into the wall, the pivot point somewhere below the floor, and there is a loud *clunk* noise.

And nothing happens.

I wait and look around. Mr. Lark walks back to stand by me.

Still nothing.

Perhaps feeling my unasked question, "This stasis well has been here for ten thousand years. It is not going to blink out like switching off a light."

"So, if electrical stuff won't work in there, how did that switch turn it off?"

"The switch is a levered beam pushing a long rod that extends to the center of the stasis well. The rod mechanically switched off the EPS. Now, we wait."

Mr. Lark leaves me to go talk to Illych. Not long after, the team sets up flash-bang trip wires at the other entrances.

And then, we wait...

CHAPTER FOURTEEN

Two hours pass with no visible change to the stasis well's distorted mass at the center of the chamber.

The others engage in quiet small talk while we wait. Every so often, Mr. Lark consults his *oculus*.

Having become bored and tired of standing around, I find a relatively flat spot along the wall near the floor, not far from our exit. Backing up to the wall, I slide down into a sitting position on the floor.

With my right-hand index finger, I begin making circles on the smooth, black stone.

Lifting my finger, I look at how clean it is. There is no dust.

Looking at the rough stone of the chamber walls, I

can see dust built up on every upward-facing surface, every thin ledge. Looking across the chamber, I observe there is no dust on the floor anywhere.

That is odd for a chamber that has been here for ten thousand years or more. Is there a cleaning crew?

"Mr. Lark, there is no dust on the floor. Why is that?"

Mr. Lark looks at me, and after a pause, his head cocks to the side, his eyes scanning the floor of the chamber. His head straightens, and his eyes close while he consults his *oculus*.

His eyes open, "Curious, there is no mechanism for keeping the floor clean."

I am standing now and move closer to Mr. Lark, "Then why is the floor clean? The walls show signs of dust accumulation."

Mr. Lark's expression changes, "Something does not want anyone knowing they walk through here?"

"That greenish glow back at the bowl chamber?"

"Possibly. Illych, we may have visitors soon. Switch the door security to lethal, including the way we arrived."

The four men spring into action. Each doorway has its non-lethal security changed to combined-motion sensor, trip-wire, and directional-fragmentary explosive. Everything facing outwards from the chamber and down their respective corridors.

The preparations are completed in a demonstration of speed and dexterity.

Illych announces, "Task complete. Anything walking up on us will have a bad experience."

The distraction ends, and I look back at the stasis well. It has significantly decreased in size. The blurriness lessening, as well. The outline of a large, rectangular object the size of an automobile is visible at the field's center.

And something else. There is a figure inside the stasis well, standing near the box.

I say, to no one in particular, "Are you guys seeing this? It appears there is someone standing in the field."

Mike stands shoulder to shoulder with me, "What's that? Humanoid? God, I hope it's human. Kinda short, though, maybe five-feet. Can't make out any details."

The others join us in gawking at the shrinking field and its undefined contents.

With the stasis well's decrease, and the proportionally increased visibility of what is inside, Mr. Lark consults his *oculus*.

His eyes open, and he announces, "Amal Halluk is on his way. He is coming via the direct route from the temple complex above. I take his casual pace to indicate our presence has not been detected.

"Regardless, I estimate we have, at most, two hours before a Djinn walks through that doorway." Mr. Lark points to the exit to the left of the one we came in through.

"Our proximity to the stasis well has slowed time for us significantly. If there are hostilities, we will not survive. In one hour, we leave, no matter what."

The seconds then tick by while we wait.

After just enough time to get bored again, the stasis

well event horizon collapses. In an instant, the stone box in the center of the room becomes visible. The humanoid figure also snaps clearly into view. Human, male, dressed in brightly colored, primitive cloth and leather. His skin is a dark brown. His left hand holds a bronze cylinder.

The man begins to move in slow motion. His head turns towards the team. Realization shows on the man's face, his expression changes to fear, and he begins clumsily running away from us to the opposite side of the chamber.

Illych barks, "Stop him!"

Four men surge forward as one towards the man, closing the distance quickly.

It is not enough.

The former prisoner of the stasis well stumbles his way into one of the booby-trapped doorways, immediately followed by a loud thump and boom. My colleagues and I dive for the ground. After waiting a moment, we all stand and cautiously approach the exit.

Illych and Held flank the doorway and look in, around, and down the corridor, shining their torches in for a better view. Illych starts shaking his head from side to side.

Mr. Lark walks over to look. After pausing at the doorway, he steps through it. A moment later, he comes back into the light carrying the brass or copper cylinder the now-dead man from the past had been carrying. It is covered in dripping blood, but otherwise appears undamaged.

He says, "That was unfortunate. A conversation with whomever that was would have been enlightening."

The magnitude of what happened washes over me, "That man could have been in there for thousands of years. Think of what was just lost."

The team is silent for a moment, perhaps out of respect for the dead.

Mr. Lark moves first, stuffing the bloody cylinder inside a leg pocket on his trousers.

The team collectively gathers around the stone box.

Illych says, "He was only a couple of feet in front of the mine when it went off. It was quick, but what is left looks like it went through a blender."

Mr. Lark consults his *oculus*, "We cannot go back the way we came. The explosion woke something up. It is not coming this way, but I think it prudent we not get closer to it. To further complicate matters, apparently our competition also heard the explosion. They have increased their pace. We need to leave soon."

I ask, "How do we leave? Our way back is no longer viable, and the other path has Amal Halluk between us and the exit."

Mr. Lark smirks, "Ye of little faith. There is another way out that will still give us credible deniability before we translate. Our escape route is down the hall that man was just blown to bits in."

Mr. Lark shifts his gaze to the stone box, "First, we need to get the lid off of this. Then we liberate everything we can carry in the next thirty minutes and run."

Illych says, "We have plastique. We can blow it open."

Mr. Lark shakes his head, "I suspect some of its contents will not respond well to explosions. We might detonate something that leaves us in the same condition as that man who just ran away from us."

Held says, "How about we run a line of plastique along the edge of the stone lid? If we're lucky, it shifts the lid enough to get at the box's contents?"

Mr. Lark is quiet for a moment, and then nods, "Do it."

Illych and Held work quickly, taking blocks of plastique explosives and ripping off smaller chunks, rubbing them between their hands into long ropes. The ropes are then pressed onto the edge of the stone box's lid. The natural stickiness of the plastique holding it in place. A blasting cap crimped on a long piece of detcord is pressed into one end of the plastique rope.

The detcord is fed out until all of us are sheltered in the gore-spattered corridor. The end is cut and fitted with an ignitor. Held gets the nod from Illych, pulls the ignitor trigger, and drops it. We all move further back into the corridor, away from the chamber.

A loud bang later, and we jog to the stone box to observe our handiwork.

The plastique worked, sort of.

The edge blasted apart, combined with the lid shifting across the box about a foot, opened up enough room to comfortably get at the contents. Looking inside, I see the box is half full of strange-looking artifacts, and half of *that* is taken up by a single object: a metallic-finned, bronze-copper, engine-looking contraption.

The other half of the box contains two of those Egyptian-style, high-voltage lights, smaller versions of what is attached to the dome above us. Five unmarked, small stone boxes of differing sizes round out the contents of the stone crypt.

Disappointed, I step back. My expectations were diamonds or bars of gold. Instead, the contents of the box more resemble what would be found in an automobile service shop. More functional than anything else.

Mr. Lark says, "Illych, we are running out of time. Take everything we can carry. We must leave now."

Ilych is already lifting out what he can and handing it off to his colleagues, who promptly store them away in the black bags.

I look at the metallic machine taking up almost half of the box's interior, "What about that big engine thing? It looks interesting and technical."

Mr. Lark says, "That is a Thorium pile. I wish it were possible to take it with us, as well as the EPS underneath the sarcophagus. Unfortunately, it is too heavy and bulky to take with us in the next few minutes."

Illych saves the Egyptian light bulbs for last. As he starts to lift the first one, Mr. Lark stops him.

"We have everything we have time for and can reasonably carry. It is time to go."

Illych nods and puts the glass cylinder back down.

Each of us shoulders a bag while Mr. Lark points to our exit, indicating we should leave.

He then says, "I will bring up the rear."

No sooner does he say this, and his eyes close to commune with the *oculus*.

Illych is first into the corridor, followed by Tank, Mike, and then Held. They move quickly, with one hand supporting a loaded bag, the other holding a drawn pistol.

It is easy for me to keep up since my teammates are carrying the heavy stuff. After carefully negotiating the initial slippery part of the corridor – slippery from the guy who was just blown up – we then pick up the pace to almost jogging into the dark corridor. There is no leaving lighting pucks on the walls. Our goal now is to escape before a Djinn finds out we are running off with the loot.

We arrive at an expansion in the corridor. It continues straight forward, but there is also a set of stairs to the left as we enter.

Illych notes Mr. Lark has not caught up and signals for him on his COMDAT.

"Mr. Lark, we have a choice."

"Take the stairs; I am right behind you. Just needed to leave a surprise in the event we are pursued."

Illych starts up the narrow, claustrophobically low-ceilinged stairway. The stair tread height and depth obviously not meant for human feet makes for slow going, and the stairs seem to ascend forever into the pitch-black heat.

The others charge up after Illych, leaving me sweating and puffing while trying to keep up. At one point, I stumble and almost fall.

My misstep is noticed, and Mike's voice from above says, "Don't fall, Thomas. These steps are so small and steep, you might just keep going. And it's a long way back down."

Jerk.

A rustle on the stairs behind me, and I look down and back. Mr. Lark is climbing up the stairs at a terrific pace, almost skipping upwards. When he catches up to me, it is obvious he is not even breathing hard.

He stops, "Please continue upwards, Thomas. Now is not the time to dawdle."

Fortunately, it is not much further, and we catch up with the rest of the team.

The stairs end in a square chamber with a low ceiling of not more than four feet, ink black, hot, and cramped. I feel like an animal caught in a trap.

We have been climbing at a quick rate, and everyone – except for Mr. Lark, of course – is breathing heavily.

Being the closest to Mr. Lark, I ask, "What is the surprise you left, if you do not mind sharing?

"Flip-trap, just after the remains of that poor fellow from the stasis well. Amal Halluk is too far back for his mortal servants to catch us. If he wants us, he will need to advance alone. The trap will slow him down long enough for us to escape."

Illych says, "About that escape, which way?"

There are several passages out of the room we are in.

Of course, Mr. Lark points at the smallest of them.

"That way."

The escape route entrance is so small that Illych has to get down on his hands and knees, dragging his bag behind him. As he enters, he asks, "How far?"

"Less than a hundred yards, and it opens into a large cavern. Be prepared when you get there. You might have company."

That last part gets everyone's attention. Then, one-by-one, they get down on their hands and knees and crawl single file into the hole in the wall.

Mr. Lark is communing with his *oculus* and pauses to say, "Wait a moment, Thomas."

A terrible hissing noise can be heard coming up the stairwell, followed by a loud boom that can be felt through the floor.

"Interesting, the flip-trap did not hold him long," Mr. Lark is speaking with his eyes closed.

A male voice echoes up the stairwell, dark and melodic, almost mesmerizing.

It is Amal Halluk.

"This world has traveled around its sun many thousands of times since such disrespect has been shown me. This has always been a problem with mankind's short-lived existence. They are always forgetting to whom respect must be shown. Give me what I have come for, and perhaps someday, I will let you go free."

Mr. Lark appears to be considering Amal Halluck's words, "I beg your pardon, elder one. I have no wish for conflict. I merely wish to escape with my skin intact."

"Manners and polite respect, in this age?" You can almost hear the humor in the Djinn's reply.

Mr. Lark's voice becomes harsh, "Do not enter onto the stairs. I am comfortable talking at this distance. Come closer, and that will change."

That ancient voice again, "Who are you?"

There is a long, silent pause.

Amal Halluk continues, "What are you?"

"The one next to you is as weak as any man, but you are not the same."

"What are you?

"You… smell different…

"It matters not. I will take you back to my estate, and we can discuss the particulars at my leisure."

Mr. Lark's hand fishes what appears to be a very large gold coin from a pocket.

"No, we will not," Mr. Lark's voice has a distant quality to it, like the calm before the storm. He then makes a motion down the stairwell.

The metallic ping of the coin striking stone steps echoes upwards back to us. Two more such notes follow. Mr. Lark pushes me off to the side, and we both move away from the stairwell.

Even in the dark, with only the light of my torch, I see the distortion boiling up out of the stairwell. A twisting, blurred vortex that appears for only a second and then is gone.

The final result is the stairwell's four surfaces melted and drawn together, effectively blocking it closed. The Djinn's howling coming through the small openings still left in the stone conveys his rage.

Mr. Lark says, "He was caught in the flowing stone down below, not far from where the stairwell begins. It will take time, even for a Djinn, to claw his escape through several meters of solid rock. Let's get out of here."

The others did not stop crawling away during our encounter with Amal Halluk. They must have made it to the end of the crawlspace because the roar of gunfire from multiple weapons comes rumbling back through the tunnel. It goes on for what had to have been a complete magazine's worth of rounds for the whole team. Then, silence.

Illych's voice comes over the COMDAT, "Your warning was spot-on, Mr. Lark, something was here. It's dead now, though, so feel free to crawl through."

Mr. Lark gets down on his hands and knees and crawls into the exit corridor, and I follow right behind him. Being the last person when traveling deep underground is unnerving. Behind me, the Djinn's howls can still be heard in the darkness.

To distract myself, I ask Mr. Lark. "What is a flip-trap?"

"A *flip-trap* is what I call a device that, once activated, is invisible. When someone or something enters the flip-traps location, it is triggered. The captive is pushed into other-space, imprisoned in a featureless, spherical cage. They work well against living things. Not as well against the Created."

"So, people just disappear?"

"Yes, instantly."

That is really disturbing. An invisible trap that makes people disappear. I am regretting asking.

"Is there a way to escape?"

"With the right equipment, like an *oculus*, you can avoid being trapped all together. Otherwise, some specialized methods will allow you to escape. Or, apparently, a Djinn can just burst free."

I take that to mean if you are Mr. Lark, then yes, you can escape. For the rest of us mere mortals, probably not.

Our discussion has kept the panic at bay during the crawl to our destination. My aching knees may never be the same, though. We crawl out into a domed chamber, walled with rough-hewn stone. The others already placing the light pucks on the surrounding walls.

The stone floor we crawl out onto is damp. Not much further and it slopes down, disappearing into the blackest water I have ever seen.

Halfway out of the water is a creature the size of a grizzly bear and so pale that albino almost does not describe it: a perverse, unholy combination of octopus and lobster with a carapace main body. Long, articulated tentacles ending in vicious-looking claws splay out around its corpse, the floor, and into the black water. Its body is perforated with dozens of bullet holes still leaking pale blood.

"Please tell me we are not swimming out of here."

"No kidding," quips Tank, "I may need clean shorts after seeing that thing come crawling out of the water."

Tank is taking the light pucks, twisting them on, and then skipping them like flat rocks across the water. They eventually lose momentum and sink down into the inky depths below. The water has a milky-green shade to it, and the lights already under the water resemble the pale eyes of an ancient leviathan lurking below.

Mr. Lark says, "No, we translate from here. However, if it were required, we could escape through the water. We are far enough ahead to maintain plausible deniability to not have to do so. This was the alternative to the other entry route. The way we came in seemed the more comfortable."

Looking at the dead abomination lying in front of me, I agree.

Mr. Lark looks around while pulling a *dongle* out. "Shall we?"

We crowd in. A moment later, the six of us and our newly acquired loot receive a jolt of freezing air and nausea from our return to the Compass.

Without pause, Mr. Lark starts walking towards the Citadel. Illych and the others, in spite of the translation nausea, fall in behind him. The pace is again blistering, and we soon pass the guardians through the main gate, into the white light and warmth of the Citadel.

As soon as the gates close behind us, Held and Mike put down their black bags and sit down. Tank strips off his gear and stretches his massive form. Illych combines both, slowly removing his gear, stretching, and then taking a seat upon the stone floor.

Mr. Lark demonstrates no fatigue while standing

silently for a minute surveying the scene. I am hunched over from exhaustion. It is weird how it sneaks up on you, so I join the others sitting on the floor.

Mr. Lark says, "Place the artifacts we retrieved in the Library. Do not otherwise touch them until I have inspected them. I have business to attend to and will return in a day or two." He turns and walks out the opening gates.

As he leaves, it occurs to me Mr. Lark is the only one who walks back and forth between the Compass and the Citadel alone. The rest of us being required to travel in pairs…

After fifteen minutes of sitting and drinking water, we collectively push ourselves to our feet. A quick stop at the library, then the armory, followed by the cafeteria, and we can finally head to bed for some well-earned sleep.

Tomorrow is another day in the service of Mr. Lark.

CHAPTER FIFTEEN

We leave the next day, returning to Charleston to supervise the ship refit. I have little to do with this, other than to be brought along every day to the shipyard and watch. Everything in this experience is new to me, and I find it a stimulating and relaxing way to pass time.

In less than two short weeks, it is time for me to go on holiday like the rest of the team. From what I am told, Mr. Lark figured out a long time ago that 24/7 missions and lethal hazards slowly breaks people down. My colleagues are unsure how he came up with the current solution, but the schedule for years now has been ninety days on followed by thirty days off.

Those last two weeks pass without incident while soaking up the warm South Carolina sun. Holiday begins, and I say my goodbyes as the team disperses. I take a flight to San Francisco. Return tickets for thirty days from now already in my luggage.

The month in San Francisco ends up being the best holiday I have ever experienced. In the past when I went on holiday, everything was budgeted. At first, I was a little shy with the credit card, but after a couple of days, I decide that if I am stuck working for Mr. Lark, a good time is in order. The fun you can have in a major metropolitan city when you have virtually unlimited money is only limited by your endurance.

I do the usual tourist things. I also find a group of people to spend time with while visiting the book stores in the city. American women love a man with a British accent, and a few of them are willing to discuss books, go for a walk, and have dinner together, followed by spending time in my hotel suite…

The days pass quickly, and I soon find myself boarding the plane back to Charleston.

■   ■   ■   ■   ■

It is a bright, sunny day in mid-afternoon Charleston, and I find myself standing, soaking up the penetrating sunlight after walking out of the airport terminal.

Returning to the same hotel. I check in and wait for a knock on the door.

It is not a long wait. Illych visits to inform me dinner is a planned team event in a private room. Joining the others, I find Tank, who had not been with us in Charleston prior, is here now.

Tank slaps me on the back, "We're back together. Looks like the new guy survived in one piece. So, Thomas, how was vacation?"

I nod, "Well spent, but I did not get the tan you did."

Tank raises an arm and curls it to display a bulging bicep, "Spent some time on the beach polishing the guns."

Mike, also sporting a deep tan, shakes his head, "Yah, I was on the beach too, but it wasn't my guns I was polishing."

A visibly relaxed Illych says, "It looks like everyone took full advantage of their vacation. There'll be more time to chat later. Now, we earn our pay. The contractor working on the ship left an update on the progress at the front desk."

The room is silent as everyone focuses on Illych.

"The ship is ready. They finished the work a week ago and took it out for a shakedown cruise. It's ready for inspection and acceptance. That's tomorrow's task."

■　　■　　■　　■　　■

After dinner, we return to the hotel to find Mr. Lark waiting for us. He collects Tank, and the two of them disappear to the Compass.

The next day consists of me standing around, mostly bored, watching the others inspecting every part of the ship. A process that continues into the evening.

We check out of the hotel, and by mid-morning of the next day, Illych signs off on the work and accepts the ship. We then motor it across the bay to a dock and tie it up.

Illych explains we are checking out of the hotel and relocating to the ship to help us acclimate to the conditions.

Accepting the situation, I take in my new surroundings. Below deck, there are only two rooms: the engine room in the rear third of the boat, the front two-thirds a wide-open space with a high ceiling. The boat's superstructure is a single pilothouse with stairs down and a ladder up to the crow's nest.

The below-deck room has bunks, storage lockers, tables, and a simple kitchen. The floor is steel plate with an epoxy coating mixed with sand to provide friction even when it is wet.

The pilothouse has a single chair bolted to the deck. The radio and navigation equipment are the minimum required by maritime law. Having the *oculus* renders them somewhat redundant.

Below deck, Illych opens a duffel bag, taking out nine stone cylinders, each about a foot long and six inches in diameter. Each stone has a strong magnet at one end. Illych sticks the stones to the deck floor in a rough circle about ten-feet across. He then hands each of us a bronze translation *dongle*, explaining it is keyed to the stone circle now laid out on the deck.

The rest of the day and most of the evening are

spent with Illych and Held translating back and forth to the Compass for equipment. Mike and I remain with the ship and unload what is brought in.

Weapons, clothing, medical supplies, food, water, and so much more come in sealed, square plastic containers. Each one to be unpacked, and the contents stowed in their preplanned locations.

Late into the night, the work is complete, and four tired men fall into remarkably comfortable bunks.

The next morning, Illych shares more of the plan. We are going to conventionally motor out to about maybe fifty miles from the coast and then translate the entire ship, with us on board, to another point in the North Atlantic, close to where I had approximated Hy-Brasil should be located.

The ship's engines rumble to life and Illych navigates us out of the Charleston harbor. Once we were out on the open ocean, Illych throttles up to cruising speed. The dual marine diesels drive the ship at a respectable pace, leaving a wake behind us more approximating something from a speed boat.

Not long after leaving the Charleston harbor, the sway of the ship makes me nauseous, followed by projectile vomiting over the railing into the sea. Of course, none of the others are affected.

Held takes pity on me and returns from below deck with medication. The nausea calms, but I still do not feel completely well. Illych tries to improve my mood by explaining that eventually I will get my sea legs. He is a little vague about how long that will take.

Prior to meeting Mr. Lark, my only experience with vomiting was when I had the flu. Pocket dimensions, violent Faeries, and repetitive nausea. I am now understanding better Illych's comment about '*it is all about the suffering.*'

During the voyage out, all of us change into tactical dress. Magazines are loaded and weapons prepared. When Illych's *oculus* determines we are far away from any outside observers, we all take turns test firing the arsenal.

Piracy this close to the American coast is an unlikely scenario. Still, I find myself speculating about how shocked modern pirates would be if they tried to board this ship. The others are experienced soldiers who rarely miss what they aim at. Indeed, pirates would be very surprised.

Illych announces we have reached safe distance. The engines throttle down, bringing the ship to a standstill in the ocean. We are surrounded by nothing but miles of empty water in every direction. Illych is motionless in the captain's chair while he interfaces with the *oculus*.

He pulls a *dongle* from a pocket, unscrews it, flips the ends, and screws it back together. The now familiar flashing black of translation replaces the bright, sunny day reflecting off the mild swells of the ocean's surface. Then the black changes to overcast grey.

And we fall.

Or I should say the whole ship falls almost ten-feet onto the ocean below. I lose my footing and fall down onto the deck, staying there until the translation sickness passes.

While I am picking myself up, I can hear Illych's remark, "Must be a tide thing."

I say, "What just happened?"

Illych replies, "The *ouiblet* doesn't compensate for moving objects or surfaces. It's good at moving things between stationary points and will make sure we don't arrive encased in solid objects. This is why Mr. Lark scouts every arrival point with an *oculus*."

"We arrived exactly where the *ouiblet* was supposed to put us. Unfortunately, the ocean is lower now than when the *dongle* was setup. That's also why the stone circle is set up below deck. The *ouiblet* can't translate into a moving target unless it's marked. The only way to translate to the boat is to setup its own circle."

That is all good to know, I guess. At least we did not translate ten-feet down into the water.

The calm ocean and sun-drenched day we just translated from had been replaced by overcast and grey, with a cold breeze and swelling waves that bob the ship up and down.

The nausea of translation is worse this time. I realize we just translated without either the origination or destination being a prepared stone circle. Apparently having one on the ship does not count. I had been warned, not that it helped, about how awful it would be. It occurs to me that something that makes you feel this bad must cause cancer or something.

The others are similarly affected, and it takes a few minutes for everyone to recover. Illych then throttles up the engines and steers the ship into the waves. Although we have no plans to use radar or anything electronic to find Hy-Brasil, we do plan on using GPS to plot the search pattern. I pull out my notebook and write down our current GPS position. We are right where we had planned to start.

The translation moved us four time zones east and significantly north. What had just been a nice, early summer afternoon had been replaced with a cold, grey late evening. The sun will be down in less than two hours.

We start our search where I had determined Hy-Brasil would most likely be and then search outwards in a spiraling, square pattern. The *oculus* will see the Hy-Brasil distortion if within at least twenty kilometers, making the search pattern forty-kilometer stripes on the ocean map.

The rough ocean is challenging the seasickness medication that I am taking to its limits. Mike and Held take turns piloting the ship while Illych searches with the *oculus*. I watch the GPS and make notes of where we have searched and when to change direction.

Night arrives, and the ship's running lights are switched on. The part of the ocean we are in is not along a shipping route, and the *oculus* detects nothing on the ocean surface anywhere nearby.

The hours pass, and I find my feet getting sore from standing on the steel plate floor near the helm for so long. Sometime around midnight, Illych pauses the search. Due to the roughness of the ocean, the ship cannot just be halted in place. The bow has to stay into the waves and keep going, so we split up the piloting duties to get some rest.

Held and I have the last watch together. We switch off piloting every hour to give one of us time to sit in the captain's chair. Turns out, all I have to do is keep the bow into the waves while maintaining a low throttle.

When the others wake, the search continues. Four hours of sleep is all we are going to get, and I felt less than rested. The sea sickness had lessened to the point I can eat, and breakfast improves my outlook.

The sun is hidden by cloud cover too thick to let in much light. The black of night turns into a cold, dark, grey morning, and it feels like rain is coming. The search pattern continues, and I am starting to doubt my estimated location for Hy-Brasil.

With noon approaching, Mike goes below to prepare lunch. Not long after, Illych breaks from his *oculus* reverie to announce he found something. He points ahead and to the left.

Held notes the compass heading indicated and steers the ship in that direction. Perhaps ten minutes pass when Illych announces we are close. Looking out the pilothouse window, all I see are grey skies and waves.

We take lunch while motoring about where the *oculus* says Hy-Brasil may be. Afterwards, Illych announces he needs to check in with Mr. Lark. He goes below deck and translates back to the Compass. While he is gone, we continue piloting the ship in circles.

Everyone has a holstered sidearm on them since

Charleston harbor. Now that we have arrived at our destination, everyone takes turns going below and gearing up. Body armor and slung rifles, the same space-age-looking carbines used in the Hoia forest mission.

While searching for Hy-Brasil, my shipmates have been watchful. Exhibiting that same hyper-vigilance I had seen back in Hoia forest. There is not much talking, and when I try starting a conversation, I am told this is not a good time to talk.

If we were near something like the portal in the clearing at Hoia forest I am told, then maybe something could come out of Hy-Brasil like that faerie that attacked us. Visions of sea monsters from mythology tug at my imagination, and I check that the door to the outside deck is closed and locked.

Now the changes to the ship begin to make sense, the railing around the perimeter of the deck, the crow's nest above me being only accessible from the pilothouse, the small windows and steel reinforcement. This ship has been turned into a fortress against boarders.

"Is there anything that might come out of the distortion? Like that faerie back at Hoia forest?"

Mike says, "It's possible. I've never done anything on the ocean like this, but anytime a portal is involved, something may notice us and come out to play."

"Um, what might come out?"

Mike shifts his gaze from looking outside to looking at me, "Think about it, Thomas, probably nothing good."

Held says, "This place has a history of people

visiting and returning without any mention of problems. We shouldn't have much to worry about, but it's best to stay alert. I like to visit the Doctor as little as possible."

Silence settles into the pilothouse, with everyone intently watching the ocean around us.

Illych charges up the stairs from below, two at a time, and catches everyone by surprise.

Seeing us jump, he says, "What? Are you guys telling ghost stories while I'm gone?

"Mr. Lark gave me a key that should get us to the island. We just sail to where the *oculus* points us. There'll be a dense fog that we sail through, and the island is on the other side."

I watch Illych close his eyes and concentrate on the *oculus*. He points forward and left while whispering a compass heading. Held changes heading and increases throttle.

An impenetrably dense fog coalesces around the ship. What had been open-ocean is now a grey wall limiting visibility to not more than a few feet from the ship. From the pilothouse, even the bow of the ship is a vague outline in front of us.

Mike says, "That was quick."

Illych nods, "We were right on top of the coordinates when I activated the key."

Mike moves his face close to the pilot house window, "So what's up with this horror movie fog?"

Illych shrugs, "I'm sure Mr. Lark has an explanation for it none of us would understand."

Held throttles down, and we continue forward at

only five or ten miles-per-hour. Illych and Mike climb up into the crow's nest, weapons at the ready. The fog is thick to the point of being a wall. The ship could be headed straight into a cliff, and we would not know it until the last second.

Held's eyes are focused dead ahead.

I say, "What happens if there is something right in front of us?"

Held must have been thinking the same thing and flips a switch, turning on the deck lights and front running lights for forward illumination. He immediately turns them back off, as the reflection back from the fog is blinding, reducing what little can be seen to nothing. There is no choice but to slowly continue blind into the fog.

I hear and feel something bump the ship. Something that gives way to the ship but pushes back enough for us to know it is there.

I suck my breath in through my teeth, "Anybody else feel that?"

Held has his face right up to the window glass looking out, "Yah, I felt that."

Looking up through the hatch to the crow's nest, I see Mike and Illych scanning in opposite directions.

Illych sees me looking up and says, "Did you feel that?"

I nod, "Held and I both did."

Returning to looking out the pilot's window, I jump at the sound of shots fired above. Mike is firing towards the stern. Turning, I look out the pilot room door window.

He keeps firing in short, controlled bursts. A grey, translucent thing is pulling itself over the railing on the starboard side, close the stern of the ship. It has a bulbous head, larger than a human's, attached to a husky, square body. Its four thick tentacle arms ending in large, opposable flipper fingers. The thing has a pair of leg-like, flipper-shaped appendages. Even in the dim fog, the wrongness of it is repellant.

Mike's shots are finding their target. The reason for why the deck had been refit with steel plating from bow to stern is now apparent. Whatever that thing crawling onto the ship is, it is not bullet-proof. Every shot punches straight through and impacts on the deck. Sparks fly, and without the steel plating, we would sink our own ship.

Mike is focusing his fire at the creature's head. After it pulls itself onto the ship, it turns towards the pilothouse and opens its mouth. The creature's thin lower jaw hinges down far back on its head, its jaws open similar to a shark's, revealing a huge open maw with rows of sharp, square teeth. The black teeth reminding me of the obsidian swords used by the Aztecs. Swords lined with razor-sharp shards of black volcanic glass, all the better to hack someone to pieces with.

Illych is now shooting towards the bow of the ship. As soon as Mike's first target falls down and stops moving, he reloads and starts shooting at another of the horrors. I swivel between looking forward and aft. There are at least six of the creatures in the process of heaving themselves over the rail. Illych and Mike switch from controlled bursts to full auto. They aim at one creature and empty a full magazine, putting a single creature down. Then reload and target the next one. Their carbines controllable in their expert hands, they are putting the things down in good order.

Unfortunately, the rate these things are surging onto the deck is faster than they can be destroyed. Held tells me to take the wheel and maintain the same heading on the compass. He then grabs a duffel bag from the floor of the pilothouse and ascends up the ladder to the crow's nest. I keep my eyes forward and watch the deck fill with wide-mouthed monstrosities. The gunfire from above is now a continuous thunder.

One of the things makes it to the pilothouse front window. So close that I can see there are just sunken pits where its eyes should be. The thing's slimy, grey flesh is translucent in places with pulsating organs visible inside its body. The first one to make it to the pilothouse makes a tentative swipe at the window, leaving a slime trail behind. Its next swing has force to it, making a loud booming noise.

One of the shooters, Illych I think, leans over and unloads at almost point-blank range into the thing's head. Slime and goo, as well as chunks of its head, splash off the window. I am piloting blind now, using the compass as my only heading reference. There are so many creatures on the deck, climbing over their dead kin, as well as so much ichor coating the window, that I cannot not see directly forward. Not that there is much to see in this fog.

Something forcefully hits the pilothouse door behind me. The pounding continues, but the shooters have too many targets to stop the attack on the pilothouse door. I watch in horror as one of the things waddles up to the front window. Stepping on the headless dead body lying there, it stretches its flipper arms upward, out of my ability to see. The thing begins pulling itself up to the crow's nest. Its legs actually stick to the window, giving it support to begin stretching upward again. Then there is a gunshot with a deeper report. The creature's body peels off backward, falling flat on the deck, its head blasted open.

I risk a look up to the crow's nest and see Held holding a drum-fed shotgun with smoke wafting from the end of the barrel.

Looking out through the gore-covered window, it is not as dim outside as before. The fog is thinning. Apparently, this is the signal for our attackers to leave. The mass of those still alive move quickly to the railings and flop over the side, into the sea.

As soon as the monsters start leaving, the shooting from above stops. In seconds, the things are gone. What is left are carnage-covered decks fore and aft. Every now and then, an empty brass cartridge case rolls into the hatchway above me and falls into the pilothouse. I look around my feet and realize there are hundreds of empty casings on the floor.

The fog dissipates as if a curtain is pulled aside. Unlike the grey, cold, windy weather we had been in before entering the fog bank, the weather here is sunny and calm. The thermometer showing a comfortable temperature outside, warmer than what we had been in less than ten minutes ago.

Only now, I realize my hands hurt from gripping the wheel so tightly and are cramping up. Held climbs back down into the pilothouse.

He looks me over, "Okay?"

"Physically."

I have no intention towards humor, but Held smiles and says, "We're through. Those things either don't like the light or are limited to the fog bank. Regardless, look at their corpses." Held points out the window. I look and see smoke rising from the dead creatures as they visibly melt away into smoke. Just like the ciorii in my apartment or the faerie back at Hoia forest. That means the sea monsters are a form of Created, not living things.

Held takes my place at the helm and increases speed while switching the sonar on.

"Look, Thomas. The island is right there."

The goal of the mission is outlined above the ocean. We are kilometers out, but it is there.

Sonar shows the undersea slope leading to the island is clear. When the ship is close to shore, Held makes a ninety-degree turn and begins circumnavigating the island. Not long after making the turn, Illych comes down from the crow's nest and consults his *oculus*.

Mike and I sweep up the shell casings and walk around the deck to inspect the damage. The first thing we find is the pilothouse door out onto the deck is bent.

It still opens and closes, but it requires some shouldering in both directions now.

Other than dents and grooves from bullet impacts on the deck, the ship is undamaged.

Returning to the pilothouse, Mike goes below to reload all the empty magazines. This leaves me in the pilothouse with Held and Illych. We are cruising at a good speed and circumnavigate the island in about half an hour.

The coast is rocky with cliffs too high to reasonably go ashore. Only one place presents the possibility of a landing without needing a helicopter. A stretch of beach with a cluster of structures nearby. We stop within sight and consider our options.

Grabbing a pair of binoculars, I scan the island. A massive stone pier a battleship could moor at juts out from the beach into the ocean. Looking beyond the pier are outlines of buildings overgrown by vegetation. The tree line starts where the beach ends, and there are no signs of human activity.

Illych announces, "I scanned the *oculus* over the entire island, and it's just trees and rocks. There are some old, stone buildings clustered not far from the stone pier. Everything is overgrown and there's a road leading into the island."

Illych ends this with a pregnant pause.

Mike looks at Illych, "And?"

"Something close to the center of the island is blocking the *oculus*. The best I can tell, there's a structure that's shrouded."

I ask, "Is that a problem?"

Illych shrugs, "Shrouding is rare. It means there's something unusual there, and it doesn't want to be observed."

"Does that mean more trouble?"

Illych says, "It could be something or nothing. Probably an artifact left here when this place was created. However, since the stories of this place talk about a wizard living here, we'll proceed like we might meet someone."

We pilot the ship up to the pier and tie off. Rather than rush onto the island, we take a break. It is mid-day yet, so we clean weapons and take some rest, including a leisurely lunch.

After preparations are complete, we split up. Held will stay with the ship, locking himself in, while following us with his *oculus*. Illych, Mike and I will travel the stone road into the island and explore.

The pier construction is constructed from massive, polygonal, stone blocks perfectly fitted together. No stone the same size as another, and the shapes of the stones vary immensely. It strikes me as a strange way to build a pier. The end of the pier ends with a stone-block road running past several stone buildings, all overgrown from what appears to be ages of neglect. Empty doorways and windows, like the eye sockets in a skull, watch our passing. The stonework of the buildings is precise and quite beautiful. I ask Illych about looking around inside the buildings. He declines, saying he has already looked with the *oculus*, and they are all empty.

We walk the road into the interior of the island, finding it surrounded by a forest of ancient oak trees of impressive girth. The forest floor is clear, with not a stump or fallen tree in sight.

Some of the trees grow right at the edge of the road. Even the ones some distance from the road canopy over our path. The result is a shaded tunnel through the forest, much dimmer than the sunny sky above.

The forest is quiet. There should be squirrels and birds making noises, instead the silence is deafening. Though dimly lit, it is still not foreboding. Our walk through the woods is more calming than anything else.

"Illych, is it just me, or are these woods relaxing to walk through?"

"You noticed it, too? Yeah, this is a pleasant walk in the forest. The *oculus* doesn't see anything that's trying to influence us, but it sure feels like it."

"Influence us?"

"Like, to sedate us. You saw the Wizard of Oz? The field of poppies scene? This isn't like that. It's just a pleasant day out," Illych smiles and shrugs.

Not long after entering the forest tunnel, we can see the light at the end, so to speak. The road is flat, straight, and clear, so we can see all the way to where the road exits the trees into the sunlight.

Even before reaching where the forest ends in a circular tree line, a stone structure becomes visible. In the middle of the clearing is a polygonal stone wall. The wall forms a circle, arching away in both directions and around. Nothing can be seen atop the wall. Inside, a central building can be seen jutting up.

The road continues into the clearing, straight to the wall, and through an arched opening. Illych halts our advance and consults his *oculus*. After a few minutes, he says, "I can observe everything on the island with the *oculus*. Everything outside those stone walls in front of us is normal. The *oculus* can't see inside past the stone walls, though. I've scanned things in the past that revealed little, but they at least revealed *something*. This is different. The *oculus* reveals nothing inside that stone perimeter. I also get the impression that something is looking out at us. We won't be alone when we go inside."

After speaking, Illych shakes his head, an involuntary reaction to disconnecting from the *oculus*. He makes a hand gesture towards the arched opening in the wall, and the three of us proceed through the gateway.

During the walk and even now, as we pass through the gateway, Illych and Mike hold their carbines by the pistol grip while still slung from their harness. This grip keeps the weapons at the ready but not in an overtly threatening way.

The gateway passage walls are vertical up to a man's height and arch overhead. The gateway is as wide as the road, and the walls are thick.

Walls this overbuilt? What are they keeping out, dinosaurs?

The road continues straight through the gate to the stone building inside. Between the walls and the central keep is a well-tended lawn of short, green grass.

For an ancient abandoned fortress on a secret, hidden island, they sure have up-to-date landscaping. The neatly kept lawn is also confirmation of Illychs' belief that someone is in here.

The warm sunlight and green grass reinforce the positive vibe this place gives off.

The team stands in the road about halfway between the wall and the keep, looking at the large double doors on the building where the road ends. The doors are set in a raised arch like the gate in the wall. The stonework of the keep is mostly a light grey. The doors are black stone with fine carving work upon the surfaces. My looking closer to work out the carved details is cut short when both doors swing open and away from each other.

The doors opening reveals a four-foot tall, gangly humanoid standing inside. It is a goblin, and an exact copy of the Doctor back at the Citadel. It is clothed in servant's attire reminiscent of the renaissance era, and both its hands are in front of it with the palms up.

Illych and Mike instinctively space themselves away from each other. I am now standing in between them, gawking at the creature. The goblin takes several small, slow steps outside. The glint of the sun reflecting off its oversized, solid-black eyes.

Then it speaks, in a high-pitched male voice, like an adolescent boy. "My master offers a peace bond during your stay within the walls of this place. He wishes to extend his hospitality to you as guests in his home. If you accept his offer, you will be under his protection during your visit." The goblin's English is flawless, if somewhat archaic, in its pronunciation.

Illych, Mike, and I stand still for a moment. I decide to reply. The goblin is offering something old and not readily understood in the modern era.

I say, "The peace bond is accepted. No violence by our hand will be committed in this place. Your master's hospitality is welcome, and we look forward to meeting with him in peace." Illych and Mike look at me but say nothing. I hope I have not messed up the formalities. If whomever is here has really been on this island for hundreds of years, their idea of social niceties will be old-world. We need to be careful to not give offense by saying something that could be interpreted as rude.

"Please, wait here for my master." The goblin turns and walks back into the keep.

CHAPTER SIXTEEN

A moment after the goblin disappears inside the keep, a man, short by modern standards, walks out of the shadowed doorway. Deeply tanned and of Caucasian heritage, his clothing is simple. A black linen shirt belted at the waist and black linen trousers tucked into black boots. I would have thought the all-black color choice odd if not for the knowledge of why we monochromatically match.

A golden skull cap covers his scalp half-way down his forehead and all the way down the back of his head, giving the impression it is as much a part of his head as hair would have been.

The sleeves of his shirt stop at the elbow, his forearms banded with silver and black bands tight on his skin from wrist to elbow. Eyes dark and bright with intelligence regard us. His exotic appearance includes a neatly trimmed moustache and goatee. The lines on the man's face betray his advanced age, but he carries himself as a fit, young man might.

He says, "Peace be upon you. Welcome and be at ease. You are guests within my home. My name is Balthazar" he then bows deeply at the waist. His English is easy to understand, but I am unable to place his accent.

"Peace be upon you, Balthazar. Thank you for your welcome. I am Thomas. My companions are Illych and Michael," Indicating each of them in turn.

"Let us go inside, out of the bright sun, and partake of my humble hospitality. It has been a great while since I have received visitors," He then turns to walk inside.

Illych looks at me, smiles, and waves me forward. I follow Balthazar inside, with my companions close behind.

The ground floor of the keep is a single great room. One corner is taken up with an ornate spiral staircase going up. A stone railing in the opposite corner protects the opening of straight stairs going down. An immense fireplace dominates one wall. Curious looking objects of metal and crystal, or maybe glass, decorate a mantle of beautifully carved wood

A high ceiling is supported by beams carved from single stones. There are no windows at the ground floor, as should be expected for a fortified keep. The center of the room is taken up by a dining table capable of seating ten. Between the dining table and the fireplace is a sitting area with a semicircle of padded wooden chairs, heavily built from a lustrous, dark wood and gleaming in the light. Each chair shares, or has, their own small table made from the same rich wood.

Illumination is provided by crystal lamps overhead emitting a pure, white light. They do not appear to be burning anything, and I see no wires attached to them. The light touches everything in the room while producing almost no shadows.

Balthazar continues into the room to the semi-circle of chairs, waiving for us to sit, "Please sit with me, and we can have a conversation."

Illych and Mike look uncomfortable at sitting in a potentially hostile situation.

I say, "We must sit and talk; otherwise, we are snubbing the offered hospitality. If something was going to happen, it already would have."

Illych and Mike carefully set their weapons down within easy reach, leaning them against the chairs they choose to sit on, picking spots with at least one empty chair between them and Balthazar.

My curiosity gets the better of me, and I choose to sit next to Balthazar, at a slight angle to face him.

"I must apologize for the attack on your ship when you crossed the boundaries to this island."

Illych blurts out, "Those things follow your orders?"

"Yes, they are posted as guards against unwanted visitors. There are few who know how to come here without my opening the boundaries. Those like myself know how to pass over the guardians. Anything else coming in is more likely to be an Adversary."

I say, "What about the others who have visited? None of the accounts I have read from visitors to Hy-Brasil mention guardians."

"Unfortunately, my visit to this place was not planned. I did not bring certain… tools with me and am only able to open the boundaries every seven years for a month's time. If I am fortunate, someone will be sailing in the area, and I will receive a visitor."

I say, "So, you could leave if you wanted to?"

Balthazer's expression shifts slightly more serious, "Let us share stories. Please, tell me what brings you to my refuge, and I will tell the story of how I came to be here."

"An exchange of stories, then?"

Balthazar nods.

"We found the journal of Captain John Nesbit in a faerie lair in Romania. The Captain visited you many years ago. His journal spoke of this place. The captain's possessions included a map showing this island. An expedition was organized, and now we are here." No reason to give away too many details. Like how we translate around, or what an *oculus* is.

Balthazar appears saddened by the news, "I remember the good captain's visit. He was a decent enough fellow. Not long after I came to this place, he wandered in, and I commissioned him to get a letter to my residence. I concluded he had failed, as none came to help me leave.

"The tools and weapons you carry, I have never seen their like before. It has been over seventy years since someone else last set foot on this island. You were not sent by one of my brothers. Who are you, and how did you know how to get past the boundaries? This is secret knowledge, ancient and unshared outside the brotherhood of the Magi. Whom do you serve?" Balthazar's body language does not change. He is obviously completely confident in his safety. The question, however, makes something shrivel up in my chest. I am sure the wrong answer will have consequences.

I say, "We are bound in service and cannot speak of it. I do not know our master's affiliation or association. I say to you: we were not sent here to harm you. Our discoveries made us curious, and we came here to see what there was to see. As to our crossing of the boundary, our master provided the means to do so. We do not know its workings," I speake truthfully, hoping it is the right answer.

"I can see that your minds are warded against being touched. The workmanship is excellent and performed by ancient hands. Regardless, I can still faintly perceive your thoughts, and you speak the truth."

Balthazar must be referring to the crown the Doctor back at the Citadel installed to shield our thoughts and emotions from outside observers.

"I will now share with you how I came to be here."

I raise a hand, "Please forgive my interrupting. Before you begin, could you share how you can speak the language we are comfortable with as if you were born to it? English was very different over three hundred years ago. I mean, if you have actually been here that long."

"I am Balthazar and a Magus of old. My line stretches back in time almost to the beginning. It is useful to speak as a native when one travels. You are shielded from my learning your language from you. But the last to set foot on this island spoke your language in its more recent form. I learned it from them. How exactly is a story for another day.

"Now we will discuss how I came to be stranded on this hidden island. In the year of Our Lord 1645, I decided to journey to what was being called the 'new world.' My brothers and I have known of the continents across the sea since the beginning. But neither myself, nor any of my brothers, had walked there since the ice retreated. After some consideration, I decided to make the journey and witness what was unfolding.

"Shortly after setting out from my residence in the Caucasus mountains, I came to believe I and my caravan were being followed. The sensation of pursuit disappeared when I arrived in Vienna and stayed with one of my brothers for a short time.

"Towards the end of 1646, I set out for England, planning to purchase a ship for the journey across the ocean. Not long after leaving Vienna, the sensation of pursuit returned. Something was indeed following me. I tasked two of my mortal servants to stay behind, so that I might observe what followed. Both servants were destroyed a week later. I then knew I was being followed by something that had ill intentions towards me.

"I decided trying to return to Vienna would bring a confrontation sooner, and perhaps, on terms to my Adversary's advantage. Instead, I pressed on with the belief that once at sea, the pursuit would end. A pause was necessary in Paris, as my mortal servants needed rest and resupply. Wards were set and guards posted. We were attacked, really more of a reconnaissance, I believe. I will not discuss the form of the attack, but it told me much of the nature of my pursuers. The position in Paris was untenable. Another attack would be much larger, endangering the city. We completed our resupply and quickly left for Calais in order to cross to England.

"There were several attacks along the way. The Adversary was trying to slow us down and weaken those travelling with me. Half my mortal servants perished between Paris and Calais.

"The attacks were unfocused and of a particularly vicious and vile nature. Mortal men of that day were ill-equipped to defend themselves. The people living in the areas we traversed suffered in our passing.

"We crossed the channel with due haste. Upon arriving in England, I could feel the pursuit diminish. Our pursuers were delayed by the channel.

"I did not rest in London, though. A ship was immediately purchased, provisioned, and crewed in less than two weeks. It was very early spring, and we should have waited a month more to let winter fully pass; however, the pursuers were now on English soil, and I needed to put some open ocean between us.

"The night before we set sail, we were attacked again. I was forced to become personally involved, as the attackers were legion. Many mortals near to the pier where my ship was docked perished in fear and pain. Only two of my mortal servants survived. After destroying the attackers, I instructed the two remaining men to travel quickly to Vienna and tell my brother what happened. My hope was that they could slip away while the Adversary was regrouping. Since then, I have concluded they were likely not successful.

"Earlier that day, the crew had boarded the ship in preparation to leave. Terrified by what they had just seen, they demanded to be released and allowed off the ship. I forced them to remain aboard and instructed the captain to cast off and head for open ocean. Our course was north up the channel. Then past Scotland and Northern Ireland. Once we made the turn southwest past Ireland, there was another attack. The Adversary now had ships, three of them, manned by vile creatures and propelled by unnatural means. We would not be able to outrun them.

"Since leaving London, my new destination was here, Hy-Brasil. I could not shake the pursuit, and my Adversary was preventing communications to my brothers. I ordered the captain to maintain the heading that would bring us here. We were less than a day from Hy-Brasil when the Adversary's ships became visible to the crew.

"Although my mortal servants had perished, I had hidden aboard the ship several ancient servants. Called 'goblins' by those unfamiliar with their true origins. They are ancient creations from when the world was young, and they have served the house of Balthazar for eons. Although they are incapable of affection or emotion, I am still fond of them.

I took the one best-suited for the task. Even though ancients may look the same, they are all unique in one way or another," Balthazar is showing the faintest emotion as he recalls the events from three hundred and fifty years ago.

"Once an ancient servant is properly aligned with a new master, it can be commanded in a language other than the one of its creation. But for the task I was sending my servant on, it would require I speak its true and ancient language to it. This is difficult and requires time. With pursuit so close, time was limited. I commanded it to attack our pursuers, to rend and unmake them. The ancient did as commanded. I did not witness what happened, but it worked. My pursuers were forced to stop and fight. The delay was long enough for me to make it to Hy-Brasil. I have been here since."

Illych interrupts, asking the question I was thinking, "I thought the physical form of an ancient could only be temporarily destroyed? That over time they would remake their form in our world? From your story, it sounds like the goblin was forever lost."

"When its physical form is destroyed by weapons forged in this world, then yes, its spirit will find a place to rest and remake its body. However, I could feel the end of the battle even at a distance. The enemy unleashed a terrible weapon, and the ancient was unmade. It was a horrible crime. Such creations cannot be made again. Those that exist now are all there will ever be."

I say, "You have been here ever since? For three hundred and fifty years?"

"Yes."

Balthazar smiles, "Enough of the past, let us speak of the future. I wish for your master to visit me. He must be powerful and wise to be able to send you through the boundaries unbidden to this island. Such a master I wish as an ally, so I might leave this place."

While I was considering what Balthazar just said, Illych says, "We can't speak for our master. He'll expect a report of what we experienced during our visit. I'll inform him of your request that he visit you."

Balthazar nods, "Unfortunately, that is too much uncertainty. Your visit is a unique opportunity. Thomas will remain here as my guest and hostage."

Illych and Mike visibly tense at Balthazar's statement, their hands instinctively going to their weapons.

Balthazar commands, "Stop! No harm will come to Thomas. If necessary, my servants will disable you and return you to your ship."

Two goblins materialize, as if out of thin air. One is almost close enough to touch Mike, and the other is positioned similarly to Illych. They stand unmoving in their outdated attire, looking straight at us. So close, we can see our reflections in their solid-black eyes.

Balthazar says, "There will be no violence in my house after a peace bond has been given. By either of us."

I say, "Illych, taking a hostage to initiate a discussion is an old-world practice. It is not accepted in the modern era, but for someone with Balthazar's experience, it is quite normal. I am sure nothing will happen to me. Go back and report. We will see what happens from there."

Illych shakes his head, "This won't be well-received when we get back."

I can't think of anything else to say. Balthazar is holding all the cards. Plus, I feel positive about our meeting with Balthazar. He is friendly, but not overly charming, and has made no overt threats, other than that the peace bond would be observed by both parties in spite of my kidnapping.

Illych and Mike stand.

Illych says, "We'll take your message to our master."

Balthazar nods and waves a hand towards the doors out to the courtyard.

Illych looks at me and says, "Good luck."

I nod and try to look confident, as the weight of what is happening begins to sink in. Even though my experiences over the last few months have been a series of life-altering events, I realize that if Karl Lark does not come for me, I will spend the rest of my life on this little island with an ancient sorcerer and his pet goblins. This is not the life I foresaw for myself, even after Mr. Lark had already altered my previous vision for my future.

Illych and Mike stride out through the opening

doors. I stand up from my chair but do not follow as they leave. The doors then close, leaving me alone with Balthazar and his two goblin servants.

"How long do you think it will be until they get the message to your master?"

I have to think about that. Walk back to the boat. Sail out to the open ocean, putting some distance to the island before translating to the US coast. Then someone would translate back to the Compass and get a message to Mr. Lark.

Perhaps, it would be best to be vague.

"Difficult to say, I am not aware of my master's whereabouts," It is a truthful statement. I haven't a clue as to how Karl Lark will deal with the situation.

Balthazar smiles, "Sometime, then? That pleases me. We will have plenty of time to visit."

Mentally shrugging, I decide to make the best of a unique situation. Glass half-full and all that.

"Yes, Balthazar, let's sit and talk for a while."

Balthazar says, "Since you are now my guest, perhaps you should pick a topic to discuss?" He sits back comfortably in his chair. Obviously, he is enjoying having another person to talk to.

He continues, "You are not the same as the other two. They are accomplished soldiers. Proud, brave and disciplined, somewhat rigid in their thinking and prone to solving problems with violence. I also believe they are elite soldiers, perhaps grenadiers or a nobleman's personal guard?"

I consider Balthazar's words and how to start such a

conversation. "They are elite warriors, even among the elite. My master chose them carefully."

Balthazar nods, "You are not rigid as they are. Your speech shows a focus on learning and knowledge. There have been many visitors to this island over the last three hundred and fifty years, but your small party is unique among them. The soldiers I understand. But what are you?"

"I am a librarian." A truthful statement, if not completely descriptive.

"Yes, a learned man. You are not a 'scientist,' though, as I believe they are calling men these days who seek knowledge. More of a wizard's apprentice perhaps? This will make our discussion while we await your master even more stimulating."

Since I am a captive already, and Balthazar seems in good spirits, I am going to risk some questions.

"Balthazar, my apologies for asking such a direct question, but what are you?" I flinch inside a little after asking the question. If Balthazar interprets the question as rude, the tone of the discussion might change abruptly.

Balthazar does not stop smiling. "That is the first question. It is a good question and politely asked. I am a Magus, part of a brotherhood, originally seven in total. Each of us apprenticed to the former in our line. When our master's age finally takes their last strength, they pass the burden of their line to another. The Magi were founded eons ago, long before any current recorded history.

"When you ascend to take the name of your line, you leave your old name behind. I became Balthazar, with memories and knowledge spanning back to the beginning of my line."

"You can remember that much?"

"Digging deep into the past is not done lightly. Only by deep meditation can memories be reconstituted from ancient times. At my place of power, there are also vast libraries with much written down by the long line of Balthazar."

"Seven Magi? I have read many old books on the occult, and there is no mention of you."

"In the beginning, there were seven. Over time, fate challenged transferring the mantles of two of us. Those mantles were then each broken into three. Each of the three passed to a worthy champion, and they became the Illuminated. Thus, there are five Magi and six Illuminated.

"When you live as long as the Magus does, you tend to disconnect from the outside world. The successors chosen to ascend are carefully observed over decades of service. Anyone who would choose to enjoy a public life cannot ascend."

I shiver a bit when Balthazar says, *'cannot ascend.'* That statement gives the impression the candidate is done away with versus finding other pursuits. Perhaps a version of how Karl Lark remains anonymous? Keeping the pool of those who know too much small…

"We are quiet. The Magi were created to balance out the efforts of the Adversary."

"The Adversary? What is the *Adversary*?"

"It is not known. The Adversary has never been revealed," Balthazar says this with a faraway look in his eyes.

"In eons of history, you have never figured out what you are fighting?"

"We do not fight the Adversary. We facilitate human survival, typically by unmasking the Adversary's efforts. The Adversary cannot be defeated by conventional means. He is ancient, even more ancient than the Magi. The Adversary's knowledge and abilities are beyond our understanding. He cannot be bested in any arena or endeavor. All that can be done is to prevent him from winning."

"So, you watch and intervene as needed? Is that why your name appears in the New Testament of the Christian Bible?"

"Yes, Balthazar was there. Not my personal form, but my predecessor after whom I ascended. A gift was given to make the Adversary's machinations less effective. Unfortunately, efforts to remain anonymous failed, and the visit was written into history. Perhaps through some unfathomable scheme of the Adversary. The Magi are not perfect and still remain human, and thus, capable of error."

"This is quite the history lesson. What are your plans when my master arrives?"

"I can leave anytime I wish, but I believe whatever pursued me here is still waiting outside the boundaries of this island. Hundreds of years mean nothing to them.

Based on your account of Captain Nesbit's efforts, visitors to this island are leaving unmolested. If this is true, then I can escape when visitors leave if I am not seen among them."

"Pardon my lack of understanding. Your plan to escape is to not leave?"

"It is a brilliant plan, isn't it?" quips Balthazar with a chuckle.

"Thomas, did you see any gardens on the island? Animals for food of any kind? This is because I am still living off of the provisions I brought here with me three hundred and fifty years ago."

I find this difficult to believe, "No ship could carry enough provisions for one man for three hundred and fifty years."

"I have an ancient artifact called a '*quixault*.' The inside is much, much larger than the outside. I can store a fantastic amount of anything and retrieve it as necessary. It is convenient when travelling and the local provisions are questionable."

"You have something like a tesseract? An actual tesseract? That you have hundreds of years of supplies stored in? How do they stay fresh? Even preserved food will not keep for hundreds of years." All those years of watching Dr. Who as a child just paid off; Balthazar keeps a TARDIS in his pocket.

"They have a word for a *quixault* in the current era? That is unexpected. Regardless, there are parts of the *quixault* where degradation of materials is essentially stopped. I have stored a marvelous selection of foodstuffs, as you will see at dinner this evening." Balthazar appears nonplussed after announcing he has a magical box with infinite storage that a person can carry around with them.

I think about what had just been discussed. Putting the pieces together, I come to a conclusion. "You'll put yourself in the *quixault*, and we carry you out of here? Is that your plan?"

Balthazar nods, "You are quick, and yes, that is my plan. Unfortunately, it is not as simple as that. Things inside the *quixault* cannot leave of their own accord. They have to be recovered by someone in possession of the *quixault*. I will need to trust your master will release me when we have put enough distance between me and this island.

"The inside of the *quixault* is unnatural. A human placed within will find their senses assaulted by the impossibility of the experience and be quickly driven insane. Fortunately, I am not a normal man. With proper preparation, I am be able to withstand its unnaturalness for days. I will find the experience unpleasant, but I will emerge with no permanent infirmity."

"How big is this artifact?"

"It is a small box that fits into one's hand."

"How do you get things out? Do you reach in and get what you want?" I know the answer will be much more complicated, but I have to ask.

"When you hold the box properly, you can see in your mind what it contains. Choose what is desired, and it will be released to you. It sounds impossible, but translating things from inside the *quixault* to the outside world does not have them physically leaving the box."

Balthazar said translate. I wonder if the *quixault* and the *ouiblet* have something in common?

Balthazar and I enjoy a long conversation that goes on for hours while his servants serve us wine and food. I cannot remember a more relaxing or mentally-stimulating experience. Balthazar is an exceptional host, and I am genuinely surprised when the tenor of the discussion changes suddenly.

One of Balthazar's goblin servants materializes and moves to stand beside Balthazar's sitting form. No words are exchanged, but some sort of message is delivered.

Balthazar says, "It is possible your master is coming for you. The same mark used to enter the boundaries when you first arrived is being used again."

"What about the things guarding against entry?"

Balthazar waives a hand, "I was not prepared when you first arrived. This time I am. Your master and his companions will pass unmolested."

From my own experience, I know whoever is coming will be here within the hour.

"Perhaps it would be best if you greet them as they pass through the outer walls, a show of goodwill and your good health?"

I nod, "As you wish."

Balthazar and I resume our discussion.

He stops mid-sentence, pauses, and then says, "An individual man approaches, who I assume is your master.

Perhaps it is time for you to go out and greet him?"

I stand and walk out through the keep doors, traversing the neatly-kept lawn to the wall gates.

When I originally arrived at the keep, it was mid-morning. Now it is afternoon but still sunny and warm. No sooner do I approach the gateway, when a single figure emerges from the edge of the tree line, walking out into the sun: Karl Lark.

I feel a surge of emotion. It appears Mr. Lark is not going to leave me on the island. My emotional response and train of thought briefly causes me to wonder if I am suffering from some form of Stockholm syndrome. The realization that Mr. Lark coming to my rescue makes me feel better is a little weird.

Mr. Lark faces me while keeping perhaps twenty-feet between us, and I wait to speak until spoken to. He is wearing banded, black armor, made from some sort of reflective, glass-like material that resembles obsidian. The armor covers his whole body while leaving his face exposed. An *oculus* is mounted into the left shoulder of the armor. The bands are finely interlocked, and does not appear to weigh its wearer down, nor limit his dexterity. I have seen many different suits of armor from across history in the museums of Europe. What Mr. Lark is wearing does not resemble anything I have seen before. I also cannot fathom the purpose of wearing it in this age of firearms.

During the pause while we stand apart from each other, Mr. Lark's face has that look I have come to associate with using the *oculus*.

After a few minutes of awkward silence, Mr. Lark says, "Thomas, you appear none the worse for wear. Where is this Balthazar that kept you from returning?"

"He is inside the keep. I was held hostage in order to bring you here, but my stay has been actually quite pleasant. Balthazar gave me a history lesson, and I have a good understanding of why he is here and what he wants. He has a proposal to make."

"Illych indicated something about his being unable to leave due to some malevolent pursuit. I plan to hear him out."

The two of us walk together back through the gates to a point half-way between the walls and the keep. The keep doors open, and Balthazar walks out still dressed in his simple clothes and carrying nothing in his hands.

Balthazar speaks first, "You are the master."

Mr. Lark nods, "Yes. But we do not call it such. Thomas is permanently bound to my service, though."

"Yes, I can see the mild *geas* of secrecy upon him but no stronger *geas* of binding. Why not bind him more permanently to your will?"

"I prefer to keep my people able to perform at their best. The skills they possess making them useful to me would not function as well if they were more tightly bound."

The conversation pauses while the two men regard each other.

"Your English is modern for someone trapped here for hundreds of years."

"Recent visitors have kept me up-to-date on the

language of the day.

"Let us be formally introduced. I am the Magus Balthazar." He bows at the waist, arms stretched out, and hands palms-up. "You are welcome in my house. The peace bond extended to your servant is now offered to you."

Mr. Lark watches this with a neutral expression, "My name is Karl Lark. I accept the peace bond, but we must move past the use of hostages."

"I understand. At the time it was a necessary tool and not my preferred way of opening a dialogue."

"You say Magus? I am familiar with the term. You must be old indeed if you are the Magus Balthazar spoken of as visiting Christ at the time of his birth?"

"That was my master. To whom I was apprenticed," Balthazar looks serious as he says this. He is now looking Mr. Lark up and down, observing his suit of armor.

"Do you know the history of the armor you wear?"

"You have seen armor similar to this before? I found it on an expedition years ago. It took some time to learn its secrets, and it has served me well ever since."

"That armor is old, truly ancient. There was a time when humans ruled over all. There are things that still walk this earth that remember that time and the tyranny that armor represents. You should take care whom, or what, sees you in it."

He then smiles, "Let us get inside, out of the sun, and converse in a more cordial environment," he turns and walks back inside the keep.

I follow Balthazar in, with Mr. Lark trailing last. Three comfortable chairs have been arranged in the center of the room. Balthazar stands by one, I walk to a second, and Mr. Lark takes the remaining. In spite of his armor, he is able to sit comfortably.

"Perhaps some refreshment while I explain the history of my predicament?"

Mr. Lark says, "Some refreshment would be excellent."

The goblins appear, offering wine and whiskey. Mr. Lark's reaction to the appearance of the goblins is noticeably less than Illych's had been.

Balthazar says, "The brotherhood, of course, knew of the existence of all the continents since ancient times, but no living Magus had set foot there since before the ice came. Ever curious and titillated by the recent European discovery, I met several of my fellow Magi, and we determined that one of us should go. Being the junior of those in attendance, it fell to me, as I knew it would.

"I prepared my household for an extended absence. In the traveling company would be: my ancient servants you have seen here, plus one whom I have lost; my three apprentices; and several other bound, mortal-body servants. It was certainly not an army, but a formidable company to be sure.

"My residence is ancient and storied, as befits the name Balthazar, and not far from the Caspian Sea, at the base of Shahgah Mountain. My soul yearns to be within its cool walls again and to travel to the Caspian

Sea and look upon its waters. It has been too long I am afraid.

"We traveled by horseback. My ancient servants required no such accommodations, of course, only those of us who were mortal. We had some extra horses to carry provisions and those comforts as I deemed necessary. We travelled north of the Black Sea. My goal was to visit the centers of power and culture in Europe during my journey to the new world. Stops at Vienna, Paris, and then finally London. In London, I was to secure a ship and crew for the journey.

"Upon passing into the wilds of Walachia, something began following us at a distance. Or, perhaps, it had been following my company since our journey began, I do not know. It was there, though, and my augurs could not clearly see or understand what it was.

"I drove my company hard to get from the wilderness to Vienna, where one of the brotherhood resides. He would give me shelter."

"Whatever was following moved away upon my company's arrival in the more civilized parts of Austria-Hungary. My brother met us on the way, miles out from his residence."

Balthazar then gives the history of his arrival at Hy-Brasil, as he had explained to me earlier that day.

"This brings us to the question at hand. I would like to escape this prison, Mr. Lark. How can I persuade you to assist me?"

Mr. Lark says, "A direct question deserves a direct answer. It would be a challenge, to be sure. To begin, we must discuss what would be exchanged in return for my organization's services. Also, I need to learn more of the nature of your pursuer and the attacks you experienced."

"Yes, you should know what you would face in assisting me. Most of the attackers were strongly bound humans. *So* strongly *bound*, their minds were broken. In large groups, with the weapons common at the time, they were a threat to us. Even my ancient servants can be overcome by enough blades and fists.

"There were other creatures, ancient servants of a lower order, leading the bound humans. Also, abominations, created by the malformation of living people and animals, were part of the assaults. The enemy's ancient servants, goblins as you call them, *bound* any person encountered along the way, thereby increasing the strength of what followed us. Those ancient servants are what gave the ships pursuing me their unnatural speed."

Mr. Lark says, "These are all threats my organization can meet and overcome. I am not a man to wait long in making a decision and am inclined to assist. However, such an undertaking will be at great expense and risk to myself and the members of my organization. What can you offer to persuade me in making my decision?"

Balthazar nods, "Of course, remuneration for any and all expenses, of course. In addition, a significant additional sum in gold upon completion and a weregild to the families of any lost in the venture.

"However, I do not believe you are a man for whom

money holds much sway. I would venture an explorer such as yourself would want something more valuable, knowledge perhaps? Knowledge I have and will share, in exchange for your service.

"My residence has many ancient artifacts and a grand library unlike any you have ever seen. Payment can be in money, the answers to questions you may have, or even choices among the artifacts I am willing to part with. Time for study within my library can also be made available. My generosity should you get me to my residence safely will be significant.

"More importantly, you will have me as a future ally, perhaps? I have been observing you while we have been talking. Such things are not casually discussed with outsiders, but I see you have been elevated by a great blessing, to be sure. It must be a terrible burden at times."

"It is a blessing and a curse, and I do not share knowledge of it with my servants."

That is interesting. Balthazar just said Mr. Lark has some sort of secret about being elevated, whatever that means.

"Understood. Should you ever wish, I can help you better understand it."

Mr. Lark says, "Perhaps, but for now can you share something of who the Magi are? I know almost nothing of them, and I have searched across the globe for many things and have never met one, nor met someone who has even mentioned the Magi. Outside of the Christ story, there is no written history of the Magi. There is very little that can hide from my gaze on this world, but whomever the Magi are, they are indeed well hidden."

"We do not wish to be known or disturbed. Our places are the most hidden and difficult to find. I would very much like to return to my place of power and to receive the company of my brothers. I will explain more should you return me to my residence.

"Mr. Lark, would you wish for more time to consider my offer? My taking Thomas hostage was only to bring you here. You may both leave at any time."

"That is not necessary. I have made my decision. You will be returned home. I must leave now to make preparations. You should prepare for an imminent departure. Thomas will remain here until my return," Mr. Lark says this while standing up and moving towards the door.

"I will return in a few short days. Perhaps as a show of your intention to make good on payment for my services, you can begin Thomas' education. Teach him things that might be useful for my organization to be aware of."

Mr. Lark finishes speaking as he approaches the doors leading outside. He turns, gives a short bow to Balthazar, turns again, and walks through the now-open doors outside.

While they are open, I see the passage of time during our meeting has continued until it is night.

The doors then close, leaving me alone with Balthazar.

CHAPTER SEVENTEEN

Three days pass before Mr. Lark returns. During this time, I discover that Balthazar often wanders the island alone during the day and at night. While I need sleep, and Balthazar provides a bed to do so, I never hear Balthazar indicate he needs rest. He never yawns or looks sleepy. As far as I can tell, the Magus does not sleep.

Balthazar produces selected texts from his library in his *quixault* for me to read. Of course, the English is Old English.

The books provided are histories. I have always been curious about history when combined with my love of old books. Reading Balthazar's offerings, I discover much of what is written differs from modern archaeological orthodoxy. In most cases, the misalignment is striking.

Reading more of what Balthazar's books represent as true history, I learn that civilized human history did not start maybe twelve thousand years ago. Instead, they represent a spectrum of activity: cities and nations on earth for millions of years; humanity almost extinguished from existence several times; wars, super volcanoes, shifting of the earth's poles, meteor strikes, etc. Each and every time, humanity bounces back, but the destruction often so complete that humanity's own history was lost. Except for the Magi. They had always been here, in the shadows, keeping the history and preventing humanity's extinction. Preventing the Adversary from winning.

Woven through this history is the influence of the Adversary and the Greater Created, or elder ancient servants as Balthazar calls them. Often entering mythology as a pantheon of vengeful gods. Other times as angels, or daemons, who appear and push humanity in one direction or another.

Even the Magi do not know the origin of the elder ancient servants. How, or by whom, they were created. What is shared by Balthazar describes them as immortal, indestructible, intelligent, and wise beyond mortal comprehension. Neither the greater, nor lesser ancient servants have free will. They are essentially androids created for a magnificent purpose eons ago. Greater ancient servants demonstrate a level of complexity mimicking free will or choice. All the ancient servants were created with the urge to take action. A compulsion to keep busy, as it were. This drive to do something, even when instructions are lacking, causes a great deal of mischief for humanity.

The last of the greater ancient servants created, the youngest, is also the most complex and magnificent. Created just before humanity came into being and imbued with a flexibility bordering on free will. It came to resent humanity's existence and has plotted against us ever since. This is the *Adversary*. This tiny bit of history is the only direct knowledge of this great being known.

What I learn is the current modern run of human history goes back approximately 12,000 years. A cataclysm shattered the planet-spanning civilization that existed at the time. The survivors established footholds to attempt to recover, but too much had been lost. The fight for survival consumed those who remained, and most everything was lost in the descent into barbarism. For the most part this matches what Mr. Lark had only recently explained.

Throughout all this, the Magi watched, giving only the slightest assistance when needed. These books contain the answers to so many mysteries. The purpose of the pyramids in Egypt. What the red-haired giants of antiquity were. Flying machines, curiously similar to Vimanas in description, are even briefly mentioned. Between my time conversing with Balthazar and the continuous reading, I am exhausted each night and easily fall asleep.

Being around the ancient wizard is strangely

comfortable. He is easy to talk to and never seems bothered by my questions. What I can't get used to is the presence of the goblins. The two of them appear and disappear without warning, and their presence makes me feel ill at ease.

Time passes quickly, and I am surprised when Balthazar interrupts a reading session to inform me Mr. Lark has returned, suggesting we go out to meet him.

We walk out through the gateway in the surrounding wall and meet Mr. Lark and Illych halfway between the forest opening and the wall. It is dawn, and the sun has not cleared the surrounding trees.

Mr. Lark speaks first, "Preparations are made. Let us sit and discuss the details before we begin. It is time for a war council."

■　　　■　　　■　　　■　　　■

Upon returning to the keep, the goblins have already prepared a small table surrounded by four chairs. All four of us take a seat with Mr. Lark opposite of Balthazar.

"Balthazar, is your interest in leaving this place still true?"

"Yes, I wish to leave."

"Excellent. Preparations have been made, and Illych will share those plans with you now."

Illych says, "There are several phases in the journey from here at Hy-Brasil to Shahgah mountain in the greater Caucasus mountain range in Russia. First is the exit from Hy-Brasil by boat to the coast of France.

"Air travel has been ruled out due to the vulnerability while airborne. Also, we don't have core air assets as part of our organization. The opposition can probably easily knock a plane down and with less chance of us fighting back.

"Instead, we go by sea and then by land. Fifteen hours from Hy-Brasil to Le Havre, France. In Le Havre, we have vehicles and additional team members waiting. You'll be released from the *quixault* once we make landfall. Due to the European Union Shengen Agreement, travel from France to the border between Slovakia and the Ukraine won't require passports.

"We have the good fortune to have extra-legal assets available to facilitate our journey. In exchange for a financial consideration, additional assets will be made available to us through the Ukrainian and Russian legs of our journey.

"Our caravan will consist of three vehicles. All are security-upgraded and tough to take out.

"Mr. Lark and I will be in the lead. I'll be driving. The middle vehicle will be an SUV with Mike driving. This is where Thomas and Balthazar will be. The rear vehicle will have Tank driving with Held as shotgun.

"The vehicles are new and carry German plates. We'll change plates at the Ukrainian border and again when we reach the Russian Federation.

"Each vehicle has water, medical supplies, food, some consideration for personal hygiene, and weapons. Expect almost no sleep or rest until Balthazar has been delivered to his home. Stops are to be kept to a minimum, mostly to refuel. These vehicles are all diesel and have a long range between refuelings.

"Any questions?"

There is an awkward pause in which no questions are asked.

Mr. Lark says, "Balthazar, is your household ready to travel?"

"It is. I just need to place my servants and myself within the *quixault*."

"Please do so."

From the edge of my vision, I witness the two goblins appear and walk towards Balthazar. Once in front of him, they bow and disappear from sight. Once both of the goblins are gone, Balthazar hands the *quixault* to Mr. Lark. Balthazar then disappears as abruptly as the goblins.

Mr. Lark pockets the small box and nods to Illych. The three of us walk out the keep doors. The pace back to the ship is blistering. No one speaks, and Ilych has fallen into a watchful vigilance as we pass through the towering, silent trees.

In no time, we are back on the pier. The ship is docked, pointing away from the shore. Without delay, Mr. Lark and I board the ship while Illych casts off. We join Held in the pilothouse as he brings the marine diesel engines to life and a sound like the purr of a great jungle cat rumbles through the ship.

No sooner does Illych leap aboard, and Held opens up the throttle and that purr changes to an angry roar. The ship leaps forward, leaving a white-capped wake behind us.

This is when I discover that Mike and Tank are not aboard and are to be waiting for us in Le Havre.

During the trip from Charleston, we never opened the throttle up this far, riding high in the water with the bow angled up. The two screws drive the ship like it is a speedboat.

Held does not throttle down as we approach the fog boundary. The ship punching through in less than a minute.

On the other side of the boundary, in the real world, it is a sunny, calm morning. Much nicer than the day I first arrived at Hy-Brasil. The sun is warm, and the breeze created by the ship flying across the water is comforting.

For the first six hours of the trip, nothing changed. The rumble of the engines and the wake behind the yacht are continuous. No one goes out on the deck, and there is always someone up in the covered crow's nest. There is only a silent watchfulness in anticipation of what might be to come.

As we round southern Ireland, the weather begins to turn. The sky changes to overcast, blocking out the sun. Perhaps an hour later, a heavy, drenching rain begins.

Held shares that there was nothing about a storm or rain in the weather forecast.

The weather degrades with each passing minute. The temperature is cooling, and the clouds grow thicker, darker, and lower. The grey of an overcast, rainy day turns decidedly black, in spite of it being not even mid-afternoon yet.

The wind intensity builds, and venturing onto the deck is no longer an option. By the tenth hour of the journey out from Hy-Brasil, the crosswind batters the pilothouse. The calm water from the beginning of the journey has been replaced with great swells the bow plows through. Salt water spraying the pilot house windows. The up-and-down motion of the ship has me reaching for seasickness medication.

Keeping someone in the crow's nest is no longer possible. It is abandoned, and the hatch is sealed.

The effect of such inclement weather and heavy seas will only lengthen the duration of the sea leg of the journey.

Held monitors the maritime weather radio. The English voice coming from the speaker reports the sudden change in weather is not local. The southern coast of the UK and the western coast of France are reporting sudden, severe, inclement weather.

The ship shudders and rolls through the ocean, and my seasickness medication is at its limits. No one is speaking, and everyone is intently watching the gloom around us.

Due to the intensity of the weather and the challenge of piloting the ship, the helm changes hands every hour.

I notice Mr. Lark in the pilothouse next to me, consulting his *oculus*. I ask him, "Does the sudden change in weather mean something?" He opens his eyes and nods, saying, "It does. I just do not know what, though."

The last hours of the trip along the south of England and across the channel see howling winds buffeting the ship. Going out on the deck would be suicide with the almost surety of being swept off the deck into the roiling sea.

The temperature has dropped to almost freezing, and the maritime radio is sharing crackling calls of multiple mayday distress signals.

None of us is an experienced mariner. More than once, the man piloting the ship judges the sea and wind improperly, and the bow plows right into a wave, submerging the ship halfway up the pilothouse window.

It is the dead of the night when we finally plow into the Le Havre harbor. Pitch-black out, the wind howling, and the rain is coming down in sheets. Fortunately, once past the harbor entrance, the menace of the high waves disappears.

There is no need to try to pilot straight to the dock. Instead, the ship is positioned to the north side of the dock, and the wind does the work, quickly pinning it to the dock.

Illych and Held disembark to tie up the ship. No sooner than the ship is secured, Mr. Lark is off the boat and striding down the dock. I follow him, and not two steps out of the pilothouse, the driving rain soaks me from head to toe.

Shuffling across the pier, I grab hold of the rope railing along one side. Illych and Held follow. The three of us carefully walking to land, making sure to keep a firm hold on the rope. The wind and rain could easily take us off the pier and into the water.

When we reach land, the reason for why this dock was chosen becomes obvious. There is a road right down to the dockside. Parked in a row are two sedans – one black and one silver – and a grey SUV. All three are late-model Mercedes. We will be traveling in style.

Mr. Lark walks down the dock much more quickly than the rest of us and without the need of the railing. As the three of us work our way off the dock, we see him ahead, standing next to the SUV with the *quixault* in his hand. Balthazar appears just as suddenly as he had disappeared back at Hy-Brasil. Mr. Lark hands the *quixault* to Balthazar as I walk up to both of them.

Mike hops out of the SUV just long enough to hand the key for one of the sedans to Illych. He then jumps back inside, in a vain attempt to stay dry.

Tank does not get out of his car. Instead, he waits inside for Held, apparently deciding to stay dry. When Held tries to open the passenger door, it is still locked. He pulls on the handle and then knocks on the window and points. Tank looks and makes a show of trying to unlock the door. This attempt at humor plays out several times until finally Tank gets it right, and Held is able to open the door. After he is inside, the dome light illuminates the interior of the car long enough for me to witness Held punching Tank in the arm. Apparently, some pranks are funnier than others.

The flash of multiple lightning strikes turns night into day.

They are close, and the thunder is deafening. The show of light and sound continues for more than a minute and then dies out. We are frozen in place in awe until it ends. It is as if Zeus, the God of Lightning himself, joined the rage of the storm.

Engines start, headlights illuminate, and the lead vehicle pulls away. Inside the SUV, it feels good to be out of the wind-driven rain and cold.

I find myself in a comfortable, leather captain's chair. To my left is Balthazar. Driving our transportation is Mike.

Thankfully, there are heated seat controls at hand, and I switch them to maximum. The rain dripping off of me puddles in the bucket seat, forcing me to lift up and brush it onto the floor.

I glance Balthazar's way and stare in surprise. The Magus had been outside in the rain for only a few moments before getting inside the vehicle. Even those few moments would have left him drenched.

Balthazar is sitting there completely dry. Apparently it is good to be the Magus.

He notices my amazement and smiles without explanation. Then he begins adjusting the electric controls of the seat for his comfort. For being in a horseless carriage for the first time, he seems very knowledgeable.

Balthazar notices my wonder and says, "This is not the first time I have been in a conveyance moved by means less than obvious."

Our convoy leaves the harbor and merges onto a

main road.

Tank's voice can be heard from a COMDAT attached to the front center console, "Is it just me, or is the rain letting up?"

It is true, the hurricane howling of the wind has been reduced to a brisk buffeting. The sheeting rain now an unremarkable downpour. An hour of driving later, the rain stops. It is still the dead of night and pitch-black out, the water on the asphalt reflecting the black sky. If not for the painted stripes on the road, it would appear we are flying through the night.

Mr. Lark and Balthazar begin conversing on possible threats we might encounter. Both agree the most likely problem would be bound, local constabulary. This would pose a significant problem, as it could keep us locked at a specific location for a dangerously long time.

Balthazar explains he will be able to identify bound humans when they are a distance away. An ability for which Mr. Lark can provide some redundancy. Balthazar also explains he can shroud the caravan from any bound adversaries, making us appear as something other than what they seek.

I find myself waving my hand in front of me and thinking *These are not the droids you are looking for.* Balthazar looks at me for a second with a raised eyebrow and then returns to his conversation with Mr. Lark. I had not spoken out loud. Can Balthazar hear my thoughts in spite of the crown?

Balthazar's prior experience of being pursued

involved foes chasing down a group mounted on horses. Plus, his team's long layover in Austria had, in retrospect, been a mistake. It had given his pursuers more time to prepare.

Balthazar feels the team has a significant advantage now. Whoever had been watching and waiting probably had not expected Balthazar to come flying out on a fast boat, straight to France, then mount up and head for home so quickly and in such an organized fashion. Our Adversary had probably figured Balthazar would come stumbling out alone, trying to find his way back home.

Whoever, or whatever, is after him is probably regrouping and being forced to react instead of just putting a prearranged plan into motion. At least that is the optimistic opinion being shared.

Dawn's pale light dispells the black night around six in the morning. I have taken to stripping off individual pieces of clothing and drying them in front of a heat vent. Balthazar eyes my clothes drying enterprise then sits back and closes his eyes.

"Your fidgeting is distracting," he says.

Mike had only been out in the rain for a few seconds and had not soaked through the way I was. It is uncomfortable until the last item of clothing is dried. At some point after this, we pass into Germany and accelerate onto the autobahn.

Mr. Lark's voice comes over the COMDAT, "We have company. Behind us, about ten kilometers, coming up fast. Two bound individuals inside. Scouts, perhaps?"

Balthazar closes his eyes and says, "We are now

shrouded from their thoughts." His statement apparently meant to be one of fact.

I say, "At least we are in Europe. Access to firearms will be more difficult." Perhaps this detail might have been missed by the Americans.

Mr. Lark says, "I am not worried about being shot at. We are on the autobahn, and the real concern is our opponent binding someone and having them ram us. If our vehicles are disabled, it will give them time to pin us down. Mobility is key to the plan's success."

Mike says, "So we are going to Mad Max it down the autobahn?"

"Yes, that is one way to put it."

Minutes pass in silence.

Mr. Lark says, "The scout car behind us will be in visual range soon."

I find myself trying to look out the back window.

"Polizei ahead, less than ten kilometers, and he has radar. Balthazar, could you shift someone's attention from us to our pursuer if they were close enough?"

"Yes."

"I am requesting you not shroud us from our pursuers. I want them to see us and give chase."

"It is done."

"That caught their attention. They are accelerating. Everyone, increase your speed and keep ahead of our pursuers. We are going to race past the Polizei. At that speed, they will give chase. Balthazar will then redirect their attention solely onto our pursuers."

We accelerate, and sure enough, in less than a

minute, we rocket pass the Polizei parked on the side of the road. Its police lights turn on immediately.

Turning my head and body, I can see the Polizei rapidly accelerate onto the road, just behind our pursuers. Whoever is after us is close enough for me to see they are driving a dark-colored sedan.

The scout sedan is gaining on our convoy, with the Polizei's late-model BMW right behind them. After chasing our pursuers for a bit, the officer must have come to the conclusion the bad guys were not going to pull over. He or she pulls alongside, apparently to give hand signals.

The dark sedan swerves into the Polizei, driving its front wheel into the rear quarter panel of the BMW. This forces the BMW into a spin, and it slides off the highway, slamming into a concrete barrier.

Our pursuer's sedan had apparently been damaged in the maneuver. The front of their car is shaking badly, and they are slowing down.

The good news is we are no longer being pursued by the Polizei or our opponent's scout. The bad news is the Polizei are going to be swarming the autobahn soon. And our pursuer now has a pretty good idea where we are.

Mr. Lark's says, "Return to normal speed. The Polizei are not searching for us. Let's not give them a reason."

Through the window, I watch Germany passing by. The adrenaline eventually wears off, exhaustion takes over, and I doze off.

Mr. Lark's voice wakes me, "We have company. Increase speed to delay our new pursuers catching up."

Illych says, "At these speeds, we are burning diesel faster than anticipated. We'll need to refuel sooner than planned."

Mr. Lark's says, "I will make a call." I can't see him, but my guess is he is using a cell phone to call ahead for something.

Balthazar says, "Possessed, our pursuer is not under *geas*. They are possessed."

He continues, "A conveyance with three passengers, the same two bound that were previously chasing us, and one possessed."

I say, "What is the difference between bound and possessed?"

"The difference is significant. A person under *geas*, or 'bound', as you say, is still a normal man or woman. Possessed are people whose bodies have been given over to a spirit not of this world. Possessed have human bodies but use them in superhuman ways. They each have the strength of six men and will be much more difficult to deal with.

"I cannot shroud us from the mind of a possessed. When it is close enough to see us, there will be nothing I can do."

Mr. Lark says, "Held, we will slow down and let them catch up, and then you will disable them."

Looking behind at the car driven by Tank, I watch Held stand up in the now-open sunroof and stand arms-free above the car. He then pulls a carbine up out of the car and puts it to his shoulder.

Our pursuers are closing fast, virtually flying up the autobahn towards us in a late-model, high-end, luxury sports car. Held waits to fire until they are close enough you can see the people inside. I see the recoil of his weapon and hear the report of it firing.

Watching for the effect, I am surprised where the bullets impact. He is not aiming at the driver, instead his fire is directed at the engine. He keeps firing, and bullet holes appear in the hood.

A magazine swap later, and the engine begins to release smoke or steam. Our pursuers have closed to no more than four car lengths. Held switches to full auto and empties the magazine into the windshield, in front of the driver.

The target car swerves a little bit back and forth. Then it sharply turns right. Instead of spinning out, the tires must have caught a good bite of the road because the car flips and begins a high-speed body roll down the autobahn.

Taking a deep breathe in relief, I am glad to be putting distance between ourselves and the smoking wreck behind us. Looking out the side window, I resume watching the countryside and the occasional automobile passing by.

Balthazar says, "The possessed has resumed its pursuit."

Mike says, "Yah, I'm willing to bet someone pulled over to help, and they took the car."

Balthazar nods, "It is the same possessed. Your

speculation is likely correct."

Mr. Lark says, "I am picking up police radio chatter with the *oculus*. This highway will shortly be getting a lot more attention from the authorities."

Illych says, "We're two hours from the Austrian border."

After a pause, Mr. Lark's says, "Time for plan B. Illych and I will fall back and deal with those who are following us. Mike and Tank will continue on and take the next exit. Follow the alternate route, and we will meet up on the Austrian-Slovakian border."

Tank and Mike's voices over the COMDAT reply in unison, "Roger Wilco."

The lead car with Illych and Mr. Lark inside veers into the left lane and slows down. They fade from sight as we rapidly leave then behind. It is not much longer, and we exit the autobahn.

The next hours pass as we navigate back roads and small towns while strictly obeying traffic laws. Over the COMDAT, Illych and Karl Lark can be heard commenting on what they are doing. Illych slows down until the possessed catches up with them. Then they lead them on a merry chase. Apparently, Illych is an excellent driver, a talent further enhanced by the excellent German engineering of the vehicle he is driving.

Eventually, the possessed's inhuman endurance and reflexes narrow the gap. Their opponent then try to run them off the road. They are not successful, being ignorant of the increased mass of the armored sedan Illych and Mr. Lark are in.

Turnabout is fair play, and Illych succeeds in forcing the other car off the road, into a ditch. The sound of car doors opening can be heard over the COMDAT, followed by the familiar boom of rapid firing .45 ACP weapons.

In the distance, faint police sirens can be heard, followed by the car doors closing.

Illych says, "That thing was fast and tough. That was a lot of punishment for a body to take."

Mr. Lark says, "The possessed threat has been dealt with. Any trouble on your end?"

Held replies, "Negative, smooth sailing."

"How far are you from the meeting point?"

"Perhaps three hours."

"See you there."

"Roger that."

It is a tense, if quiet, three hours. Balthazar spends most of the time in a trance, and Mike focuses on the road. We finally meet up at a fueling station on a main highway into Slovakia.

While the vehicles are refueling, everyone gets out and stretches while remaining vigilant. Our convoy reconstituted, the journey resumes.

The drive through Slovakia is smooth and uneventful. At one point, Illych speculates aloud about how the scouts had probably reported who we were back to our Adversary.

Maybe...or maybe not.

But I appreciate there is no one trying to kill us, no back roads maneuvering, and no high-speed, death-defying stunts on the autobahn.

Soon we are leaving the western world and entering Ukraine. Ukraine is a big country, and it will be rougher going. I am curious how Mr. Lark plans on crossing zones in the ongoing civil war and then dealing with the presence of Russian military.

We refuel again in Slovakia, just before crossing the border. Nobody on the Slovakian side is interested in our crossing, but on the Ukrainian side, we stop at the checkpoint.

Ukrainian military silently inspects our vehicles. Illych passes paperwork to the Ukrainian customs, which apparently explained everything because we are immediately shunted into our own lane, away from the other commercial traffic. We are directed to turn off our vehicles and stand outside.

The silence is deafening. No one speaks, and no effort has been made to hide the weapons in our vehicles.

I am waiting for a shout, or whistle, followed by our arrest. When nothing happens, I default to waiting calmly while standing next to the SUV. It is not like this is my first journey into weirdness with Mr. Lark. My guess: this is what Illych meant when he said "*extra-legal assets.*"

A military truck arrives while we were waiting, and what I am guessing to be a military officer gets out and walks into the border guard building. Shortly after, a uniformed border guard comes out yelling in a language I do not understand.

This is apparently the signal for us to continue on. License plates are switched. No words are spoken while we mount up. A gate is raised, and we drive into Ukraine.

Austria is a modern, wealthy country. Slovakia is former eastern bloc and noticeably poorer. Driving into Ukraine is like crossing into another reality. The modern mixed with the old, and signs of poverty are everywhere. The quality of the roads varies from smooth and modern to poorly maintained and strewn with potholes.

We have to stop for rest after being on the move from Hy-Brasil for over twenty-four hours now. Arrangements for this need had been made ahead of time, and I marvel at the organizational skills of Mr. Lark and the team. In three days, they had acquired vehicles and outfitted them, researched the path to Shahgah mountain, and made arrangements for rest along the way while bribing our passage through a rough part of the world. I am part of a first-class, organized crime team.

Our rest area is a compound surrounded by concrete walls and razor wire. We drive in and position the vehicles for a quick getaway.

A handful of locals are present, and they have prepared food and places for us to sleep in a warm, dry building.

An exhausted group, we eat in silence, even Tank.

Balthazar and Mr. Lark sit together, away from everyone else, talking in hushed tones about who knows what. I do not care; my belly is full, and I fall into a bed.

Consciousness returns with Illych shaking me awake. Looking at him with bleary eyes and a pounding head, I say something impolite.

His expression is serious, "Trouble."

I roll my eyes, "Really? I just want to sleep."

Illych slaps a hand on my shoulder, "Get up."

Lifting myself from bed, I look around at the others. They are all up, armed, and looking through windows into the compound where the vehicles are parked.

Where are Balthazar and Mr. Lark?

"What's happening?"

"Ukrainian military in company strength."

"Balthazar and Mr. Lark?"

"They must have left while we were sleeping. One of our hosts woke me, and they were already gone."

I look out the window. There are armed, uniformed, soldiers everywhere. Parked in the gateway is an armored vehicle with a big gun on it.

One of them, an officer or senior NCO, is talking to one of our hosts I recognize from earlier. He points towards our room, and the two men start walking towards the door. Six soldiers fall in behind them.

Illych says, "No fighting. We're massively outgunned. I'm guessing Mr. Lark is nearby. Play it cool and say nothing."

The door opens, and the eight men enter.

"I am Captain Toloy. You are under arrest. Surrender your weapons. Now!" The captain's English is heavily accented but passable.

We comply, and the soldiers take our weapons and

empty our pockets. Our arms are pulled back and our wrists put in restraints.

What the hell is going on and where is Mr. Lark? I am used to us getting in and out undetected and unsuspected. Instead, we are being arrested. This is new for me, never having been arrested before, and the soldiers are not gentle.

There is a bit of macho interplay as the soldiers arrest my colleagues. One of them engages in a stare down with Tank. Tank's muscled form and broad shoulders dwarf any of the soldiers. At first, they act like Tank is nobody, until they receive the look of restrained violence he gives them.

They are a little more respectful after that. Getting the job done but without any added discomfort.

We are walked single file out to a waiting military truck and loaded in. This leaves us sitting on the metal floor of a truck, surrounded by ridiculously young-looking soldiers with very real rifles.

The drive lasts for what had to have been hours. The road is rough, and the suspension of our transportation is not designed for comfort. The discomfort taking away any possibility for going back to sleep.

No one is talking. Us or the soldiers. This leaves plenty of time to think. How does a librarian find himself under arrest in Ukraine? Where is Mr. Lark? With Balthazar gone, are we still being pursued?

By the time we arrive at our destination, wherever that is, I ache all over. We are half pushed, half carried out of the truck. Between the sleep deprivation and the prolonged sitting on the steel bed of the truck, I feel more than half dead. If someone gave me a corner on a dirty floor to sleep on, I would take it.

Night has fallen, and I am pretty sure we are in a military base or prison. There are concrete walls, razor wire, armored vehicles, and armed soldiers everywhere. It is like something out of a war movie.

We are hustled single file in through a door and down a poorly lit corridor. Steel doors open and close. At one point, we are walking down some narrow concrete stairs, and the smell of the air becomes increasingly dank. As we are being separated, Illych says the first words I have heard from him in hours, "Relax, Thomas." Then I am alone.

I soon find myself thrust into a dirty, concrete prison cell. A cube of a cell consisting of concrete surfaces and a steel-barred wall and door. A tiny sink and toilet, both filthy, and a raised concrete slab with a thin mattress and blanket on it. Carved into every surface is graffiti in Cyrillic characters and pornographic images. A single, dirty, caged light bulb illuminating all of it.

The guards remove the restraints once I am in the cell.

The bars are rusty, and apparently the lock does not work, because my jailers wrap a length of chain around the bars of the cell door to hold it closed and secure it with a padlock. They leave without speaking a word.

Thirsty, I try the water in the sink. What comes out does not look like water and vaguely smells of gasoline.

I say to myself, *"Relax. What the hell does that mean?"*

After thoroughly shaking out the bedding, I lay down on the hard bed. It is amazing what enough exhaustion will do because I fall asleep instantly.

The sounds of steel-on-steel wake me. A door down the hall has been opened. Without moving my body, I open my eyes and see a metal tray with two bottles of water and a small bag of potato chips just inside my cell door.

What is written on the bottles and bag are indecipherable, but the water tastes clean and pure. I rip open the bag to discover some sort of pretzel bread inside. I drink one bottle and eat the pretzel immediately.

Lying quietly, I listen for noises that might tell me something about where I am or what is going on. A low frequency throbbing, like a generator, is nearby.

"This is Thomas. Can anyone hear me?" There is no reply.

This place has no windows, and without a watch, it is not possible to know the time. There is nothing to do but catch up on sleep, so I nap some more. After that, there is nothing to do but think.

The sound of a steel door opening interrupts my thoughts, and I look up to find four Ukrainian soldiers crowding around my cell door. They remove the padlock and chain, and two of them enter the cell to collect me.

They half push, half carry me quickly away from the cell. We turn a few corners and go down at least one long hall. It all happens so fast I cannot keep track. The guards are silent, and I suspect my saying anything will not change that.

The short walk ends in a concrete room with several tables covered in the gear from our vehicles. I am strapped into a chair, facing the equipment-strewn tables. As soon as I am restrained, the soldiers exit, leaving me alone in the room.

There is no clock in the room, so I cannot say how long I wait until the door opens and a uniformed man enters. He is shorter than average, blocky, muscular, and bald.

"You are Thomas Davies?" The man's voice is deep with a heavy accent.

"Yes."

"Why your trip to Ukraine?"

"Business?" I really did not know what else to say.

"Too many guns for business. You paid bribes at border, why?"

"I am traveling at my employer's request. I do not know anything about any bribes."

The man picks up the blocky metal form of a COMDAT and waves it in front of my face. "This is a communications device. How does it work?"

"I do not know."

He puts the COMDAT down and picks up a *dongle*, one of many confiscated from the team and the vehicles. I unconsciously hold my breath.

The man looks at me and can see the change in my demeanor. He smiles. Grasping the *dongle* with both hands, he twists the ends apart. The *dongle*s in the team's possession at the time we were taken into custody are escape types set to return us to the Compass. If my interrogator flips the ends and reattaches…

He examines the two separate pieces closely and then flips the one end and slides them together, giving a final twist…

And nothing happens.

The man has been watching my expression while he reassembles the *dongle* and is almost as surprised as I am when nothing happens.

The rest of the equipment on the table is non-Karl Lark normal, and I am not asked about any of it.

"We will talk again soon. Take this time to think about where you are and how helpful you will need to be."

The door to the room opens as if on cue, and I am un-restrained and hustled back to my cell.

Once there, I think about what just happened. My guess is they selected me first for interrogation because they see me as the weak link in the group, which was probably very true.

They wanted to see my reactions when they handled the two pieces of equipment no one could explain. As they had expected, my body language gave away the items' importance.

At some point in my reverie, I hear thumping noises, perhaps explosions in the distance. Not long after, the faint sound of machine gun fire can be heard. Everything is muted but probably not that far away. Starting out as sporadic, the tempo increases. The sound gets louder, like the first shots were more distant and are getting closer.

The now-familiar sound of metal doors opening echoes down the hall, and another young-looking Ukrainian soldier holding keys walks to my cell door and unlocks it. He waves me out and does not attempt to restrain my hands.

For a moment, I consider trying to overpower him. He is alone, rifle slung, with his focus on taking me somewhere rather than my being a prisoner. The reality of the situation is that attacking the soldier would most likely end with me injured on the floor. At worst, I would be shot.

My journey away from my cell is the reverse of my arrival. One by one, Tank, Mike, Held, and Illych join me by the time we are going back up the stairs. We nod at each other in greeting, and no one looks the worse for wear.

Halfway up the stairs, there is a nearby explosion. The ground shakes, and dust and bits of concrete fall from the ceiling. What the hell is going on? Russia and Ukraine are engaged in some sort of a conflict, but where we were taken into custody is not even close to the hotspots.

Just as our team has been reassembled on our way out of the prison, more soldiers are joining us along the way. By the time we take an exit door out into the compound, we are a mass of men maybe twenty strong. I am wondering why the soldiers' rifles are still slung, our hands unbound, and everyone is behaving like we are not in custody anymore.

Stepping through the door into the compound beyond, I see it is daytime. The sky overcast and grey, but it is still day. The smell of gun fire and the sounds of battle are obvious. The staccato of machine gun fire can be heard coming from different directions. The walls of the compound block the view of the action.

Illych says, "This is what it sounds like when you're surrounded." The others nod in agreement.

Not thirty feet from the door are the three vehicles from our caravan. Standing between them and us is a smiling Karl Lark, holding his cane.

Next to Mr. Lark is the Ukrainian officer from the border crossing with Slovakia.

I look at Illych and catch him looking at me with the same question on his face. Where is Balthazar?

A sergeant runs up to us and starts yelling at the soldiers around us. Then he points away and starts running. The soldiers, to a man, unsling their rifles and sprint after him.

That leaves just us and the Ukrainian officer.

Mr. Lark says, "No time for questions. We need to get out of here. Your gear is in your respective vehicles. Captain Ulant here will be riding with Illych and myself to guarantee our safe passage. Quickly now, we must go."

As we load up, a team of soldiers carrying equipment runs into the compound. One of them has a radio backpack, and the others quickly set up a mortar.

The man on the radio yells something. The men at the mortar make some adjustments and fire a series of shells. This process keeps repeating. I have seen war movies before but nothing like this.

Once we mount up, and the vehicles are started, Mr. Lark's voice comes over the COMDAT restored to its mounting on the dash, "Follow closely and have weapons at the ready."

I find my pistol, confirm it is loaded, and draw the slide back to rack a round into place. Then I flip the safety on and wait.

We accelerate hard across the compound. At the last second, an armored car blocking the entrance through the wall moves out of our way, and we zoom through the gate.

Into hell.

The Ukrainian military base is huge. The compound we were in was one of many. Off to one side, several sources of tracer fire converge on a target in intermittent bursts. One switches to continuous and does not stop until its ammunition source is exhausted. This is closely followed a large silhouette striding out of the haze in the distance. In spite of the heavy machine gun fire, the thing does not even slow down.

In addition to the machine gun tracers, there is sporadic cannon fire. I can't see the source, but the flash and fire from the explosions is visible. Similar scenes play out on both sides of the road.

Our heading is west on a rough, gravel road, but we do not slow. If anything, we are accelerating.

Mr. Lark says, "The attack came from the east. Bound humans, possessed, abominations, and some

Lesser Created. Our Adversary was drawing his full strength while we had our peaceful drive across Slovakia."

Illych says, "Why the arrest? Safe passage had been guaranteed."

"Someone did not have a firm grasp of the terms of our agreement. The safe passage was not renegotiable. They have been made aware of their lack of vision."

Now it is my turn, "Does Captain Ulant understand the situation?"

"Yes, Thomas, he does. Every government in the world has people that keep track of such things. Captain Ulant understands the gravity of the situation and that breaking our agreement has led to this catastrophe. Fortunately, he was able to get to the military compound early enough to raise the alarm; otherwise, we would not be seeing the battle around us. Instead, it would have been a quiet massacre."

I start to ask another question and Mr. Lark interrupts, "Enough questions, Thomas. I need to focus on the *oculus*."

Fortunately, the road is straight and we are barreling along at high speed. The dust from the gravel road kicks up in our passing, leaving a visible wake.

Mr. Lark's says, "Slow down. Trouble ahead."

Illych asks the question on everyone's mind, "What kind of trouble?"

Mr. Lark snaps, "The maximum range of the *oculus* is approximately twenty kilometers. We are surrounded by activity, and we are traveling at a significant velocity. I can barely see anything a few kilometers in front of us. The best we will be able to hope for is a minute's warning, and that is what I just gave."

Illych says, "Slowing down." A good thing since he is in the lead vehicle. With Balthazar missing, I have chosen to ride shotgun in the SUV with Mike driving. I can watch the road ahead over the lead car and can see what we almost ploughed into.

Five military trucks, same model as the one that had taken us to the military compound, were in a convoy apparently returning to the base. The lead truck is still wheels-down, but it looks like it lost a fight with a trash compactor.

The next three trucks are scattered off the side of the road, lying on their sides, more or less intact. The last truck is lying on its side, blocking the road while looking like it came to the same violent end as the lead vehicle.

The trucks had been transporting soldiers.

Mr. Lark says, "I see no survivors."

I believe him. Corpses are everywhere. On the road, in the trucks, on the sides of the road, dozens of them. They did not die from gunfire either. Some are missing limbs, and others show massive trauma. There are bodies up in the trees on both sides of the road where they had been tossed, some still clutching their rifles.

Even in the dim light, blood is visible everywhere. Pooled by the dead and splashed across the wrecked trucks. As we drove into the middle of the scene, I notice the ground is littered with brass casings. They had been brave men who did not run, instead standing and fighting against something terrible.

The truck blocking the road is a problem. We are able to slowly go off-road and carefully drive around it. Fortunately, the sedans are all-wheel drive.

I have to ask, "What did that? Did their attackers take their dead with them? It looks like this just happened."

"It was not attackers, plural, it was a single attacker, and it is not dead *yet*," Mr. Lark's voice has a hint of resignation in it.

"Illych, stop here. We won't be able to outrun it."

All three vehicles come to a halt.

"It is coming, the thing that did the massacre we just passed."

Illych barks out orders, and the back of the SUV is quickly opened. Two large, plastic, hard cases are removed and opened. One of the cases contains two heavy rifles with large bores. Illych grabs one and Held the other. Huge drum magazines are inserted. Everything is done quickly and quietly.

Held says, "Time to slay a giant."

Tank grabs a machine gun from the other case and a backpack with an ammo feed coming out of it. With practiced ease, he shoulders the pack, feeding the ammo belt into the weapon. This is finished with the cycling of the bolt chambering the first round.

"Held, what is that?" I say while pointing at the weapon in his hands.

"Autoloading shotgun with drum-fed solid slugs. This will send maximum kinetic energy down range in a very short period of time."

Tank pops down the bipod on his weapon and rests it on the hood of one the sedans, producing noticeable gouges in the expensive luxury car that no one seems to care about.

Tank says, "Mr. Lark, what is it?"

"The mythological term is a *troll*. It is an oversized goblin. We can slow it down with Truestone, but the immobilization duration will be very short, only a few seconds. Start shooting as soon as it appears and do not let up."

A jet-engine-loud roaring erupts from the woods, off to the side of the road.

Mike pushes me so one of the sedans is between us and the sound of the approaching monster.

Good God.

What comes out of the trees is a bowel-loosening monstrosity. As tall as two men, lanky, with long arms sporting clawed hands that could almost drag the ground while it walks. Dark green and naked, its soccer-ball-sized, solid-black eyes sit above a mouth – hinged far back in the thing's head – that would have been at home on a great white shark.

The troll is also wounded – the recent encounter with the Ukrainian troops leaving a significant mark. Its torso, legs, and arms all sport holes and missing chunks. The thing is limping, definitely slowing its pace.

As soon as it bursts into view, the gunfire starts. Illych and Held fire controlled bursts from their autoloading shotguns. Tank, on the other hand, uses his bulk to pin the high-caliber machine gun in place on the hood of the Mercedes. He pulls the trigger and does not let go.

The troll stumbles and struggles under the withering fire. If it had not been wounded already, I doubt our position would be as confident.

In turn, Held and Illych each drop spent drums to the gravel, and with practiced ease, insert fresh ones. Mike supports his colleagues' efforts, firing long bursts from his carbine and then reloading.

I had lost track of Mr. Lark, instead entranced by the display of focused violence in front of me. Tank empties his backpack in less than thirty seconds. After the last round clears the chamber, he discards the machine gun, oil smoking off the over-heated weapon. He snatches up his carbine from his harness and re-engages.

The troll is uncomfortably close now. There is no more time left for anyone to reload again.

Mr. Lark appears in my side vision, sprinting towards the troll, moving impossibly fast for an old guy. The Truestone sailing through the air, hitting the troll in the chest.

Just like the ciorii back at my flat, the wounded troll falls down, convulsing on the ground. The white light blazing from the Truestone becomes a bullseye. Both Held and Illych close in to shoot at that spot from almost point-blank range.

The shotguns blow open the body of the Troll, revealing the location where the White Fang should be deployed to put this monster down.

It almost goes as planned.

As Mr. Lark predicted, the Truestone did not last long. No sooner had the chink in the troll's armor appeared, and the thing regained mobility.

One great, clawed hand sweeps around, hitting Held on his left arm and across his torso. He is violently thrown almost ten feet, hitting the side of one of the cars and crumpling down onto the ground, motionless.

The troll taking its rage out on Held left its defenses wide-open, and Mr. Lark leaps to within feet of the creature, well inside the thing's reach of being able to effortlessly shred him.

Mr. Lark stabs the White Fang into the area where the Truestone had indicated. The troll bellows, shivers, and goes still, falling to the ground as if its bones had just disappeared. Mr. Lark gets caught up in the creature's long arms and struggles for a minute to free himself.

Mr. Lark says, "Illych mount up, we must leave before we have more visitors," as he extricates himself from the dead troll's embrace.

Illych says, "Understood. Mike, put Held in the SUV and apply first aid. Thomas, you'll assist. Tank, you'll drive them. Mr. Lark, Captain Ulant and I are in the lead car. We abandon the other vehicle."

Mike and I carry Held to the SUV. I glance at the troll's corpse as we load him in. Smoke has started to rise from the body as it begins to sublimate out of existence.

After the vehicles are moving, Mike addresses

Held's injuries as best possible in the back of a speeding SUV on rough roads. Broken arm, severe lacerations on his chest, head injury, possible internal bleeding, Held is conscious but not talkative. We make him comfortable while Mike takes his blood pressure. The numbers indicate internal bleeding is a real possibility.

Mr. Lark listens to the update on Held's condition, "We are two hours from the Ukrainian-Russian border dispute. Once we cross, Held will go to a Russian hospital. Provisions were made ahead of time. It is in his best interest he holds on until then."

I think I understand what Mr. Lark is really saying. With Captain Ulant in our company, using a *dongle* to save Held is out of the question. That is if they even work. Based on what happened in the interrogation room back at the Ukrainian base, they may not be functioning.

Our race to get ahead of our Adversary continues for hours. Fortunately, there are no more run-ins with trolls or otherwise. Held becomes increasingly more pale and less responsive as we close the distance to the border.

Just short of the disputed Ukrainian-Russian border, Captain Ulant is dropped off near a unit of Ukrainian soldiers. We do the crossing through two makeshift border checkpoints, one Ukrainian and the other Russian. This time no questions are asked on either side. License plates are switched and we sail through.

Thirty minutes later, Mr. Lark has us pull over. People and equipment are moved around between the two remaining vehicles. Mike, Tank, and Held are going to a Russian hospital. The rest of us are continuing on. My guess is that as soon as they put some distance between us, the others will abandon their vehicle and translate to the Compass to take Held to the Doctor.

With Illych driving the SUV and Mr. Lark riding shotgun, we drive for another two hours.

Pulling over, Mr. Lark releases Balthazar from the *quixault*. We then mount up and continue on with Mr. Lark and Balthazar sitting in the back, occasionally talking between themselves in low tones.

I fall asleep in the comfortable front passenger seat for several hours. Illych shakes me awake when we stop for fuel. He looks exhausted.

Mr. Lark says, "Thomas, Illych is going to take some rest. You will drive, and I will give directions."

Illych passes out in the front passenger almost instantly, snoring, sometimes loudly. I ignore it and focus on the road. The best speed I feel comfortable with is slower than what Illych had achieved. The roads varying from good to fair, then awful.

We pass many Russian military checkpoints. They all seem to know we are coming and wave us through.

At some point my curiosity gets the better of me, "How is this possible? Driving around Russian Federation territory armed, and they do not seem to care?"

"They care, and they know where we are and that we are armed. They also know our business is not political or local. We are just passing through and are willing to pay for it."

"Is our passing through unmolested expensive?"

"Yes, in money and potential future favors of a similar nature."

Balthazar has been quiet and is intently looking out the windows. Now that I think about it, he has been trapped on that island for three hundred and fifty years. Hy-Brasil had been a big prison cell, and three hundred and fifty years was a really long prison sentence.

We are getting close to Shahgah mountain. The roads and terrain are getting rougher. I drive until the next refueling stop and then switch with a refreshed Illych.

Day turns into night, and we continue on with Illych and I switching every few hours. The mountain driving is treacherous, and the roads poor in quality. It is slow going.

Mr. Lark and Balthazar, of course, do not sleep, nor does Mr. Lark offer to help with the driving.

When the morning's first light reveals our surroundings, I can see we are driving along the foothills of a mountain. Our goal is ahead, the eastern end of this mountain range.

Being this close, we pull over at Balthazar's request. He releases one of his goblin servants from the *quixault*, sending it ahead to prepare for our arrival.

Balthazar is visibly excited, and he begins pointing out landmarks and naming them as we pass by.

We turn the corner of the base of the last mountain preventing us from seeing our destination, and there it is: Shahgah mountain.

Balthazar explains his home is not on – nor in – the mountain, but in what Mr. Lark calls a non-Euclidean contraction on its eastern slope, as it nears the Caspian Sea.

We pass through the last village nearest to Balthazar's residence. It is less run-down than the others we have seen this morning. There are even some older buildings, well-constructed with superb stone work evident.

Balthazar says, "I am disturbed as I see no evidence of my servants here. My household maintained relations with the local population."

The road ends in a dirt path that eventually also disappears. We are now following Balthazar's instructions, driving across open country.

A large, square pillar of time-worn stone appears on the horizon.

Balthazar points at it and says, "Continue on past that. Be warned, Thomas, there will be a brief change in scenery. Please continue forward without stopping."

A brief change in scenery is the story of my life over the last few months, so I shrug and do as instructed. Everything outside the SUV changes to a grey mist. The transition is brief, and we soon find ourselves on a flat stone road.

"Stop here!"

We are already driving slowly, so it takes only a tap on the brakes.

Balthazar says while getting out of the vehicle, "Welcome to my home!" Mr. Lark follows him, as do

Illych and I.

The stone road is as wide as a four-lane highway and at a slight incline, ending at a Sumerian-style ziggurat perhaps a mile away. The road is bordered by massive, carved pillars on each side at regular spacings.

Through the pillars on our right, we can see a forest with trees of ancient and massive proportions. Tall and straight, they climb for the heavens. I am reminded of the redwood forests in North America. These trees are on that scale in dimensions.

To the left of the road are fields that have lain fallow for who knows how long.

As the four of us stand looking around, the goblin servant Balthazar had sent ahead reappears. Arriving by the usual method of shifting into the edge of my vision next to Balthazar.

The two speak to each other in an odd language. I could not have repeated its utterances in any way if I wished to. The words spoken in a staccato with each syllable brief in duration.

After the brief exchange, Balthazar looks at Mr. Lark, "We are safe here. This place is secure and unmolested. My defenses are in place.

"Let us walk the rest of the way. Mr. Lark, you have done as I requested, and we must discuss your payment. I have other matters I would like to engage you in if your interests allow for it."

Mr. Lark nods, and Illych and I follow.

The four of us stroll towards the ziggurat, Balthazar appearing to be in no hurry, walking slowly while looking around. He is normally a difficult man to read, but I believe anyone seeing him now would realize the man is on the edge of tears seeing his home again after so long.

As we near the ziggurat, it is evident this is not a featureless pile of stone. There are windows, some big enough to fly a helicopter through. Balconies can be seen at different elevations.

The massive gates match the dimensions of the road leading up to the ziggurat. Their surfaces covered in reliefs and carvings. Visual representations of different events, others are written language. It has a beauty to it, and I find myself drawn to looking upon it.

My reverie is broken when the gates open. The similarity to the gates of the Citadel is not lost on me. They move silently and without any overt signal to open.

Inside is a courtyard with a high-vaulted ceiling. Around its perimeter are other smaller gates, doors, and windows. In one corner are several human-sized stone benches.

Balthazar leads us to the benches. "Please remain here for a time. If you agree Mr. Lark, a peace bond will be upon you while you are on my land. No hand will be raised against you, and I pledge to protect your person and those of your household while you remain here. In return, you will guarantee no aggression on your part. Agreed?"

Mr. Lark nods, "I agree. I and those with me will not provoke, nor act aggressively, while under your roof or on the grounds of your estate."

"I humbly suggest, Mr. Lark, you return to your conveyance and leave all weapons there. I assure you they would be of little use to you here. There are things in my household that may startle you and will not take the uselessness of your weapons into account when they react.

"I must investigate my residence and understand what has happened. The gates will remain open if you wish to retrieve something from your conveyance. You are free to walk the grounds of my estate and take shelter here in this entryway. Do not attempt to enter into my residence. My home has its own spirit, and until you are known to it, traveling beyond this entryway will result in much unpleasantness."

That said, he turns and walks through a gate to the interior of the ziggurat, its doors swinging open without any verbal command and closing swiftly behind him.

The three of us return to the SUV and leave our weapons there. Mr. Lark believes what Balthazar said about the uselessness of conventional arms in what is most likely a supernatural fortress.

While we are dropping off our weapons and grabbing what we will need while we wait for Balthazar, Illych hands me my emergency *dongle*.

I take it while commenting. "I don't think these work. During my interrogation back at that military compound, one of the officers activated the *dongle* and nothing happened."

Mr. Lark is standing right there and hears my comment, "Of course not. Each *dongle* is keyed to either an individual in my organization, or any grouping of them. I can't have some random person finding a *dongle* that falls out of someone's pocket during a mission and have them arriving alone at the Compass."

That is a relief, mystery solved.

We bring wool blankets, water, and food back with us. We eat and chat a bit about the events of the last two days. Then, Illych and I find benches to sleep on.

The last thing I see before drifting off to sleep is Mr. Lark sitting quietly, consulting his *oculus*.

CHAPTER EIGHTTEEN

I am able to sleep until I wake on my own. My eyes open to see the night above. Starlight shines down through the great windows set high in the walls above the entryway and the massive skylights built into the domed roof.

The entryway reveals its own illumination. Evenly spaced pillars, set high up midway to the domed ceiling, that appear to be solid stone during the day, luminesce in the dark of night. The reflected soft, white light makes the white stone of the entryway floor glow. This is a pleasant sight to awaken to.

Illych is already up and talking quietly with Mr. Lark. I stand up to join them and quickly realize a visit to the loo is in order. Where are the facilities? Such a mundane topic did not come up before Balthazar left, and I do not want to defile a corner of his home.

My internal struggle must have been playing out across my face because Illych chuckles, "One of Balthazar's goblins visited not long after we went to sleep. The bathrooms are over behind that door." He points at a man-sized door close to the gate we entered through. "They're not modern. It's more of a squat toilet thing. I am sure you'll figure it out."

It is weird alright. A single room almost as big as my whole flat back in London. The center of the room has a low platform with a hole in it.

The same glowing pillars are evenly spaced around the room. Two of the corners have running fountains. The fountains' edges are populated by carved nymphs. At least I hope they are carved nymphs.

My goal achieved; I rejoin my colleagues in the entryway. As I walk in, Illych calls out, "That was different, wasn't it?"

I nod, "Apparently, they did things differently in the old days."

Quiet is the order for some time after that. Entranced by the architecture and light of the entryway, time passes easily. Night eventually fades into morning, and the pillars' illumination reduces as the sun's rays find their way in.

After studying the walls and pillars around me, I see things I would like to write down. A sketching notebook would have been nice to have to be able to record all of this for future review.

Walking in through the same gate, Balthazar returns as the sun reaches mid-morning. His simple, black peasant clothing has been replaced by a bone-colored cloak with the hood down. His right hand carries a bronze-colored staff, and there is a complicated looking crown upon his head seemingly attached to his scalp plate.

"Mr. Lark, Thomas, Illych, I thank you again for your efforts in returning me home. My household is more or less in order now. We will enter and sit in one of my schools. Perhaps, you would call it a library. I must warn you before we proceed – the spirit of this place has a physical form, and it awaits us within. Please be at peace. It will not harm you."

He turns, and we follow through opening doors.

A grand hall of marble and granite extends some distance in front of us. Alcoves line the hall with complex scenes of activity displayed in metal and stone. As we journey down the hall, we pass arched openings to other halls or rooms. All are darkened such that nothing can be seen within.

Halfway down the hall is a tall figure, at least seven-feet tall or more, of lean build, and wearing silver-grey robes; its feet unshod and consisting of two large toes and a claw to the back. The thing's arms hang far down its body and end in large, strong-looking hands. Its face is shadowed inside a deep hood, but I swear I can see a glint of light on large, solid-black eyes. It is an unnatural and terrifying figure.

Balthazar walks quickly down the hall without

pause. The spirit of this place turns and follows Balthazar closely. I trail behind, gawking at the wonders around me. I have to jog at one point to catch up.

We continue straight through an archway at the end of the hall, entering into a library.

It is a place of beautiful architecture. Wood, metal, and stone carved and wrought for every pillar, arch, and window. The chairs, desks, benches, and tables strategically placed between alcoves recessed into the walls all around us. The walls soar straight up as high as the main gate entryway. Skylights let in sunlight, supplemented by the same clear, white crystal lamps I first saw at the keep on Hy-Brasil.

There are no ladders evident, and I can only guess at how books from the higher alcoves are retrieved.

In the center of the room, four padded chairs have been circled facing each other over a low table.

Balthazar moves to stand in front of one chair. Mr. Lark takes the opposite. I sit to Balthazar's right, and Illych takes the remaining chair. The monstrous thing representing Balthazar's residence silently positions itself close behind the Magus.

"Coffee?" Balthazar waves his hand to the table, and his goblin servants appear with silver cups and a coffee set. With supernatural dexterity, four cups of coffee are poured from one decanter. A goblin offering a cup with a bow to each of us in turn.

I take the offered cup and wait until everyone has been served. Balthazar lifts his cup and says, "Thank you, please enjoy." He then takes a sip.

I smell the brew first, not out of suspicion. I like good coffee – especially the smell of good coffee. This coffee has a heavenly aroma. I sip and almost choke. The taste is wonderful, but it is brewed in the Arabic tradition and is as thick as motor oil. Smaller sips are needed.

Illych has a similar reaction. Mr. Lark goes last, learning from our missteps, and takes a small sip, "This is truly excellent coffee, Balthazar. I have never tasted its equal."

Mr. Lark's compliment appears to please Balthazar to no end.

"Thank you. Now to business. I have fully assessed the state of my household. During my absence, my mortal servants eventually despaired of my returning and left. Families who have served the house of Balthazar for millennia are gone.

"This and other things I do not understand. I have attempted to contact my brothers and found nothing. Since my exile to Hy-Brasil, some great tragedy has played out. I do not know what has happened, but it is my duty as a Magi to repair whatever breach has occurred.

"I cannot leave my household now. If I am the last of the Magi, I must remain safe here and work through others. My household must be reconstituted. I have much to learn of the outside world and the changes over the last centuries.

"To this end, I will look to you, Mr. Lark. I will pay you handsomely for my rescue. I have come to understand you are not motivated by the love of wealth. To men such as yourself, wealth is only a means to an end.

"You have proven honorable in the traditional sense, and I wish to employ your services further. I sense an alliance would not appeal to you. However, a mutually beneficial collaboration may allow you to better achieve your own goals."

Mr. Lark waits a moment before replying, "Balthazar, I do understand the value of what you offer, especially now, after having walked the halls of your home. Such collaboration would require a better understanding of the roles you may ask me to engage in."

Balthazar smiles and nods, "Your approach shows wisdom. Yes, you should know more before we continue forward. Normally, I would work through my ancient and mortal servants. Please do not interpret my words as disparaging, but the Magi do not employ mercenaries.

"I have watched you, Mr. Lark, and spent days in discussion with your servant, Thomas. You do not seek power beyond what is needed to keep you free. I believe I know what you desire, and I will not speak of it in front of your servants.

"I will ask you to be my eyes in places I cannot see. There are places that need to be visited. Questions answered. I will need assistance finding out what happened to my mortal servants and help bringing new ones into my service.

"I will not ask you to fight. However, I cannot promise you will not need to defend yourself. Some of the paths you will follow are dark and less than safe.

"With my direction, you will walk paths rarely seen. Some have not been trodden for many, many years. Ancient wonders you will witness. And plenty of gold, of course, to pay your way."

After Balthazar finishes, we sit there staring at each other for several minutes. Whatever the Magus wants us to do, it will be an experience.

Karl Lark finally nods, "Not all of my time will be available to you. That which is available, I will offer."

Balthazar grins, obviously pleased, "For my rescue from Hy-Brasil, in what form should your gold be in?"

Mr. Lark does not miss a beat, "Bars."

"Will a single ton of gold be appropriate?"

"That will suffice, thank you."

Wow! I did the math in my head. It worked out to a considerable sum of money. No matter how the ton is calculated.

Balthazar says, "I cannot move the gold beyond the road to my residence. You can take it all at once or in small amounts over time. It will be kept in its own chamber as yours to be retrieved at your leisure. Should the unfortunate befall you, it will go to your heirs. The sun will go black and cold before the word of Balthazar is broken."

Balthazar's tone changes with that last sentence. There is iron resolution in his voice.

"As for the promise of knowledge, bring any artifact of old you possess to my residence, and I will tell all I know. Will this offer be sufficient payment?"

Mr. Lark says, "Let it be said the House of Balthazar is upright and true. Your word has been kept. I will take one-fifth of my gold when we leave today. The rest will remain safe in your vaults until I return for it.

"As for mutual cooperation, how shall we begin? I believe you have a place in mind for us to start?"

"Your words are pleasing, thank you. And yes, I have a place to begin. I have four brother Magi. There are also the others, the Illuminated, of which there are six. Whatever calamity has befallen them, they would have left messages and evidence. This is not the first time the Adversary has moved against us.

"I would suggest following back along our recent path from Hy-Brasil. The numerous abominations and those under *geas* are disturbing. I wish to know more about how they came to be here and from where they originated.

"Abominations are living things. Most are relatively short-lived. The ones sent against us in the last few days were not from my original pursuit three hundred and fifty years ago. Regular replacements would be required, held in reserve in anticipation of my attempted return. That place needs to be found and destroyed."

Mr. Lark says, "Then that is the next place we visit."

CHAPTER NINETEEN

Dr. Elizabeth Chatzas was a creature of habit. After a long day at the museum, she would come home and play some soft music to relax, change into something comfortable, curl up in her large, four-poster bed, and read a novel. Something fictional, preferably a combination of murder-mystery and romance.

It had been two weeks since her time with the abominable Karl Lark and his goons. They had used a stun gun on her, injected her with sedatives, then injected her with God-knows-what to cause that awful anxiety.

Thomas Davies was working with them. He and Higgebotham were both supposed to be killed when Lord Halluk's men came to take the book.

She had woken up in her own bed. That meant they had been there, tucking her into bed. An unacceptable invasion of her privacy.

A few days after returning, she had visited her doctor for a physical. Everything checked out. Still, the experience might have long-term consequences.

Tonight, she was going all out. A bath drawn and waiting. After adjusting the music selections, she entered her bathroom and disrobed.

No sooner had her foot slipped into the warm, comforting waters, than her doorbell rang.

Too late now. Whoever it was could call another day. The rest of her body slipped under the water, and she resumed reading her novel.

The door to the bathroom was still open when he entered. She would have screamed if pure terror had not gripped her first.

"Lord Halluk!"

Her exclamation was not in the respectful tone she had been taught to use in addressing him. Nothing could be done about it now, though. To see him silently enter, dressed all in black with a blood-red tie, and those too-large amber eyes looking through her, was unnerving.

She had first been introduced to him at his estate in central England. The estate a massive, sprawling affair, older than history, and beautiful. Britain had its share of creations made by people for which money was no object. Lord Halluk's estate eclipsed them all, magnificent beyond compare with attention to every detail.

One of the things she had learned on the estate is that immortality can create great beauty; beauty to the point of painfulness. Immortality can also create magnificent opportunity, and an immortal in pursuit of vengeance can be cruel beyond imagining.

There had been three visits. The third visit had seen her swearing loyalty to him. This cemented her position at the museum. She had been true to her word since.

That was years ago. Communications since had been handled by a courier who reported to one of Lord Halluk's secretaries.

She knew he was not human. On his estate, none attempted to hide it. There were *things* there, things other than Lord Halluk, which made it obvious.

"Elizabeth, we will talk now."

Djinn never apologize; they had taught her that. And one does not ask it of them.

She knew she must stand in his presence. Reclining in a bath would give offence. She curled her legs under her and lifted herself into a standing position, bowing her head.

"Lord Halluk," her tone proper now.

She could not detect if her nudity affected him, or if he even took notice.

"You will tell me everything now. I must decide your loyalty and whether you will continue to enjoy your ongoing service to me."